BREAKWATER

An Ellie O'Conner Novel | Book 5

JACK HARDIN

First Published in the United States by The Salty Mangrove Press

Copyright © 2019 by Jack Hardin. All rights reserved.

Cover Design by Collier Vinson (http://www.collier.co/)

This is a work of fiction. Names, characters, businesses, places, events, locales, and incidents are either the products of the author's imagination or used in a fictitious manner. Any resemblance to actual persons, living or dead, or actual events is purely coincidental.

No part of this book may be reproduced in any form or by any electronic or mechanical means, including information storage and retrieval systems, without written permission from the author, except for the use of brief quotations in a book review.

For Heidi

*Because you named your dog after Ellie.
And because you're my sister. I guess that's a bigger deal.*

CHAPTER ONE

It looked like congealing blood, the way it slowly trickled down the wall.

She stepped back, and the small metal ball clicked inside the can as she shook it. Leaning back in, she gave the nozzle a quick press, and dark red paint plumed out. Satisfied, she tossed the near-empty can into a metal trash can that sat at the corner of the building. She peeled off the latex glove, now stained with a spectrum of colors, and discarded it.

A middle-aged man bearing olive skin stood next to her. His long hair was pulled behind his back in a ponytail. "You're very talented, Juanita," he said.

She ran the back of her wrist across her forehead, wiping away a bead of sweat that was creeping toward her brow. "Thank you," she said, though she didn't smile.

"He looks like me," said a small voice beside her. Juanita's little brother pointed to the image of a young boy standing next to a card table, watching two older men playing dominoes.

Alex Serrano rubbed the top of the young boy's head and smiled down on him. "That's because it is you, Junior." He looked back on the finished mural. The east-facing wall of the shelter now briefed passersby on the local culture. The men playing dominoes gave way to two children at the opposite ends of a ping pong table and a portly lady behind them frying plantains in a large pan. Further down the wall were images of men playing soccer, a teenage boy connecting his baseball bat to a ball. In the center of it all, in typical blockbuster graffiti lettering, were the words "Hope House." The drying rivulets of red formed the messy yarn hair of a doll a little girl held, clutched in the crook of her arm. Both the Cuban and American flags flew above her.

Alex had opened Hope House almost two years ago now. It was nestled in the center of the Miami neighborhood of West Hialeah. The community was comprised of nearly ninety-five percent Hispanics, making it one of the most ethnically homogeneous places in the nation. Initially conceived as a shelter for poverty-stricken, Spanish-speaking immigrants, Alex's vision had grown, and Hope House had matured into a recreation center as well. It was a safe place where kids could come in off the streets and play foosball, video games, and even learn to read or cook. The street gangs were not as invasive as they had been a decade ago, but they still held influence over some areas of the community, peddling drugs, burglarizing storefronts, and intimidating those not willing to join their ranks.

Alex stood admiring the detail in the face of the boy swinging the bat. "One day," he told Juanita, "you will do big things."

She shrugged and looked back at her brother. "I just

want him to have a better life," she said. "I'm not sure how to give him that."

Alex set a fatherly hand on her shoulder. "You keep going to school, stay focused, and many opportunities will arise. Luck, they say, is when preparation meets opportunity. Keep preparing. In six months, you could be in college."

Juanita gave a half-smile, then whistled to her brother who was now at the other end of the building picking up pebbles and skipping them across the street. "Junior!" she yelled. "It's time to go."

Alex stood with his hands on his hips, still admiring the mural. "Thank you again, Juanita. This is amazing." He turned toward her. "We're serving tortilla soup for dinner tonight. Make sure to come get some."

"Thank you," she said, then took her brother's hand and started down the sidewalk. Junior waved at Alex as they walked away. Alex smiled at the boy a final time before turning and going back inside. When they reached the corner, Juanita turned south on W 8th Avenue instead of continuing on W 37th Street, the route back to their aunt's house.

"I thought maybe you changed your mind," her brother said.

"No," Juanita replied. "I need to do this."

"Mr. Alex will ask me where you are when I come to the shelter without you."

"Tell him I am visiting a cousin. That will keep him from asking questions."

"But we don't have a cousin."

Her tone grew agitated. "I need you to do that, Junior. If you don't, they might start looking around and find out that *Tia* can't take care of us. They'll put us in foster care and probably separate us. Do you want to go live with someone you don't know?"

He lowered his head. "No," he said softly.

His little hand felt small in hers. They walked side by side, navigating broken bottles and deep fissures in the neglected sidewalk. More than once she tugged him back from stepping on a discarded needle.

"*Mami* would tell you not to do this," he finally said.

Juanita wanted to stop in her tracks. She wanted to grab Junior and shake him and remind him that their mother was dead. That she wasn't there to tell them anything. But she didn't. Instead, she chose her words more carefully. "We're alone now, Junior. I need to watch out for us. *Tia* can't do it."

He gripped her hand harder. "You could have told Mr. Alex what you are doing."

"He's a good man, but he can't get us out of here. I turn eighteen in a few months. If I can make some money before then, I can get the judge to let me take care of you, and we can move somewhere better."

She stopped at the corner of an old, condemned motel that was hemmed in with panels of temporary chain link fencing. The half-hearted effort to prevent people from trespassing on the decrepit property hadn't worked. In a dozen places, holes large enough for someone to crawl through had been cut into the fencing, and most of the room windows were busted out. Juanita personally knew half a dozen vagrants that still called the place home.

She peered around the corner of the building and saw a dark blue van parked on the curb. The side door was open, and a man she didn't recognize stood near it, waiting. He had a large beard and thick arms that were folded across his chest. His bulbous nose looked like it was made out of putty and one side had caved in.

Juanita quickly turned back to her brother. "I have to go to the van alone," she said. "Jesse told me not to bring anyone with me."

"Why?"

Ignoring the question, she said, "I'll be back in a couple of weeks."

Junior squeezed her hand harder and drew down on it. Tears were forming along his eyelids. "Don't go."

She squatted down and placed both hands on his shoulders, looked him in his eyes. "We can't stay around here anymore. But I can't get us out unless we get some money. Do you understand that? Jesse promised me it wouldn't be long. He's going to watch out for me."

"I don't like Jesse."

"He's been good to us. Just go back to *Tia's* and stay in your room until you leave for dinner. And don't tell anyone what I'm doing. You understand?"

"Yes. I understand."

She stood up and pulled him into her. His head hardly reached past her stomach. He tilted his head back and looked up at her, producing the first smile of the day. "I can hear your heart beating in your stomach. Is that where it's supposed to be?"

She wouldn't tell him it was because she was nervous. But she had to do this. Their aunt was worthless. All she cared about was her next plunge of the needle, that next fix that would send her back into the clouds and keep her oblivious to the reality that she now had a niece and nephew to care for.

"It's going to be okay," Juanita said. "I promise you."

"What work are you going to do?" he asked.

"We've already talked about this. They are going to give me some work in the fields. It will get us some money."

He nodded and scrubbed at his tears with loose fists.

She gave him one last hug before letting him go and crossing the street. She didn't look back. Seeing Junior around the corner crying just might have enough power to compel her to stay. And she couldn't stay. She was going to give that little boy a good future. And to do that, they needed money. She wouldn't get much, but this was a start.

As she approached the van, she nodded quickly at the burly man. From this proximity, she could see that his right eye was colorless. The iris, instead of a bright green to match his left, was white. "You're late," he said, as he motioned for her to get in. Jesse was in the driver's seat, and seeing him made her relax a little. He acknowledged her with a brief nod before turning back and looking out the windshield.

The back of the van had three vinyl-covered bench seats which were separated from the front by a steel mesh barrier. Three other girls who looked to be about Juanita's age were already inside. She ducked and took the empty bench seat in the back. The side door slammed shut, and the large man with the misshapen nose got into the front passenger seat.

Outside, something caught her eye, and she looked up to see a curtain move in an unbroken window on the second floor of the motel. Junior was standing there, his tiny six-year-old frame drenched in a hoodie better suited for a large adult. Even from here she could see his wet, puffy eyes. She loved that little boy with all she had.

Looking at him standing there alone made her heart hurt.

His eyes were searching the windows of the van. She set her hand to the glass, but he couldn't see her. The tint was too dark. But she blew him a kiss anyway as Jesse started the van and pulled away from the curb. She watched Junior grow smaller as they moved down the street until a billboard blocked her view and he disappeared for good.

Juanita swiveled back in her seat and faced the front. The other three girls were staring into their laps, clearly as nervous as she was. They drove in silence for the next ten minutes, passing up the airport as they rode along NW 7th Street and drew closer to downtown.

Suddenly, the van took a sharp right and cut down an alley before braking hard enough to elicit murmurs of concern from the passengers. The murmurs quickly mutated into anxious cries as both men up front reached down toward their feet and produced heavy gas masks. They slipped them over their heads and adjusted them. The larger man leaned over something that was sitting on the seat between him and Jesse. Then came a series of quiet squeaks, like a spigot was being turned, followed by a low hissing noise that became stronger with each squeak. The two girls at the front began to scream, but they suddenly stopped. One laid a hand on the window, and the other grabbed the edge of their seat as if they were trying to keep their balance. Suddenly their heads slumped followed soon after by their shoulders. Then, to Juanita's horror, they slipped from the seat and fell to the floor like someone had switched off their circuits. The young lady in front of Juanita screamed and started to call out Jesse's name for help.

Juanita's heart was pounding deep in her chest, and her throat had gone dry. She stood up as high as she could and craned her neck. She couldn't see anything. Just both men staring straight ahead, unmoving, looking like impassive aliens in those awful masks.

Juanita moved to the side door and tried the handle. It wouldn't budge. She started banging on the window with her fist, her blows now fueled by a cold terror. Then she felt it. She took in a panicked breath, and her body mellowed like a sleeping pill had begun to unfurl in her chest. Groggy, she returned to her seat. The third girl had stopped screaming and was now laid out across her seat, her eyes closed, an arm drooping awkwardly toward the floor.

Juanita's body slumped, and her face slid onto the smooth, cold vinyl of the seat.

Jesse. She had trusted him.

He betrayed her.

She blinked slowly now, her thoughts, no longer sparked by high voltage terror, were oozing, seeping from her mind like a thick syrup.

Junior was right. She shouldn't have come.

As she slipped into unconsciousness, her heart was heavy with the knowledge that she would never see her little brother again.

CHAPTER TWO

Three Months Later

He loved the darkness. He felt comfortable in it, like an old skin you didn't want to shed.

Brett Riggins killed his outboard and rode his flat-bottomed boat into a cut in the mangroves before tying off on a narrow ramshackle dock that led deep into the underbrush. He stepped out of the boat and ducked beneath reaching branches. He didn't need a light. He had passed across these old boards hundreds of times. Thousands, perhaps. Twenty yards in, he veered right, and when he pressed in on the door, it slid against the floorboards with a non-committal creak.

It was nearly sunrise, and the tiny pinpricks of light that came to the earth from violent stars could not pierce the tin roof of the small, weathered shack. Inside held the kind of thick black that could compel even the most rational adult to believe that something may have come with the darkness. But not for Brett. No one came out here, and nothing but the occasional critter ever got in. The decrepit structure sat deep in the mangroves, a few miles north of Everglades City, nestled in an like an old animal that had hidden away to curl up and die in privacy.

He stepped inside. The lantern and the box of matches sat on a short counter on the opposite end. He started toward it and tossed his keys through the darkness, hearing them clatter onto a small table in the center of the room.

"Hello."

Brett swiveled around as a halting noise escaped his throat; a malnourished scream. He jumped back a couple of feet and held his hands out in front in a frenzied effort to protect himself from the unseen intruder. He managed a weak "Wh-Who are you?"

The voice was softer, belonging to a female, but firm and confident. "I've been waiting for you to show for the last eight hours." Then, like a parent worried sick over their teenager, she said, "Where have you been all night?"

"How...how'd you get here? Nobody knows about this place."

"That's not important."

"You police?"

"Brett, there is a pair of handcuffs on that table you just tossed your keys on. Please put them on."

He spoke into the darkness. "Handcuffs? What is this? You arresting me? I've done nothing wrong."

"I won't tell you twice."

Brett didn't like her tone. It carried a quiet authority. He couldn't see if she had a weapon pointed toward him. If she had really been out here in this place all night by herself, she possessed a level of guts he thought impossible for a woman; most men too. Reluctantly, he stepped over to the table and felt around. His keys rattled as his hand slid over them, and then his fingers touched the familiar cold steel of the handcuffs. He grabbed them up and rattled them around. "Okay. I got them on."

"Nice try. Put them on. *Now*."

He growled under his breath, and the sound of the metal teeth ratcheting together echoed across the thin walls of the shack. "There. Happy now?"

"I only heard six clicks, twice."

"Come again?"

"Brett, twenty teeth lie along each track, each representing a two-millimeter width. Six clicks represent just over a centimeter."

His words now issued from an icy voice. "And your point?"

Still speaking into a context where you couldn't see your eyelashes for the dark, she said, "Being that your wrists could pass for a couple of dry twigs, I would say you owe me another five clicks per cuff."

"Well, if you don't like how I do it, why don't you come over here and do it yourself?"

She heard the creak of a floorboard as Brett began to walk toward her, followed by the cuffs rattling together, a clear indication that he still had not put on the cuffs. Her conclusion was confirmed by the clatter of loose metal on the floorboards.

"Stop," she warned.

"If you were going to shoot me, you would've done it by now." But what happened next made him stop in his tracks.

A light flashed on, streaming from a small LED

flashlight that was pointed upward and reflecting off the low tin roof. It illuminated the outline of a person seated in his only chair—a rickety old thing he'd made from driftwood years ago. She was wearing a red ski mask, a tank top, and jean shorts, her hands encased in thin black gloves.

Brett curled his fingers into fists and continued toward her. As he neared, he threw his right foot out, swinging it around and sending it toward her face. She put up a forearm and set her shoulders, blocking the kick. She stood as he brought his leg back and regained his balance. She let the flashlight clatter to the floor where its beam now reflected off the far wall.

"I don't know who you are," Brett said, his head bobbing around like an overeager boxer, "but you shouldn't have come here. This is my place." He whipped his right fist toward her face and stepped in. Just as his knuckles were about to make contact, she pivoted, leaned back, and his fist rocketed past her. She used that as an opportunity to send a knee swiftly into his abdomen. Brett sputtered and collapsed at her feet, all the air having abandoned his lungs. She pushed him to the ground where his mouth connected with the dirty floor and his upper lip split on the wood. Temporarily incapacitated, Brett felt the cuffs enclose around his wrists.

She spoke. "I saw that there was a warrant for your arrest. Something about assaulting a dancer at a club a couple of nights ago."

After he gained his breath back, he lifted his head off the floor and spat out a loose wad of blood. "I'll post bail and be out before lunch. Then I'm gonna find out who you are and pay *you* a little visit."

"Are you now? I think you're forgetting about all the back child support you owe. I think that will have to get paid before you post bail."

"Doesn't matter. I'll still get bail. I got the money."

"Mhm. And that would include the backpack full of cash I found beneath the floorboards?"

Brett twisted hard beneath her, but she dug her knee deeper into his lower back. "You're gonna *die*. That's *my* money."

"You know, it might be, Brett. But now, it's mine."

"I've been saving that money for three years."

"Maybe that's why your ex-wife isn't getting any child support payments. Didn't I see somewhere that her name was Sally?"

"That's none of your business."

"You're right. All I know is that I could really use fifty thousand clams about now. I have bills too, you know." After retrieving her flashlight, she reached into Brett's pants pocket and retrieved his cell phone.

"What are you doing with that?" he asked.

But she ignored him and stepped outside the door. Pressing the home button, she looked at the service icon. There were no bars, and tiny words against the backlight read, "No Service." But she knew that a caller within a specific proximity to any provider's cell tower could connect to the nearest emergency center. She dialed 9-1-1, and when the dispatcher answered, she put her wrist to her mouth and spoke into it to muffle her voice. "There is a recent warrant for a Brett Riggins." She gave the dispatcher the location and hung up before he could ask any questions. Before walking back inside, she tossed the phone further into the mangroves where she heard it clatter against several branches and land with a splash in the shallow water.

Walking back into the shack, she grabbed up a roll of duct tape she had brought with her and spent the next minute wrapping Brett's hands, running the tape all the way up his arms and stopping above the elbows. Then she wrapped his ankles and legs. Finished, she moved to the front corner of the shack and grabbed up a backpack, shouldered it, and walked back to Brett. "Oh. Before I go." She tapped the backpack. "That little stash of meth you had in here? I went ahead and put that in the cabinet. I'm sure the police will be happy to find that with your fingerprints all over it."

As he cursed her, tiny bits of red-tinged spittle flew off his lips. She leaned down and gave him a patronizing pat on the back. "Hang tight."

"Wait. Where're you going?"

"I have breakfast plans. You can tell the police they'll find your boat tied off a couple hundred yards closer to the Pass."

"What? You can't leave me here like this."

But the sound he heard next was the door scraping against the floor as it opened and then shut. Outside, a couple of boards creaked before the familiar sound of a small outboard puttered to life. In less than a minute the engine's drone had drifted further away until it was gone altogether.

Brett entered into a futile struggle with his bonds, finally giving up and yelling out in frustration, a thick vein pulsing down his neck as he mindlessly screamed for someone to help.

But the nearest soul within three miles was driving away in his boat.

CHAPTER THREE

Ellie O'Conner slowed her Bayliner to idle speed, reducing her wake as she made her approach into Matlacha. The sun had crested the horizon an hour ago, staining her bright blonde hair with waking shades of red and orange before continuing its ascent into the high arc of the sky.

She pulled into a temporary slip on the south end of Matlacha Community Park and tied off. The backpack lay at her feet. She grabbed it up and tossed the ski mask into the glove box, removing a blank piece of paper and pen before shutting the compartment door and locking it. Disguising her handwriting with standard block print, she wrote:

Sally, Brett is going to be locked up for a while. I'm sure he would want you to have this. He's sorry for all the times he missed his child support payments.

She signed it:

A Friend.

P.S. Probably best if you didn't mention this to anyone.

She shouldered the backpack and stepped off the boat onto the floating dock. After cutting through the park, she came out onto Pine Island Road, the only thoroughfare in and out of the island it took its name from.

At eighteen miles long and two miles across, Pine Island registered as the largest island in the state of Florida. Sanibel Island lay but two miles off its southern tip, laying claim to miles of sugar sand beaches that were noticeably absent on Pine Island. Rigorous zoning and development regulations ensured that Pine Island remained a geographical and cultural heirloom in a state that was becoming over-commercialized and overrun with seasonal tourism.

Driving west out of Cape Coral and into Matlacha made you think a gentle breeze had somehow blown you back in time to a place that still held a small town charm, that spoke softly to you and said, in some way, that you were home.

Ellie crossed the two-lane street and walked behind a long, narrow building that sat in front of a stub-nose canal. She picked out an old Nissan Sentra in the narrow crushed shell parking lot and tugged on the driver's side door handle. It opened. Moving quickly, she set the backpack on the floorboard, tucking it close to the seat, and then placed the note upside down on the seat. She locked the doors and went around to the front of the building.

She pulled on the front door to The Perfect Cup, and smells of freshly brewed coffee, blue crab omelets, and morning muffins swirled in her nose. Looking toward the far wall she saw a tall man, his back toward her, filling up his mug at one of the many coffee dispensers. He wore a beige t-shirt that fit snugly around a muscular frame and blue jeans whose cuffs slipped over ostrich-skin cowboy boots.

Ellie navigated her way past a few tables and stepped up behind him. She slipped her arms around his waist. "Whoa, there," Tyler said, trying not to slosh his coffee. Without turning around, he put his free hand over hers and gave a gentle squeeze. "You'd better stop that, Jackie. Ellie's meeting me here in a little bit, and it'd be best if she didn't see us like this." Ellie pulled away, raising her brows as he turned around.

His radiant green eyes looked like tiny blades of spring grass spun together. They met hers, and he feigned alarm. "Ellie. Uh, hi."

"Stop it, you goof."

He winked down on her, then leaned down and gave her a kiss. They had been dating for over three months now, but whenever his lips touched on hers it still felt like the first time, still made her stomach flutter. He pulled back and grinned. "I'll take that over a cup of coffee any morning."

As her gaze moved to his head, she frowned. "Where's your hat?" His sandy brown hair fell just over his ears and the top length, which wasn't quite right, was finger-combed to the side. Ellie had known Tyler for over a year, and she struggled to remember a time that he had appeared in public without his red, sun-faded ball cap. Something was truly out of place, the world tilting slightly off axis.

"Couldn't say," he said. "I'm starting to think someone snuck in my place last night and stole it."

"And left your television and all your guns?"

"Precisely. That hat is the best thing I own."

"Where do you think it is?"

"Not a clue. I thought maybe I left it at your uncle's bar yesterday."

"Did you call Major about it?"

"I did. He said it hasn't turned up."

"Well," she said, "if it doesn't show soon, then you, sir, need a haircut."

Tyler ran his hands over his head. "Is it that bad?"

She grimaced. "Think late 90s boy band."

"Ouch." Tyler looked up toward his hairline and self consciously moved some hair off his forehead. "Noted," he said.

"Nick and Tiffany here yet?" she asked.

"In the anteroom," he said. "In and to the left. I'll be right over."

Ellie found their friends talking over cups of coffee. Nick Barlow was nearly as tall as Tyler's six-foot-two frame but slimmer, and his black hair was cut close to his scalp, reminiscent of the seven years he spent in the National Guard. Nick and Tyler had been best friends since high school and roomed together at Texas Tech fifteen years ago. Tiffany had grown up in Naples, a half hour south, and the Barlows had recently relocated to Fort Myers to be closer to her family, with Nick working as a subcontractor for a local construction company.

Ellie pulled out a chair. "Hey, guys." Tiffany stood and gave Ellie a friendly hug across the table. Tiffany's short brown hair was cut just above her shoulders, and her lively, hazel eyes never failed to convey her zest for life. Nick and Tiffany had one child, Kayla, who was the same age as Ellie's niece, Chloe. Both six-year-olds were already best friends, co-conspirators in all things rainbows, unicorns, and sparkles.

Ellie took her seat as the waitress appeared and placed an empty mug in front of Ellie. "There you are," she said. "They said you would turn up at some point. Sleep past the alarm?"

"Something like that," Ellie smiled.

"What can I get you?"

Tyler returned to the table and took his seat next to Ellie while she ordered Irish Eyes: poached eggs on a bed of seasoned spinach, with feta cheese and diced tomatoes on the side. The waitress's rosewood lipstick and powdered cheeks could not conceal the melancholy that resided in her narrow face or hide that her mind was somewhere else, far away from coffee, omelets, and muffins.

Ellie reached out and touched her hand. "Sally. Everything okay?"

Sally straightened while her mind rode an invisible path back to the present. "I just got a text from a friend down in Everglades City. She said Brett just got arrested for drug possession. Someone had wrapped him up in a cocoon of duct tape and called the cops on him." She shook her head angrily. "I thought he was done with all that."

Everyone at the table expressed how sorry they were. "It doesn't matter much, I guess," Sally said. "He's always been as bent as a fish hook. Just would have been nice if he could have helped with some of the bills. You know?" Sally tapped her paper pad. "Let me get this in for you, Ellie."

"That's too bad," Tiffany said after Sally left. "She's such a sweet lady."

Nick leaned back and tried to stifle a large yawn. "You awake over there?" Ellie asked.

"Yeah," he said. "Sorry. Just trying to wrap my head around some things at work. You know how a new job can be."

"He hasn't been sleeping well these last few nights," Tiffany said. She reached around her husband and ran the flat of her hand across his upper back. "He has meetings at a construction convention in Miami the next couple days and has been up late prepping for them. I told him if this job is going to keep him this amped up, then we need to have a talk."

Tyler said, "Well, as my mama used to say, work the work, don't let the work work you." Tiffany took a sip of coffee and set her mug down. Looking at Tyler, she said, "You know, you need a haircut."

Tyler sighed. "Good grief. I lost my hat, okay?"

"Well, you'd better find it quick. Or get another one."

Tyler shot a glance at Nick, looking for backup, but Nick only shrugged. "I'm with her on this one. Your hair. It's not right, man."

"Ellie," Tiffany said. "Have you given Jet an answer yet?"

After spending the better part of a decade with the CIA, Ellie had stepped away from fighting global terrorism a year ago and come back home to Pine Island with no pressing plans to find a new career. When she was presented with an opportunity to join the Drug Enforcement Administration, she had been slow to accept. But she finally had and over the next several months experienced the satisfaction of bringing down three local drug organizations. But a tangled mess of bureaucracy and lies ultimately led to them letting her go.

Now she was back to helping her uncle at his bar and marina, The Salty Mangrove. At thirty-six Ellie had already learned what most people don't until late in life, and what some never do: that life doesn't always have to be run at full throttle, that you're not wasting your life if you step back and enjoy the sand between your toes and the wind in your hair. In this new millennium the tyranny of "being productive" was a real thing, and Ellie was fairly certain she wanted no part of it.

Tim Jahner—"Jet" to many—had put in over three decades with the DEA. He had recently retired from the agency, stepping away from his role as the head of Fort Myers' Special Response Team, and was in the process of opening up an investigative agency. He had been courting Ellie on a professional level, trying to convince her to join him.

"Not yet," Ellie replied. "I haven't ruled it out, but I'm not in a hurry to jump into anything either." She excused herself and went and filled up her coffee mug. When she came back to the table, Tyler and Tiffany were laughing hard. Nick, on the other hand, was rubbing his forehead with his fingers, shaking his head.

"What'd I miss?" Ellie asked.

Tiffany was holding a small piece of paper, dogged-eared with a crease down the center. She handed it across the table. Ellie took it and turned it around. It was a picture: a clearly much younger Nick was wearing gym shorts and no shirt. His skin was shiny with sweat, his arms spread eagle. And across his chest in thick black marker were written two sloppy words: *Not Tom*. The same was written across his forehead. He was looking up at something.

"What is this?" Ellie asked.

"I was rummaging through an old box and found that gem," Tyler said. "Nick, you want to tell her?"

"Go ahead, old buddy. Just remember turnabout's fair play."

"So," Tyler said. "Tiffany, Ellie, you want to take a guess at what that's all about?"

"A hazing," Tiffany said.

"Nope."

"A dare?" Ellie offered.

"Not a hazing. Not a dare. This, good ladies, is a picture of Nick Barlow trying to win the heart of one Jenna Price. That was, let's see, sophomore year at Tech. Jenna was a senior, and Nick was infatuated with her. He'd done everything to try and get her to date him, even though she had been dating Tom Ellis for the last year. This particular night he got a little toasted on bourbon and conceived a bright idea." Tyler looked at Nick. "You want to finish?"

Nick sighed, trying to keep back a smile. "Sure." He took a sip of his coffee. "So I told Tyler to find a marker and write 'Marry Me, Jenna' on my chest. I didn't bother to check it, and Tyler told me to let him write it on my forehead too. Then..." Nick rolled his eyes and motioned for Tyler to finish.

"Then he runs a half mile across campus and stands in the grass outside Jenna's dorm room balcony. Turns out Jenna wasn't there. But her roommate was and wasted no time getting her camera. That picture was taken about three seconds before Nick emptied his stomach on the lawn."

"You wrote 'Not Tom'?" Ellie laughed.

"Yep," Tyler said. "Nick hated Tom. But the best part was that picture right there made the front page of The Daily Toreador, the campus paper." Tyler held up a hand, indicating he wasn't finished. "To top it all off someone started taking in donations and within two days had like a thousand t-shirts made up that said 'Not Tom.' The rest of the year you'd show up to class and see some random student wearing their Not Tom shirt. If it had happened today, he would have had his own hashtag trending."

Both ladies were nearly bent over in laughter. "A real Casanova," Ellie finally said.

"I can see why you've never told me that one," Tiffany smirked.

"Tyler," Nick said, a warning in his voice, "you'd better watch it. I've got plenty on you, my friend."

"The pictures are what hold the magic," Tyler said. "You've got stories. You have no pictures."

"Don't be too sure of that."

Through the laughter, Ellie noted that Nick was smiling, but it wasn't reaching his eyes.

FORTY-FIVE MINUTES later Ellie and Tyler said goodbye to their friends and hung back outside the front of the restaurant. Tyler assessed the row of cars hugging the sidewalk. "You park in the back?"

"No, I rode the boat in. Docked it across the street at the park."

Tyler studied her for a moment. "Your boat? You

overslept and took your boat? Driving would have taken half the time."

She shrugged. "It's a beautiful morning."

"You know, when Sally mentioned Brett, you seemed caring but not surprised. And I've never known you to oversleep anything except maybe an early morning dental appointment."

She raised her chin and looked him in the eye. "Your point?"

Tyler produced a pack of gum from his pocket and tossed a piece in his mouth. He worked it between his teeth as he studied her. "You know, one of these days you could invite me along. Overslept my ass."

Ellie looked out toward the Matlacha Pass Bridge where plenty of hopefuls had nearly two dozen lines in the water. "Noted."

"How'd you find him?"

"I have my ways."

"All right, Miss I-have-my-ways. What did you do it for, other than your general disdain for low-lives?"

"I had a hunch, and it paid off. Literally. Sally should be good on money for a little while."

"You're joking?"

"I am not."

His eyes narrowed on her. "You're not normal. You know that, right?"

"You like me this way."

"I like to side with the honey badger."

"You think Nick's okay?" she asked. "Something's off with him. I think it's more than just him being tired."

"Not sure," Tyler said. "He didn't seem like himself to me either. When he gets back from Miami, I'll take him fishing out in the Sound, get a few beers in him, and see if I can get him to talk."

"Take him fishing? On a boat?" It was a well-known fact that Tyler liked to be on a boat about as much as Ellie liked tolerating drug dealers. That aside, Ellie still loved him, even in the face of such a monumental flaw.

"Did I say the Sound?" He winked at her. "I sorta meant the pier." Then he looked at his watch and pulled out his truck keys. "I've got to run. Have a handgun class to teach."

They said goodbye, and Ellie called over her shoulder as she crossed the empty street. "And find your hat."

CHAPTER FOUR

The card reader accepted the magnetic strip and beeped, illuminating a tiny green diode above the handle. Nick Barlow pushed open the door to his downtown Miami hotel room and wheeled his travel suitcase in behind him. The door slapped shut as he jammed a finger behind his collar and loosened his tie, a bright orange tie Tiff had gotten for him just last week. Orange was his favorite color, so it followed that this was now his favorite tie. He sat down on the bed and ran his hands across his face. Even from this side of the balcony door, he could hear the muted sounds of the city—the thin whine of car brakes, a police siren, a child laughing loudly.

Beads of nervous sweat were popping up along the back of his neck and underarms and forehead. He came back to his feet. Anxiety huddled deep in his abdomen, and he started to pace the floor like a caged animal.

He wanted to tell Tiff. He had wanted to tell her yesterday. And the day before. He'd wanted to say something all week. But he couldn't. He just couldn't.

It was all getting to be too much.

Opening the door to the mini bar he reached for the gin. But he stopped midway and withdrew his hand. Alcohol wouldn't make this go away. He tried swallowing back the dread that had taken up residence in his chest like a malignant tumor.

He removed his wallet and phone and set them on the desk along with his car keys.

Nothing would make this go away.

* * *

Retirement was not unlike an extended summer vacation. Just this morning he had taken two of his grandchildren to the beach. The day before that he had taken another to a movie. He was learning things about the grandkids and even his wife that he hadn't paid mind to before. Two weeks on three days off meant you didn't get a lot of time with those you love. It meant you had to tailor your entire life around the job. But now everything was a little surreal. No more spending his nights alone in a sleeper cab while vehicles sped by at eighty-miles-an-hour. No more spending another night away from the lady who'd grabbed his eye and his heart way back at Eagle Mountain High.

That's what Walter Bennett was thinking as he held his wife's hand and strode down the sidewalk with her. After thirty-eight years of driving a big rig for North American, Walter had finally turned the keys in and retired to South Florida. He and Mary were still enjoying the experience of waking up together and realizing that they had all day to do everything or nothing at all. Tonight he was walking her to the Miami Symphony for a performance of Beethoven's 5th. Walter himself preferred the likes of Johnny Cash and Merle Haggard over Beethoven, but he'd learned over the years that keeping a healthy marriage meant doing things for your loved one that you might not choose for yourself.

They crossed the street and headed east on NW 39th Street. Suddenly, they heard a muted scream from across the street. Muted because at their age everything sounded muted, as if swimming underwater. Scuba divers in a world absent of water. Another scream issued from somewhere behind them just as something tumbled out of the sky and punched into the concrete five feet in front of them. A sickening thud raced down the street, and blood from the man's head slung against Walter's pants legs.

Mary screamed; that rare type of howl that comes out half wild animal and half pure terror. The kind of scream that most people can go through their entire lives and only hear in the movies. Mary's hand left her husband's and went to cover her mouth as she stumbled backward. Walter couldn't move. He just stared bewildered at the man's body before a vibrating tingle worked a track down his arm and he began to feel a tightening in his chest, as though someone was ratcheting his ribcage in toward his spine. He tried to speak, tried to tell Mary that he was having a heart attack, but before he could open his mouth, he pitched forward, his own head hitting the pavement just inches from the body of the man wearing a bright orange tie.

Four stories above, the curtains in Nick Barlow's room danced past the threshold and onto the balcony, stirred by a cool evening breeze.

CHAPTER FIVE

It wasn't easy, walking into someone else's nightmare. Ellie sat behind the wheel of her Silverado holding Tiffany's hand across the console, staring at the trunk of a palm that stood just off her front bumper. "I don't want to go in," Tiffany said resolutely. "This can't be happening." She let go of Ellie's hand and used the inside of her hands to wipe the tears from her cheeks.

"I know," Ellie replied softly. It hadn't been twenty-four hours since she Tyler, Nick, and Tiffany had breakfast together. No one foresaw that the very next morning both ladies would get up before dawn to drive across the Everglades to sit in the parking lot of the Miami-Dade morgue before they opened at eight o'clock.

Ellie waited for Tiffany to open the passenger door before turning off the truck and stepping out. The air was cool and moist, the breeze calm, the morning mocking them as they walked toward the building with heavy hearts and damp eyes.

They entered the lobby, and Ellie gave the receptionist Tiffany's name. A row of chairs lined the entrance hallway, and they were asked to take a seat while they waited.

Five minutes later an older gentleman with bowed shoulders and a receding silver hairline came down the hall and stopped in front of them. He introduced himself as Harold Wilson, one of the medical examiners. His facial features were sharp and handsome, his gray-blue eyes kind. He reminded Ellie a little of her father, and for a brief moment, she was overcome by how much she missed him.

Harold shook hands with both ladies and asked them to follow him. He led them to the end of the hall where they turned and entered a small space that looked a little like an interrogation room. A table sat in the center of the linoleum with two chairs on each side. Harold pulled out one for Tiffany and then took the chair beside her and brought out an iPad that had been tucked under his arm.

Ellie stood behind Tiffany and remained silent.

Tiffany turned toward the older man. "Do we not view the body in person? I'm sorry. All I know about this kind of thing is what I've seen on television."

"I understand. No, we don't do that anymore," he said. "Most counties don't. The floor in the morgue is hard, and I'm afraid we had too many people pass out over the years. Some were injured in the process." He smiled kindly. "A few years back we started taking pictures and just show them to you here on the iPad." He pressed the home button on the device and swiped a finger across the screen several times. "If I may prepare you, Mrs. Barlow. When your husband fell, he landed predominately on his right side. His head hit just before his body. So the right side of his face is, well…" He drifted off before continuing. "We've laid a cloth over the crown of his head and taken the picture of the left side of his face."

"I see," Tiffany said. Then she steeled her jaw before nodding to indicate she was ready.

Howard tapped the screen a final time and slid the device in front of her. From behind, Ellie watched Tiffany's body stiffen as she looked over the image. Ellie leaned in, and her stomach fell as she saw Nick resting on a cold metal table.

"Mrs. Barlow?" Howard finally asked.

"That's him," Tiffany choked out.

Howard nodded respectfully, the way a funeral director might. "I'm very sorry," he said. Then he tapped the glass a couple more times and asked Tiffany to use her finger to provide a digital signature identifying the body as belonging to Nick.

"What happens now?" she asked.

"We'll turn his body over to the mortician, and I believe he'll have your husband's ashes ready by the end of the week. You can come pick them up, or we can ship them to you."

"What about an investigation or something?"

Howard gave a small shrug, and Ellie laid a hand on her friend's shoulder as he spoke. "A detective will be assigned to your husband's death and will look at all the possibilities involved. They should be in communication with you as early as today."

"All right. Thank you." Tiffany nodded pensively and stood up.

The entire ordeal was over in less than ten minutes.

"I'm sorry you had to see that," Ellie said as they arrived back at the truck and got in.

Tiffany buckled and leaned against the door. Her fingers were busy picking nervously at each other as they lay in her lap.

"What happened, Ellie? Since Kayla was born, I haven't seen Nick get drunk. There's no other explanation for him falling off that balcony. Other than someone...pushing him." Her voice trailed off.

"They'll look at all the angles," Ellie replied, "and see if they can locate any video footage."

"He was acting strange the last few days. I even asked him about it, but he said it was nothing. But he wasn't himself."

Ellie started the truck. "I know. Let's see what the investigation turns up, alright? It was probably just a freak accident." She hated that term. Freak accident. It sounded like a clown had gotten in a car wreck. But she couldn't think of anything better off the top of her head.

"Yeah, okay," Tiffany said. "Ellie?"

"Yeah?"

"I'm scared. And I don't know how to do this."

"I know." Ellie reached over and gave her hand another squeeze. "We'll do it together."

CHAPTER SIX

The darkness incumbent in the human heart, the raw lust to achieve selfish ends at the cost of another human's blood or dignity or life, still astounded him. Even now as he entered his sixth decade of life.

He held a printout of the teenage girl's photo in the palm of his hand. Her hair, the color of night, reached nearly to her waist. She looked past the camera, expressionless, her hands at her side. She was pretty—full lips, small nose, and high cheeks. A face which, in that single moment of time, reflected a simple beauty. It was her eyes that harbored the pain. Two dark pools of sadness.

Jet Jahner laid the photo in the center of his desk and drummed his fingers across the wood. He sighed, and his gaze drifted to the framed quote hanging on the wall near the front door.

"Bad men need nothing more to compass their ends, than that good men should look on and do nothing." In its more popular form, the quote read, "The only thing necessary for the triumph of evil is for good men to do nothing," a faulty rendering that even John F. Kennedy had once mistakenly attributed to Edmund Burke. But Jet had chosen to display the quote as it stood in history, penned by John Stuart Mill. It summed up not only Jet's entire career but his personal view on life. Evil men, as it were, never slept, always scheming fresh ways to get ahead on the backs and blood of others.

They needed to be stopped.

He had been in his early thirties when he stood over Pablo Escobar's bullet-riddled body on that red tile rooftop in Medellín. Watching members of the Search Bloc huddled in front of Escobar's cooling body, Jet had learned what many never do: even the worst of men are still, in the end, just men. And as men, they die and leave everything they have acquired behind for someone else to possess. Jet understood that day that even the worst of humanity—men like Escobar—were not invincible. They were not gods hailing from Mount Olympus. No, what set them apart was their ability to skirt the law and bribe those enforcing it. They were simply wise in the doing of evil, and the world remained full of men and women who woke up each morning and decided afresh to wipe their dark brush over the canvas of the world all over again.

Jet's hair was gray now, nearly silver, decades away from the chestnut brown of his youth. This time last year he had been quietly entertaining the idea of stepping away from the agency, considering whether or not it was time to turn in his badge and put the DEA behind him. But when Garrett Cage, Special Agent in Charge of the Fort Myers office, had brought on Ellie O'Conner as outside support to assist in finding local drug dealers, Jet had been all in. Over the course of the next several months, they found success, taking down three separate drug operations as well as a smaller syndicate that dealt in illegal arms. With those victories behind him, and knowing that the county in which his grandkids were growing up was a little safer, he decided to hand over his badge. He had put in his time fighting drugs, and it was time to step aside so the next generation could take their place in a war with ever-changing faces and foes.

But leaving the DEA had not been an invitation to retirement. Not yet, anyway. Spending most of his time between the putting green and his fishing boat was still a few years out. He had spent his entire professional career acquiring an extensive repository of skills, and he wasn't quite ready to shelve them.

After whittling down his options, Jet had, with certain parameters, decided to step into private investigation. He had no plans to stare down cheating spouses with his camera or assist defense attorneys in helping to exonerate potentially guilty people. Defense attorneys had to operate on the assumption that their clients were innocent. Jet did not. He had spent his former career putting people behind bars. He wasn't about to cross the aisle to work for the defense.

The decision to become a PI had not been made in a vacuum. Florida's new governor, Judy Ratcliffe, had recently campaigned on a promise to raise clearance rates across the state. The clearance rate was the percentage of cases in which a suspect was arrested and charged for a particular crime. Over the last decade, violent crimes had seen clearance rates of just over fifty percent, a number that was slowly declining on a year-by-year basis. Simply put, of all the murders, rapes, robberies, and assaults across the state of Florida, half of them never laid a charge to anyone for the crime; no one was ever arrested.

Police departments countered these statistics with a legitimate argument: standards for charging someone had become too high, with many prosecutors demanding that detectives deliver "open-and-shut cases" that would lead to quick plea bargains. Cases, however, tended not to wrap themselves in pretty little bows. Alibis were checked and rechecked, witnesses questioned, evidence examined, indicators followed and pursued. Still, in the end, you handed the DA the best you had, even if that translated into more work on their end to get a conviction.

Eight years ago, Governor Ratcliffe's own daughter had been murdered in Orlando as she walked home from her job at Altamonte Mall. Her killer was never caught. After taking office, Ratcliffe had followed through on her promise and devised the Closure Act, a unique solution intended to drive up clearance rates by ten percent over the next five years. Often times, all a case needed was a fresh perspective. Somebody along the line missed a connection or didn't think a lead serious enough to follow up. So a team of independent investigators would be assembled to get fresh eyes on certain cases, cases that had been worked properly but hit dead ends.

Naturally, the decision had been unpopular among most in the law enforcement community. No one was interested in someone from the outside nosing around their case, even if they were supposedly on the same team. But when protocols were defined to ensure that outside help would not lead to detectives getting their toes stepped on or their cases mishandled, tempers settled and optimism rose. The new team would only handle cases flagged as suspended by the assigned detective. Only then could the case get picked up—only when the investigation had been exhausted and was still lacking enough evidence for an arrest. If the case was revived by an investigator and an arrest made, it would be the detective who received the credit.

Qualifications were high for joining the new investigative ensemble. Members were required to have at least a decade of previous experience with state or federal law enforcement and had to be approved by a board which included the state commissioner, state attorney general, and a handful of local police chiefs. Jet had received unanimous approval and a notice just last week that all authorizations had been established and that he was now clear to begin working. He would have access to case files and state databases that would allow him to conduct research and background information. Alternatively, any cases he worked outside of this purview would not give him access to state databases. For those, he was on his own. Any violation of this was forbidden and could lead to legal consequences.

Jet's new office was located in a modest, three-room suite at Pine Island Center, at the main intersection as you entered or left the island. The back room held the copier, office supplies, and a small floor safe for housing sensitive information. The additional office sat ready in the event he brought in an associate, and he hoped Ellie would be that person. His desk sat in front of the far wall from the entrance with an oak bookcase and a potted palm behind it. Most of Jet's time would be spent out of the office knocking on doors and pulling loose strings of inquiry, seeing where they led. But the office provided a stress-free environment where he could meet new clients, work through paperwork, and conduct research.

The suite's front glass door opened, and Jet's ten o'clock appointment stepped into the room. A middle-aged man with olive-brown skin who looked to be in his late thirties. His black hair was long, pulled into a ponytail behind his head.

Jet stood and came out from behind his desk. "Alex," he said, extending his hand.

"Mr. Jahner, good to meet you in person."

The men shook hands before Jet motioned toward one of the two leather chairs in front of his desk. "Please, have a seat. And call me Jet." He returned to his chair and folded his hands.

"I see you received the email I sent you," Alex said. He motioned toward the picture Jet had set down a few minutes earlier.

"A pretty girl," Jet said. "Missing for three months now?"

Alex nodded. "It will be twelve weeks tomorrow. She willingly got into a van that was supposedly going to take her to a job of some kind."

"And her brother? He saw the van?"

"Yes, he was watching from a vacant motel room window. He could only give the police a generic description of a man who got into the passenger seat. He couldn't remember any specifics about the van except that it was a dark color. No make or model."

Jet took out a yellow legal pad from his desk. "What's her brother's name?" he asked.

"Junior. Juanita told him she would be back in two

weeks. When she didn't show a few days after that, he came to me."

"You've known them for a while?"

"About four months before she disappeared. Some coyotes brought them and their mother across the Texas border a couple of years ago, if I remember correctly. The three of them ended up in Miami, living with the mother's sister who is a heroin addict. Their mother died of cancer last summer."

Jet scribbled across the paper. "Your email said something about a guy named Jesse?"

"Yes. Junior said a man by that name had been coming around as if he was interested in his sister. Like a boyfriend, I guess. He would bring McDonald's over to their house and take them to the movies. He's the one who got her this supposed job."

"Any idea what kind of work was proposed?" Jet asked.

"Not really," Alex said. "All she told her brother was that it was field work."

Jet took a sip from his coffee mug and nearly winced from the cold liquid. "I'm sorry," he said. "Can I get you something to drink?"

Alex held up a hand. "I'm fine. Thank you. I grabbed a coffee on my way up here."

Jet set his mug to the side. "Is there any chance she lied to her brother and had no intentions of coming back?"

Alex huffed in response. "Not a chance. She loved Junior very much."

"What did the case detective uncover?"

"Nothing," Alex said. "That is why I'm here. Their best guess was that she was sold. You know, human trafficking. They asked around for a few days and went through her things at her aunt's place. They even got some prints from a DVD case that this Jesse guy let them borrow. But the prints didn't return anything."

Jet noted the anxiety in the man's face. "This has been hard on you," he noted.

Alex tried to shrug it off with a half-hearted smile. "Yes," he admitted. "I started the shelter to help prevent things like this. Had someone told me that Juanita was spending time with a man, I would have made it my business to know something about him."

Jet was well aware that in cases like this there was a slim chance the victim would ever be found, assuming Juanita was still alive. Human trafficking was no longer a problem that simply occurred "over there." It didn't just happen in Thailand, or Brazil, or Singapore. The United States had seen a dramatic rise in human trafficking over the last decade. It was the new slavery, and Juanita fit the profile on all counts: an undocumented immigrant, in a poor area of town, with no parents. Unless a detective had cause for an emotional attachment to this case, after the initial inquiry, it would sit among a stack of files, unresolved and unpursued. Another uncleared case.

"Tell me more about your shelter," Jet asked. "Hope House? Is that right?"

"Yes. Hope House. We're coming up on our three year anniversary," he said proudly.

"Have you always been in non-profit work?"

Alex smiled and shook his head "No. Not at all. I am an immigrant myself. When I was a teenager, my family escaped Cuba during the Maleconazo."

Jet remembered the Cuban uprising well. In 1994,

due to the recent dissolution of the Soviet Union and old embargoes imposed by the United States, the Cuban economy had fallen into chaos. Thousands took to Havana's streets to protest the ham-fisted leadership. In the end, over 35,000 refugees fled the island, leading President Clinton to enact the Wet Feet Dry Feet Policy as a response to the massive exodus. The policy stated that any Cuban found on the waters between the U.S. and Cuba—with "wet feet"—would summarily be sent home. Anyone who made it to U.S. shores—with "dry feet"—would be given a chance to remain in the United States, later qualifying for legal resident status.

Jet nodded. "Of course. So your family became citizens?"

"Yes. But it was hard on my parents, leaving their country. Especially difficult for my father, who had been a dentist back home. Here in America, his degree was not accepted, and he struggled to find good work. When he died of a heart attack a couple of years later, I coped by joining a gang in South Miami. I was very angry about the death of my father and rose quickly in the leadership. Late one night I held up a couple coming out of a local restaurant." Alex's eyes darkened as he recalled the event. "The lady, she got very angry that her husband was handing over his wallet. She tried to slap my gun away by swinging her purse. So I shot her. Three times. They gave me twenty years for it."

"That's hard," Jet said.

Alex tossed his hands out. "We all make our choices. I made mine. Ten years in, I realized that I could stay angry or take responsibility for both my past and my future."

"That's something most people never learn," Jet

noted. He thought of all the drug dealers and pushers he had arrested over the years. All of them would recite perfectly good excuses for doing what was wrong. It was a rare occurrence when one would choose to accept the responsibility and the blame for where they had ended up. But that, as any prison psychologist would preach, was where change began. That was where the crooked paths became straight.

"You are right," Alex said. "I can honestly say now that prison made me a better person. But you asked about Hope House." He swung a leg over a knee and resettled into the seat. "A few years before I was up for parole, I decided I wanted to find a way to give back to the community I had wounded so many years ago. West Hialeah is an amazing place. It's less than ten miles from downtown Miami and has a vibrant Latino culture. Many wonderful people live there. But as all lower class neighborhoods, there are some areas that can also be very dangerous. Poverty seems to breed all forms of crime, and the gangs have started to increase their memberships again. When I was still on the inside, some good people heard about my vision and helped me get the right connections and funding for Hope House. The shelter gives them a safe place to be and keeps them off the streets. I bring mentors in too, who help to teach them what they are having trouble learning in school and for those who just won't go."

Jet set the pencil down and sat back in his chair. His gaze returned to the picture. He could feel something a little like anger growing inside his chest. "My oldest granddaughter is Juanita's age," he said, and looked back to Alex. "I'll find her."

CHAPTER SEVEN

His fingers shook as he stared at the computer screen.

He didn't want to do this. People had already gotten hurt. One, at least that he knew of, had been killed because of it all. And he wasn't even sure what "it all" was.

Doing this would endanger others, he knew. It would put them in the path of those who had already killed to cover up their secret. Whatever that secret was.

He stood up, walked to the window, and looked down at the marsh below. A ring-billed gull dove toward the surface of the water and disappeared behind the thick grasses. A moment later, the bird rose triumphantly, a small fish in its beak, then it coasted to the dock and drew up, landing its small talons on the old boards. It started in on its meal, pinching and tearing at the fish's flesh with its beak.

That's about right, he thought. And people were no different.

The anger, simmering deep in his chest, once again

began to boil within him, and for the moment overrode his fear.

He returned to the desk and sat down. What he was about to do would put good people in harm's way.

But doing nothing was no longer an option.

He took a deep breath, set his fingers on the keyboard, and began to type.

* * *

ELLIE PULLED a couple of fishing rods away from the wall and selected a tackle box from the top of the stack. Using her foot, she pushed open the storage room door and stepped out into the large, open space of the covered dry dock. Walking to the front from the rear of the building, she turned down an aisle that cut between steel racks laden with boats. She stepped into the sunlight through a side door and worked her way past a dozen boat slips before heading across the wide boardwalk to where it joined up with the pier. The Norma Jean pier was the southernmost structure on Pine Island and jutted eighty yards into the wind-blown waters of Pine Island Sound.

A father and his young daughter were bent over the wooden railing, looking down at the water. The girl brushed a strand of hair from her face and saw Ellie arriving with their fishing gear. "Look!" she said excitedly. "There's a manatee down there!"

Ellie stepped to the rail and looked over. Fifteen feet below, a sea cow was nestled up against a barnacle-covered piling, bobbing lazily in the water.

"We're visiting from Maine," said the father. "We don't get manatees up there."

"You're lucky to see him," Ellie said. "The water temperature is unusually warm for this time of year. They don't do well in cold water and by now are usually further south." A loud hiss came from below, and the young girl laughed as the manatee snorted. The father leaned back up and took the rods and the tackle from Ellie.

"You can turn them in at the bar when you're finished," she said. "And we have live bait if you're not bringing up enough with the lures."

The girl scrunched her face. "I don't like slimy bait," she said, and looked up at her father. "Can we just use the fake stuff?"

He chuckled. "Sure, sweetie."

Ellie winked at the girl. "I don't like slimy bait either."

"What's biting right now?" he asked.

"You can hit redfish and sheepshead pretty consistently right now. And if you drop at the end of the pier and have a little patience, you might bring up a tripletail. There's a guide in the tackle box that will help you pair lures with the fish you're going for."

They thanked Ellie and started making their way down the pier as she returned to the bar. The Salty Mangrove was the island's favorite restaurant and watering hole and had been owned by Ellie's uncle for the last nineteen years. It was a small wood-lapped building with a kitchen squeezed in between a tiki hut and an indoor seating area for the restaurant that was encircled by a wooden railing. Rolled patio curtains could be lowered when it rained.

It was late January, and that meant the busy season was in full swing. Sun-famished refugees from up north had completed their annual treks to Southwest Florida, fleeing the harsh winds and cold snows that inhibited golf, pickleball, and fishing.

Ellie had just opened the bar and noted how quiet it was. Fu and Gloria Wang, the only liveaboards at this end of the island, had left on a month-long cruise around the Caribbean and wouldn't be back for another couple weeks. Otherwise, they were permanent fixtures at the bar, sometimes arriving before it opened and always shutting the place down. Their absence had been felt as if someone had stolen a couple bar stools that had yet to be replaced. With Gloria around, there was rarely a quiet moment. She had a simple, but lively mind, and was prone to share whatever she might be thinking the instant it came to her. Fu's presence assured that someone was always around with a ready smile. He smiled with his eyes, and you couldn't look at him without wanting to smile yourself, like a yawn that was catching. One of the great oddities of the modern era was that Fu did not speak English, that somewhere along the line Gloria had undertaken to learn Mandarin. If Gloria wasn't around, there was just no talking to Fu. The Wangs were good people, and Ellie was beginning to miss them.

She squatted down and started to check the keg levels beneath the bar. Above her, she heard the distinctive sound of a hammer tapping a nail. She stood up. Major was in between a couple of bar stools, setting a nail into one of the pilings that formed the bar's support. The piling was wrapped in decorative rope, and he was introducing the nail a foot above the bar top.

"What's the nail for?" she asked.

He set the hammer down. "Come take a look."

Ellie's uncle, standing at just under six feet, was average in height, and his broad shoulders and thick forearms gave him a stocky appearance. His face was square, eyes set back under low brows, and he kept his graying auburn hair buzzed close to the scalp. His face held the deep, weathered lines that years near and on the water carved into a man. He wore cargo shorts and a blue, short-sleeved, button-down shirt and double-banded Birkenstocks. Without debate, he was a cornerstone in the structure of the local community. Major, whose given name was Warren Hall, chaired the Rotary Club, sponsored Little League teams, and contributed both time and money to Big Brothers Big Sisters and Meals on Wheels. More than once, he'd been nudged to take a run at the mayor's chair, but he valued simplicity too much to give it serious thought. He was a businessman and a small-time philanthropist, he would counter, not a politician.

Ellie stepped out from behind the bar and brushed past a string of year-round Christmas lights as she came around to the front of the tiki hut. Major placed a small picture frame on the nail and leaned back.

An ache surged through Ellie's chest as she looked at a photo of Nick. It was taken here at the bar. His face was turned to the side, and he was smiling as he spoke with someone off-camera while clutching a sweating bottle of Shiner, his favorite beer.

Ellie had driven to the Barlows' house early this morning and watched Kayla for Tiffany while she went to the crematorium to pick up her husband's ashes. Ellie had offered to accompany her, but Tiffany said it would be better if she did it alone. On her way back home, the detective in Miami had called Tiffany with an update.

He was still waiting on the toxicology report. They processed the room for prints and were still working through what came back, comparing any results with previous guests associated with the room rental and anyone who may have been connected to Nick in any way. Video footage from nearby security cameras or camera phones from those passing by or living in the penthouses across the street had yet to reveal a shot of Nick's balcony at the time of his fall. When pressed, the detective conceded that, unless something unusual turned up, they had no reason to think that foul play was a factor. Nick had not fallen far enough away from the building to suggest a hard push. It was, however, too early in the investigation to form a conclusion.

"Nick may have only lived down here a few months," Major said, "but anyone who met him loved him. He was the real deal."

Ellie turned to her uncle. Other than her father, she couldn't think of a better man. "That's kind," she said. "Where did you get the picture?"

"I was going through photos on my phone last night. Chloe, it seems, had swiped it when I wasn't looking and took a batch of random shots. Mostly goofy close-ups of herself."

"Chloe took that?" Chloe was her sister's six-year-old daughter.

"She did. Might be the next Leibovitz if she stays with it." He picked the hammer back up. "I'm off to get the Contender ready. Carlos and I are heading to a cut I found off Cayo Costa. There's some big tarpon hiding in there that seem to think they're safe from me."

"Well, don't let Carlos drive the boat back. And don't let him fall overboard again," Ellie said.

Carlos Hernández was the founder of HedgeTex, an electronic brokerage firm with offices in every state save Wisconsin and Alaska. His personal stake in the company put his net worth over ninety million dollars, easily making him one of the wealthiest men in Lee County. He made regional headlines last month after pledging a million dollars of his own money to food pantries across the state. His giving habits were generally kept out of the spotlight, but he had publicized the pledge in an effort to compel others to donate with him. Carlos came from humble beginnings, his family immigrating from Honduras when he was a small boy. His parents did their best to provide for their six children, but there were days they went without meals, only eating what little they received from the generosity of friends and what their local food pantries could offer. Carlos had been the only one of his siblings to finish college and start his own business. He never did forget his small beginnings, and now that he was enjoying the kind of financial success most only dream of, he had turned his attention more toward philanthropy, recently stepping down as HedgeTex's CEO and being content to simply chair the board. He was a poster child for the American dream. His only weakness seemed to be a proclivity toward drinking a little too much whenever he went out on the water.

"He still claims he meant to fall over last time," Major said, and headed for the docks. "Thanks for holding things down for me."

Ellie spent the next few minutes rearranging the liquor bottles on the back wall. Major had a habit of pouring drinks and setting the bottles back in a slipshod manner.

"Excuse me. Could I get a little service here?"

Ellie turned to see a tall man towering over the bar, an expansive smile exposing large white teeth. Carlos was nearly six-and-a-half feet tall, had the arms and chest of a lumberjack and a neck that probably wouldn't snap if a truck ran over it. The top of his bald head nearly scraped the edges of the palm fronds that hung over the edge of the hut's roof.

"Carlos. How are you?" Ellie said.

His deep voice resonated across the bar. "Well, I've fled the confines of my office, and heaven has donated its weather to us. If I can just outfish your uncle, it will be the perfect day."

"Well, good luck with that," she said. "Major's getting the boat ready. You want a drink while you wait?"

"I'll take a Miller if you've got one back there."

"Indeed." Ellie opened the refrigerator behind her and grabbed a can. She popped the tab for him and handed it over. He took a long, slow draw as Ellie spoke. "Major tells me the gala will be well attended."

Two months ago, Major had convinced Carlos to sponsor a gala that would benefit children's cancer research. He had worked tirelessly with the staff from Carlos's foundation to make the event a reality. One hundred people who were somebody in the upper echelons of the society would be attending at five thousand dollars a plate. Once the evening got off the blocks, there would be an auction, where the winner would have an opportunity, at a future date, to put Carlos underwater by means of a dunk tank, right here at The Salty Mangrove. Ellie had liked that idea, thinking that dunk tanks should be revived as an instrument for community entertainment. Secretly, she wanted a chance to get Major on the seat and have a few throws of her own.

Carlos swallowed before he replied. "It will be a fun night, Ellie. Warren has been very passionate about it. You're coming too, right?"

"I wouldn't miss it. Besides, I'm his date."

"Lucky man." Carlos looked over to his left and frowned. "Where are Fu and Gloria? I thought they were screwed down to these two stools right here."

"They unhinged themselves long enough to go on a cruise," Ellie said.

"No kidding."

"Stranger things have not happened," she said.

A shrill whistle came from the docks. Major was on the deck of the Contender, waving at Carlos. "I'd better go," he said. "When your uncle is ready, he's ready. He's left me before." He chugged the rest of his beer and set the empty can down.

"Have a good time," Ellie said. "And try to stay on the boat this time." She watched him make his way across the boardwalk and step on board, then waved goodbye to Major as he steered out of the marina and into the sound.

Katie, her younger sister by two years, appeared around the side of the building and stepped behind the bar. "Hey, sorry I'm late," she said. "I had a meeting with Chloe's teacher, and it went long."

"Everything good?

"Yeah. She's just struggling with some of her reading assignments." Katie rubbed her hands together. "So, what needs to be done?"

Major had left a notepad on the counter. Ellie ran a finger down the list. "Looks like...being on time."

Katie shriveled her nose at her. "Smartass."

"Why don't you grab some limes and quarter them for the garnishes?"

"On it." Katie disappeared into the kitchen.

Ellie's phone buzzed in her shorts' pocket, and she drew it out. The screen showed an email notification with no subject. She opened her Gmail app and waited for it to load.

She rearranged a couple more liquor bottles and glanced down. Her shoulders tensed as she read the first line:

Your friend, Nick. It wasn't an accident. He was murdered.

CHAPTER EIGHT

ELLIE STARED WIDE-EYED at her phone, disbelieving, thinking she was the recipient of some sick prank until she read on:

> *Nick stumbled onto something he shouldn't have. Go talk to Avi Narrano and ask him what he knows about Breakwater. He did some work with Nick and can be trusted. Let me know what he says.*
>
> *It's not safe to go to the police.*
>
> ***BE CAREFUL.*** *Whoever killed Nick is still out there.*

There was no signature, no name, fake or otherwise, taking credit for the correspondence. Ellie noted the sender's address: justicefornick@gmail.com. *Hokey*, she thought. But it communicated.

In the week since Nick fell to his death, Tiffany had been resolute that Nick had not killed himself. Tyler had yet to budge from the same position. And that, of course, left only two other scenarios: an unfortunate accident or murder. There were no other possibilities.

Ellie's mind was swirling as she stared at the email. Whoever sent this apparently possessed information that no one else did. Somehow they thought they knew what really happened to Nick. She rubbed her forehead as she re-read the email.

She knew that finding out who sent this would be an impossibility. Gmail accounts were untraceable, with any information that came with the email referencing Google's own servers. Only a warrant would provide access to those.

But why had they sent it to her? And how had they known her personal email address?

Ellie had worked for the CIA for over a decade, eight of those years as a black-ops agent based out of Brussels. The Agency had ingrained a full range of skills into her until she was a walking Swiss Army knife. One of those skills had been analyzing information—looking at something from every angle, attending to every detail and nuance.

Now, her mind churned as she analyzed each word, every phrase, looking for anything that might surrender a personality or even a specific person. But nothing stood out. The email was intentionally generic, and she saw no immediate clue that might help her pinpoint who the sender might be.

A voice from behind her pulled her from her thoughts. "Ellie?"

She turned around to face her sister, whose dark brown hair contrasted against her blonde. "Good Lord," Katie said. "Are you okay? I haven't seen you look that sick since I outfished you last week."

Ellie blinked. "I need to head out for a while. Are you good to hold things down here?"

"Of course. What's going on?"

"I'm not sure."

Katie eyed her sister. "You're worrying me a little bit."

"I'm fine. But you're good if I leave?"

"Go on, get out of here. Just call me later and let me know you're okay."

Ellie nodded absently. "I will." Then she walked out of the bar and down the ramp to her car.

* * *

When she pulled on the handle to the glass door, Ellie nearly bumped into a man as he came out. She smiled a hello and stepped back to allow him to walk through before she went in.

Jet was sitting behind his desk. He was fit for his age, his toned muscles filling out his polo, his silver hair giving him a distinguished appearance that complemented a sober and disciplined personality.

"New client?" she asked, using her head to motion toward the parking lot.

"It seems that way."

"He lose his cat or something?"

"Funny girl. You here to tell me you're finally going to come work with me?"

"Funny man," she retorted, settling into the seat Alex had been in moments before. "What are you doing for him?"

"He runs a shelter down in Miami. A girl in the neighborhood went missing." He picked the photo up and turned it toward her. "Two months ago," he added.

Ellie glanced at the image. "She's pretty."

"And in a situation like this," Jet said, "that's not a good thing."

"He's from Miami? Why didn't he get a PI from over there?"

"Already did. Twice. The first guy ended up flying up to New York to work an angle on an existing case and couldn't give it the time. The second guy couldn't turn up anything after supposedly working on it for a week. Alex, the man who just left, has a friend in law enforcement over there who told him about me. I'm familiar enough with the area, so it should be a good fit." There was a Keurig perched on a narrow console table against the wall. Jet pushed away from the desk and walked over to it. He pulled up the lever and removed the old pod, tossed it into a small trash can. "Coffee?"

"No. Thanks. How's he affording you if he runs a shelter?"

"One of his donors didn't like the idea that the detective assigned to the case was coming up short. As in, nothing but the first name of a guy who hasn't been seen since." Jet set a fresh coffee pod into the slot and shut the lever. He pushed the button, and the coffee maker slowly gurgled to life. He turned around and crossed his arms. "That said, you're really not here to throw in your hat with me?"

"Not yet," she said. "But you should know that the winds are blowing stronger in that direction." She held up her phone. "I need you to look at something. Do you remember my friend who died a couple of weeks ago?

"Of course. Nick, right?"

Ellie leaned forward and handed the phone to him. Jet's reading glasses hung from a thin chain around his neck. He set them on his nose and palmed the phone, frowning deeper the longer he looked at the screen. He read the email several times before handing the device back and removing his glasses.

"You first," he said.

"It helps to explain Nick's behavior before he died. He was anxious about something. We all brushed it off as stress from a new job. Looking back now, I probably should have known better."

The coffee maker stopped. Jet grabbed the mug and returned to his seat. "Any ideas who sent it?"

She shook her head. "Had to be someone in his broader work circle."

"What's Breakwater?"

"A local construction company. But I called Nick's wife. She handled Nick's books and said he hadn't done anything for them."

Jet drummed his fingers on his desk. "I'm not sure I like the note saying that the police might not be safe."

"Me either."

"That can only mean a couple of things," Jet said. "Dirty cops or whoever sent you this doesn't want any heat coming from the authorities. I assume you need me to look up who and where this Avi Narrano is?"

"I only have Google available to me these days, and that didn't return anything I can use. He doesn't exist on the internet."

Jet returned his glasses to his nose and scooted his chair in. He entered his password into his laptop, and Ellie stood and paced the office while she waited.

"Okay, here," Jet finally said. The printer hummed behind him. He waited for the paper to spit out and then snatched it up and handed it to Ellie. "That's the only Avi Narrano I could find within three counties. You're lucky you weren't told to go talk with John Smith or Jose Lopez."

The printout showed a name with basic information: name, date of birth, and, more importantly, an address in Bonita Springs. "Any work information?" Ellie asked.

"That's all I could pull up." Jet eyed Ellie. "You can't go get involved with this by yourself. If Nick really was killed, then you have no idea what you're walking into. I know plenty of good cops I could take this to."

"Take what to?" Ellie said. "We have one email from who-knows-who stating an opinion. Besides, you know how police corruption works. The good cops start poking around, and the bad ones catch wind of it."

Jet sighed. "Let me go with you."

"I can take this step myself. I'm going to someone's house, and you have the address. If I'm murdered on his front steps, send flowers to my sister." She held up the printout as she turned toward the door. "Thanks for this."

"Ellie."

She paused.

"Be careful."

* * *

The address Jet provided brought Ellie into a quiet suburban street on the east side of Bonita Springs that sat up against Bird Rookery Swamp. The lots were large, the homes small, and Ellie found the one she was looking for at the back end of a cul-de-sac. The front yard had a slight grade that slanted up toward the front porch. It was full of children's toys: dart guns, a soccer ball, a tricycle, and a few plastic cups that looked like they had been used to dig in the dirt.

When she rang the doorbell, Ellie heard a gaggle of children erupt from inside. The front blinds shuffled and parted as a small boy stuck his nose onto the glass and stared at Ellie like he wanted her to break him out. A woman's commanding voice was cause for the boy's disappearance, and the blinds returned to normal. The door opened, and a portly Hispanic woman was balancing a baby on her hip. Four small children gathered around her knees and looked expectantly at their guest. The woman looked at Ellie impassively, as if she were anticipating a sales pitch for a new cable or electric service. Gray strands shot through her black hair, and Ellie pegged her for a busy grandmother or a babysitter who was in over her head. She yelled something in Spanish to the children, and they fled back into the house. "Can I help you?"

"Yes," Ellie said. "I'm sorry to bother you. I was wondering if Avi was available."

"Avi? No. He's at work." Then she snapped at a child who was trying to escape across the threshold. "Is something wrong?"

"No, ma'am. Nothing's wrong." On the drive here Ellie had considered the best way to approach the topic. She didn't know who Avi was, who he worked for, or what kind of work he did. All she knew was that at some point he had crossed professional paths with Nick. "A friend of mine," Ellie said, "Nick Barlow—he did some work with Avi. He died early last week down in Miami.

I was hoping I could ask Avi a few questions about Nick."

Her brow creased. "Please wait a minute." She shut the door. Ellie waited patiently, enduring fresh stares from the hopeful escapee and wishing for both of them that someone would wipe his slimy nose. When the door opened again, the baby was no longer on the woman's hip but was crawling on the floor behind her, clutching a small bag of potato chips that spilled with each motion. "Avi is my husband. He's on a job site right now. I told him what you said. He said if you like you can go to the job and talk with him. I am Irene, by the way."

"Thank you, Irene. That would be great." The older lady recited her husband's location, and Ellie punched it into her phone.

"You know," Irene said, "I remember Avi telling me about your friend dying. He had a fall?"

"Yes, ma'am."

Irene smiled kindly. "I am very sorry. Avi said he liked working with your friend. He was upset when he heard that he had died."

Ellie thanked her and returned to her truck. She had just started the engine when a bright orange dart slapped the windshield and fell into the road. Ellie caught a glimpse of a small boy hiding behind a bush and reloading his plastic rifle. A little girl wearing only a diaper trotted out the front door and mounted a tricycle, her plump face full of joy.

If only the world were as simple as dart guns and tricycles, Ellie thought. Irene reappeared in the doorway and barked at the children to come back inside. Ellie gave her a goodbye wave and slowly accelerated down the street.

CHAPTER NINE

Victor Cruz sat in the driver's seat of his Toyota Tundra and debated whether to get out of the vehicle. He knew it would be easier if he didn't.

He watched through the windshield as a dozen children scampered across the playground and haphazardly distributed their time between the swing set, the slides, and the monkey bars. A little girl picked up a handful of pebbles and hurled them toward the slide. She was quickly scolded by her mother and redirected to the swings. A boy who looked to be seven or eight ran up the steps of the slide and flung himself recklessly down it as a playmate chased him earnestly from behind.

On the far side of the playground was a sandy area where children could dig for replica dinosaur bones. The sand pit was shaded beneath a canvas awning, and several adults stood along on the sidewalk or on nearby benches as they watched their children play.

Cruz put a stop to the internal debate and exited his truck. The playground was fenced in, designed to contain little balls of human energy. Cruz flipped the gate latch, stepped to the other side, and the gate clattered shut behind him as he made his way to the digging pit.

He stopped behind a lady with shoulder-length brown hair. She had a small backpack slung over one shoulder where a Power Rangers cup was tucked into a side mesh pocket. She was involved with her phone, pecking away with her thumbs.

"Abby."

She turned toward Cruz, her face quickly showing alarm. Her forehead wrinkled in irritation, and when she spoke, it was through gritted teeth. "Victor, what are you doing here?" She glanced nervously back at her boy, who was kneeling in the dirt, singularly focused on finding relics from a distant past.

"Abby. Can we talk?"

"Here? You pick here, now, to talk?"

"You won't answer my calls."

She crossed her arms across her chest. "What do you want?"

Cruz looked over her shoulder to the boy. "I want to see him."

"No."

"He's my son, Abby."

"No," she repeated. "You should have thought about that before you beat up that man. He's still in a wheelchair in case you didn't know."

Cruz felt a surge of fury rise up within him. He swallowed hard. "How many times do I have to tell you I'm sorry? That man, as you call him, his name is Mario. And *he* has forgiven me. Why can't you?"

"Now is not the time for all this."

"Then when? I want to be a part of my child's life."

"I don't want my son knowing that his father beats people until they're paralyzed. I don't want him knowing he has a father who went to prison." She glared at him. "Things are different now. You scare me. I don't want you around either one of us."

"Abby, it hasn't happened before or since. I love him, and I love you."

She huffed indignantly. "Don't ever say that again."

"Give me another chance."

"Why? So one day you can get angry enough to put one of *us* in the hospital?"

"No. That thing with Mario. It...it was different."

And it had been different. For the better part of twenty years, Cruz had managed his anger. It was something that seemed to have always been there, nearly as far back as he could remember. It started to fester when he was six, after his father left and never came back. The man who he thought loved him left him rejected and abandoned, with an ever-diminishing hope that he might one day return. So the fights at school began and, along with them, too many detentions and suspensions to count. His mother, like a bird who could only sing one tune, would tell him to shape up and get his head right before he found himself somewhere he didn't want to be. But he couldn't stop. He was angry, and a boiling pot had to vent.

He was a sophomore in high school when a man whose name he couldn't remember spoke at assembly one afternoon about taking control of your past and setting your own course. Only then did things start to change. Cruz listened, and though he left school that day unable to recall the specifics of the talk, he walked home with a fresh sense of hope about his future.

He joined a local gym, and the punching bag became his best friend. It was there that he took out his displeasure. It was there that he exorcised his demons until he had nothing else to give, and he finished lathered in sweat, his knuckles often bleeding through the cloth wrap.

The workouts kept the violence at bay even if he never discovered how to pluck up its root. He graduated high school and, after moving from job to job, finally started an auto repair shop, which he ran successfully for nearly a decade. Until his landlord sold the building to a commercial developer. Cruz had been unable to find a new location suitable for his shop, and he was left doing small repair jobs for old customers out of a friend's suburban garage. He became increasingly frustrated, desperate for something better to come along.

And it did. During a weekend trip to Miami, an old friend schooled him in the endless possibilities of stealing cars, stripping them, and parting them out to local buyers. The proposal held enough charm to compel Cruz to make the move from Orlando to Miami, and, instead of repairing cars, he went into the business of taking them apart.

And business was good. Soon he was making more in three days than he used to bring in over the span of three months. He met Abby, she moved in with him, and they were together for two years before she announced one day that she was pregnant.

Life was finally shaping into something worthwhile: money was easy to come by, he had a steady girlfriend, a child on the way, and was well respected among those in his small, tight-knit community.

There was, however, that perennial problem. When

he moved to Miami, a decent gym was too far out of the way for him to attend regularly. He no longer had that outlet of release, and now all that was needed was the right set of circumstances to make his anger blow.

And blow it did.

One Friday evening, as dusk began to set over Florida's largest city, Cruz found himself scouting a white Impala parked outside a tattoo parlor. He watched as the car's owner went inside without bothering to lock it. He would be gone in three minutes, be hidden in a garage three blocks away in five, and have the car stripped and pieced out within thirty.

He walked down the street, tools in hand, watching for passing police cruisers when Mario Diaz—his competition—materialized from behind the donut shop adjacent to the tattoo parlor. Mario was closer to the Impala, and when he locked eyes with Cruz, he smiled a silent provocation. The car would be his.

But Cruz did not redirect; he did not back down. By the time he reached the car, Mario had already opened the door and was about to slide in when Cruz grabbed him by the shirt collar and yanked him around.

The men exchanged harsh words charged with malice and intent, neither man willing to back down. Mario got in Cruz's face and released a torrent of insults amid a string of expletives. The Impala was now forgotten, and both men were seconds from blows when Mario changed tactics and informed Cruz that if he didn't walk away immediately, then Mario would be paying Abby a little visit. He concluded that, when he was done with her, the baby might be an additional casualty.

Cruz's anger had always hovered below the surface,

boiling and sloshing along caverns deep within. It was Mario who pulled the plug and sent it spewing.

Cruz unleashed two decades of pent-up wrath into Mario's body, cracking bones, tearing skin, and bruising flesh. When Mario finally lay in a pitiful pile at his feet, Cruz picked him up and folded his back across his knee. A half-dozen people poured from the tattoo parlor, but by the time three men pulled Cruz off Mario, it was too late. Mario's back was broken.

Cruz was arrested and sent to jail, while Mario went to the hospital. During Cruz's short stint in prison, Mario found religion. He came to visit Cruz and, even though the doctors said he would never walk again, offered forgiveness to the man who had taken away the use of his legs. He then apologized for his own provocation.

Now, as Cruz looked into the scornful eyes of the lady he once thought he would spend the rest of his life with, he saw only bitterness and hatred, all of it generated by, and directed toward, him.

"Please," he said again. "I've dealt with it all. I'm not like that anymore."

Her tone was defiant, if not combative. "It doesn't matter," she said. "It's in you, Victor. You just don't get rid of something like that."

In the sand pit, the little boy jumped up and looked around for his mother. When his eyes fell on her, he dropped his plastic trowel and ran to her, sand falling off him like hundreds of tiny mites.

Abby stepped in front of the boy, trying to shield him from his father. "Nino, go back and play. Now."

Nino clung to the back of her leg, and his head popped out from around her. He stared up at Cruz and contorted his face. "Who are you?" he asked. "Your eye looks creepy."

"Nino!" his mother snapped. "Go play. *Now*."

Cruz smiled down on the boy but did not speak to him.

"What happened to your eye?" Nino asked. But he was too busy ducking his mother's swats to wait for a reply. He let go of her leg and darted back to the sandbox, where the fake fossils quickly regained his attention.

Cruz silently agreed with the boy. His right eye was unsightly. Sometimes, when he looked in the mirror, he didn't even recognize himself. He went into prison with two good eyes. But those first weeks inside, when you have to choose sides, he chose wrong. Five men assaulted him in the showers, and, after breaking three ribs and bruising a kidney that had him peeing blood for five weeks, one of them grabbed him by the back of the neck and slammed his face into the shower knob. His eyes took the brunt of the trauma, and it never did heal right. The lively green that still filled his left eye had disappeared in his right, replaced by a colorless and soulless white. He was now legally blind in that eye, and some had suggested he cover it with an eye patch. It didn't help matters that his nose was swollen and misshapen—the consequence of too many schoolyard fights—and looked as if an entire hive of bees had worked it over with their stingers. He wasn't going to make things worse by trying for a pirate look.

Abby looked away. "You need to go," she said.

"Why does it have to be this way?"

"*Why does it have to be this way?*" Abby's tone was ripe with indignation. She stepped closer to him. "I'll tell you why. Because you won't be honest with me about what you do." Her eyes bore into his. "You said someone helped get you a lighter sentence. Fine. But you won't tell me who. And you won't tell me just what they have you doing. What *is* the work you do, Victor?"

"You know I can't tell you that."

And that was why, no matter what he said to Abby, he knew he would never get time with his son. He was not free. He was, for all intents and purposes, someone else's slave. And how it happened was as unexpected as Miami snow.

He had not been in jail for two weeks when his name was called by a guard. He had a visitor. A dark man in a gray suit with a cold and determined disposition. A man he had never seen before spoke to Cruz about a man he had never heard of.

The agreement was simple: Cruz would be provided the best lawyer money could buy. His sentence, instead of a lengthy twelve years, would be reduced to a bearable three. He could put his mistake behind him and no longer concern himself with cellmates, handcuffs, and prison food.

The conditions of this Faustian bargain were straightforward. The nine years cut off Cruz's sentence would now be in the employment of the man fronting the lawyer. Cruz would be paid well. He never did ask about the nature of the work. He didn't have to. There was a clear and unspoken understanding that the work would be illicit.

He said yes.

Cruz had been released nearly a year ago now, and Abby still would not let him see his son. Not once did she visit him in prison, not even after the baby was born. So he would find himself driving by the daycare during pickup or parking down the street from their apartment so he could get a glimpse of three-year-old Nino playing outside.

He couldn't tell Abby what he did. And you didn't walk away from an agreement with Miguel Zedillo. Two others had tried, and both they and their families had disappeared like a bad magic trick.

Now, Abby stood before him, glaring.

"I owe him," Cruz continued. "I wouldn't even be standing here speaking with you if it wasn't for him."

"And yet, you won't tell me who *he* is. You haven't changed at all. Leave now, or I will call the police."

Cruz raised his hands, conceding defeat. "Okay." He took a final glance at his son and turned to walk away. He paused. "You know, a lot of fathers aren't even interested in seeing their kids. I want to get to know mine. I never knew my father."

"Then you shouldn't have gotten locked up in the first place. When you can tell me what you're involved with now, then maybe I'll think about it. Until then, don't come near us again."

"I'm sorry I hurt you." Then, with a final glance at his son, Victor walked away. He got back into his Tundra and wrapped his fingers tightly around the steering wheel until his knuckles were white. He breathed heavily through his nose as his chest rose and fell in great heaves of anger.

He closed his eyes. The old patterns of anger had diminished, but he could feel them begin to stir once again. He wanted to go back out to the playground and tell Abby that she couldn't keep her son from him. He wanted to grab the boy's hand, snatch him away, and take him to go get ice cream or to a movie. At very least he would teach him that the Power Rangers were weak and introduce him to real superheroes like Batman or Guardians of the Galaxy. But the truth was, he couldn't do that. The courts sent him to prison and Nino to his mother.

Cruz started the truck and took a final look toward the sand pit. He drove out of the parking lot and forced himself to put his son out of his mind.

He had work to do.

CHAPTER TEN

It was a flawless January afternoon in Southwest Florida. The deep blue sky was cloudless, the salt-infused air a perfect seventy-seven degrees, weather that could make anyone but Tyler wish they were out on the water with a rod in their hands. In the twenty minutes since she had left Irene to suffer from the scourge of tiny children, Ellie had circulated a dozen profiles through her mind, trying to paint a mental image of the anonymous sender of her email. She had a fleeting vision of an old man in a wheelchair who lived on Ramen noodles and Diet Dr. Pepper and kept half a dozen cats in an ill-lighted apartment. She imagined a thirty-year-old with Cheetos-stained fingers who lived in the back of his mother's house and stayed up playing Fortnite until four every morning. But profiling aside, she continued to question why she was sent to do the legwork. Why couldn't the sender go visit Avi? And why get her involved at all?

Google Maps informed her that she had arrived at her location—the eastern end of an office complex whose architecture, with its insistent angles and sharply tapered roof lines, dated back to the 1970s. The one-story building before her was hemmed in with oleander, and a small yard at the front was bisected by a sidewalk leading to the front door. Several work vans filled parking spaces along the front curb, all but one of them with ladders tethered to their roof racks.

A realtor's lockbox hung from the handle on the front door. Ellie tried the door and, finding it unlocked, stepped inside to a large reception area. High vaulted ceilings inset with half a dozen skylights drew in natural light from outside. A man in dusty jeans and a gray t-shirt was up on a scissor lift, taping the seams of newly installed sheetrock. The bare concrete floors retained the scars from old glue that had been scraped up and swept away. Ellie moved further in and caught the man's attention.

He removed his trowel from the wall and looked down. "You need something?"

"I'm looking for Avi."

"Avi?" He turned and pointed to a closed door on Ellie's left. "He's down that way somewhere." She waved her thanks and turned the door handle as she went in. The room smelled powerfully of drywall compound, and Ellie noticed the walls had recently been sprayed with an orange peel finish. She passed up a bathroom and a small kitchen area before coming out into an open room where three men were busy installing new panels into the ceiling grid. A radio in the corner was blaring Tejano music, with its distinctive combination of accordion, bajo sexto, and drums filling the room. A short, thin man with dark hair and a well-trimmed mustache noticed her, and his brows lifted in some sort of recognition as if he had been expecting her.

She spoke loudly over the music. "Avi?"

He set down a stack of ceiling tiles before saying something to his co-worker, who went over to the radio and turned down the volume. He brushed his hands down his pants as he came over to Ellie. "You spoke with my wife?" His English was filtered through a heavy Spanish accent.

"Yes. I'm sorry to interrupt you on a job."

He waved her off. "It's not a problem. You were a friend of Nick's?"

Ellie observed the men still working behind him. "Can we talk down the hall?" she asked. He indicated for her to lead the way. She waited until they were nearly at the front before speaking. "I understand that you worked with Nick on a couple of jobs?"

"Yes. We mostly do framing, and he was an electrician, but we crossed paths on a lot of jobs ever since he moved here. We had lunch together quite a number of times. He was a nice man. I was very sorry to hear he died."

Ellie didn't like being in the dark. *Go talk to Avi Narrano....He can be trusted.* Maybe if she knew who was behind the email, if she knew why Nick had been so anxious before he died, then she might feel a little better about being here. Finding out the truth would require a leap of faith, hoping it didn't end with her sharing the same fate as Nick. The only way to move ahead was on the assumption that Avi could be trusted. A mental glimpse of a grieving Tiffany and a confused little Kayla prompted her next words. "Have you ever done any work for Breakwater?"

Avi's furrowed brow revealed his surprise at the question. "Breakwater? Yes. But not for a long time. Why?"

Great question. She decided to deflect. "You don't do any work for them anymore?"

"Oh, no." He shook his head emphatically. "Not for...two years maybe? They were a good company for a long time. Back then they were called Garwood. Garwood Construction. But they changed owners, and the new ones—they started doing business in a way I didn't like."

"How do you mean?" she asked.

Avi scratched at the thin layer of stubble on his chin while he chose his next words. "A couple of times they asked me to invoice them for some work I didn't do. Like once I installed some sheetrock for them in a new country club in Bonita Springs. They asked me to invoice them for some of the painting too. But I don't do painting."

"Why do you think they would ask something like that?"

"I think maybe they were having money problems and were trying to write more taxes off. But it made me uncomfortable. I was trying to get my citizenship and didn't want any problems. They asked some other people I know to do something like that too, but none of them did it either."

"Do you remember the names of the new owners?"

"No. I only dealt with one of the project managers. Caleb. But I hear he died of cancer last year. I think Breakwater is pretty small now. Why are you interested?"

Ellie decided to stretch the truth until she knew what

she was dealing with. "Nick did some work for them, but I'm not sure they were paying him fairly. His wife is just trying to collect on the final jobs he did."

Avi nodded as though he understood. "You know," he said, "if you want to know more about Breakwater, you should go see Barry Corbin. He worked for Garwood for many years. Even for a little while after they became Breakwater."

"Barry Corbin?" she repeated. The name scratched at the back of her mind like it was trying to escape from a dark room, as though she heard it before. But nothing clicked in place.

"Yes. He left after the company changed owners, but he could probably tell you a lot more than I can."

"Thank you. I'll do that."

"You know," Avi said, "Nick was telling me he was speaking at some breakout sessions at that convention in Miami. It's really strange what happened to him."

"Yes," she said, "it is." And then she decided to take a step further. "When was the last time you saw him?"

"The day before he died. When I heard what happened it didn't seem all the way real, you know? I just talked with him the day before."

"Did he seem different than usual?"

Avi thought about it for a moment. "No. He was very, you know... laid back. That is how Nick always was. I saw him right before lunch, and he seemed fine to me."

"Did you remember what you talked about?"

"He was telling me how his little girl is starting to learn piano. I told him a couple of things about my grandchildren." He shrugged. "I think that was all."

"Thank you," she said. "Do you know where Breakwater's offices are?"

"No. They moved from their old place in Cape Coral. I don't know where to. Like I said, they're pretty small now. I was not sure they were even still in business."

"Can I give you my number?" she asked. "If you hear of anything about Breakwater, would you mind calling me?"

"Sure."

By the time Ellie drove out of the office complex, she had already decided to wait and speak with Barry Corbin before sending back a reply to the email. She didn't like the idea of being someone's gopher, someone's private snoop, especially for one who wasn't willing to reveal anything about themselves. They might have a good reason for staying in the shadows, but since she didn't know what that reason was, it held no weight with her. Waiting until after she spoke with Barry would at least keep her a step ahead.

Right where she wanted to be.

CHAPTER ELEVEN

TYLER'S stilt house sat on three acres, north of Burnt Store, just south of Charlotte Harbor Preserve. Ellie turned her truck off Acapulco Road onto a pea-pebble driveway, which curved a path through thick growth on either side before bringing visitors to a wide, open area where the house was perched. The yard was full of wild grasses that Tyler kept mowed down, and his back yard sat on the edge of a marsh that overlooked Gasparilla Sound and the Gulf of Mexico beyond. A narrow dock started at the end of the yard and ran ten yards into the marsh. And because it belonged to Tyler, there was no boat in sight. When he purchased the house two years ago, it had a small front porch at the top of the stairs with barely enough room to fit a couple of outdoor chairs. He had quickly rectified that by spending the next couple of months adding a wrap-around porch to the entire house, with a shingled roof over the rear section.

Citrus, Ellie's exuberant Jack Russell, was on the passenger seat with his paws on the side of the door, whining excitedly as though he had just arrived in heaven. Ellie turned off the truck and was in the process of telling her dog to wait a moment when he leaped past her face and over the steering wheel. He misjudged his landing point, and his chin whacked the side of the door on his way down, flipping him so he landed on his head, his rear end following after. He stood up slowly, sat, and stared quizzically at the gravel. Ellie got out, and when she shut the door to the truck, Citrus startled and looked up at her, dazed.

"Hi," she said. "I'm your owner. Remember me? I was trying to tell you to wait."

He pawed at his nose and whined. A pelican drifted low overhead, and the dog's stupor suddenly vanished. Citrus's head snapped up, and he yipped at the bird as it glided toward the salt marsh. His ears perked, and he darted toward the water, onto the dock, and, like a defective windsurfer, belly flopped into the water.

Ellie took the front steps to the top, where a woodstock Ruger 10/22 was leaning against the porch rail. As she pulled open the wood-framed screen door, its rusted spring protested loudly. It was, she had decided long ago, one of her favorite sounds in the world. You could hear the sound of a screen door creaking open and slapping shut just about anywhere and feel like you had just come home.

The inside boasted an open floor plan with no walls to separate the kitchen, the living room, and the dining room. Large casement windows provided a nearly 360-degree view of the surrounding forest, marshes, and Gasparilla Sound. She could see Tyler on the back porch, leaning up against the rail, and she made her way across the tile floors and joined him.

He had an old coffee can in his left hand. It was full of pebbles, and he was picking them out one by one, tossing them lazily over the rail where they landed at the edge of the yard and bounced to the waterline. Citrus was still swimming happily in the marsh.

"Hey," Tyler said. "Your dog didn't ask if he could swim in my pool."

"From the looks of it, you haven't cleaned it in a while."

"I guess it'll be all right then."

Leaving the can on the railing, Tyler stepped over to a compact refrigerator sitting next to a wicker couch and withdrew a beer while Ellie settled into a cushion. He picked up his bottle opener—a customized .50 caliber brass casing with a tapered cut in the side—and popped the top. He handed the bottle to Ellie, but not before he leaned across and gave her a prolonged kiss. Ellie closed her eyes, relishing the warmth of his mouth on hers.

He smiled after they pulled away. "I needed that," he said, then leaned down and grabbed an open beer sitting near his feet.

"Me too." Ellie tucked her feet beneath her and for the first time tonight noticed Tyler's hair. "You get a haircut?"

"Yeah." He looked up and ran a hand across his head. "Gail usually cuts it, but she was out this week. I figured I'd go ahead though since, you know, some people thought I looked like I was in a boy band. You like it?"

It was uneven on top, and the sides didn't seem to blend well. "What was the name of the girl who cut it this time?"

"Fran. Why?"

"Is Fran blind?"

"What?"

Ellie pursed her lips together. "Maybe you should just find your hat."

"Whatever. I'll bet my mama would like it."

Ellie looked at the bottle's label. "What's this one?"

"That…is an IPA from a cool little microbrewery in Bradenton."

She took a slow pull and savored the taste of bitter hops mingled with hints of orange. "I like it." Out in front of them, a blue heron swooped down and landed gracefully at the edge of the marsh. Ellie loved it out here. She felt like she was on the edge of the earth. Dusk was beginning to set in, the sun hovering over the horizon, preparing to dissolve into the ocean as it continued its eternal dance with the darkness. Palmettos rustled against the side of the house, and the sea grasses bent and bowed in the marsh, obeying the wind. "Hey, what's the .22 doing on your front porch?" she asked.

"Some wild hogs ran through here before I left for work this morning. I waited for them so I could get in a few headshots, but they never did circle back. I set it back out after I got home." He laid his empty bottle on the deck at his feet. "I was talking to Tiffany earlier today," he said. "She's not doing so great."

"Yeah," Ellie said quietly.

"Hell, I'm not either," he said, and then sighed deeply. "I hate this. Tiff's going to have to start over, and Nick won't ever get to see his daughter grow up and get married. What the hell happened?"

Ellie ran her thumbnail across the label of her bottle. After receiving the cryptic email about Nick earlier today, she spent a fair amount of time debating with herself whether to tell Tyler about it. Tiffany too, for that matter. Tyler would worry about Ellie getting involved, and Tiffany would understandably want to inform the police. The looming roadblock was that Ellie had been told not to go to the police. And yet she had nothing substantial to go on. Nothing but an invisible hand conveying an opinion about Nick's fate.

Citrus was still below them, now sprawled out in the yard and convulsing back and forth as he scratched his back against the tough grass. On the edge of the property, a cluster of saw palmetto rustled, and three wild hogs emerged, their confident heads raised high. They were small for hogs, but more than twice the size of Ellie's dog. They pranced proudly through the yard. Ellie stood up to warn Citrus, but Tyler rose up and placed his hand on her shoulder. "Just hold on," he whispered. "They won't hurt him. He's too fast."

The hogs snorted as they neared Citrus, but the dog remained oblivious while they sniffed around him. Suddenly, his little eyes flicked open, and like some invisible cook had slipped a spatula beneath him, he flipped into the air, all four paws clearing the three-foot mark.

Ellie and Tyler laughed as they watched Citrus's ears flatten on his head and his tail shoot between his legs as a black hog started chasing him across the yard.

"Go get your gun off the front porch," she said.

"No way. This is a lot more fun."

She smiled. "Yeah."

Citrus streaked toward the property line and disappeared into the woods. The hogs followed, and Ellie reached out and grabbed Tyler's forearm when she heard a yelp from the brush. "He's fine," he said. "Just wait." Sure enough, a few seconds later Citrus shot back into the yard like his tail was on fire and disappeared around the house.

They heard a fast, methodical thumping coming from the front steps that softened as it moved to the side porch. Citrus appeared and trotted over to his owner, his troubled face conveying the full range of his emotional trauma. He shot a few nervous glances behind him ensure he hadn't been followed.

"Hey, little guy," Tyler said. "What's the word?" Citrus looked up at Tyler like he knew Tyler could have done something to stop the terrorists, but didn't. The dog jumped into one of the two empty wicker chairs and settled in, still eyeing Tyler with an irritated suspicion. The two humans returned to the couch and watched as the hogs reappeared, sniffed around a while, and then finally left for good.

"Tell me something about Nick," Ellie finally said.

"What about him?"

"Anything."

Tyler grabbed a fresh beer from the refrigerator, rid the bottle of the cap, and leaned back against the cushion. "You have a bet with someone to make a grown man cry?"

"He was your best friend. And you're not talking about him being gone."

Now it was Tyler's turn to fidget with the label. "That's because I can't, Ellie. You know, I almost called him this morning to tell him to come by Saturday and help me rotate the tires on my truck."

"I'm sorry, Tyler."

He sighed deeply but took up her request. "Nick was probably the most generous person I've ever met. He would work weekends to remodel some old lady's kitchen at no cost or buy his neighbor new tires for his car after the guy lost his job. Everybody loved him. The only person he couldn't get along with was his own brother. And that wasn't his fault."

Nick's parents had passed several years ago. Ellie met his younger sister at the funeral last week. If the brother had been there, she'd completely missed it. "I guess I didn't know he had a brother."

"Yeah. Nate. But they hadn't spoken in, I don't know, a decade? They didn't get along as adults. Nate grew up to be a pile of dog crap and moved up north somewhere. Anyway, Nick was just different. He saw people; he noticed when they were struggling or when they weren't quite right." Tyler took a final pull on his beer, draining it in four solid gulps. "When my girlfriend broke up with me the night before I left for college, Nick heard about it and showed up at my place with a six pack of Dr. Pepper and a VHS copy of Top Gun. He never said anything about it, just tossed me a can before turning on the VCR and starting the movie."

The back porch was quiet for a while, Tyler thinking about his friend, Ellie hurting for him and trying not to think about how a VCR made her feel older than she really was.

"I stopped by Tiffany's earlier," Ellie said. "She's a tough girl. But I can't imagine."

"Me neither. When I went by yesterday, Kayla was at the kitchen table drawing a picture of her and Nick together. They were holding hands." Tyler wiped at the fresh moisture in his eyes. "She handed me the picture and said she hoped Daddy would be home soon. She still doesn't get it. Doesn't matter what Tiff tells her." He shook his head angrily. "It feels like I've fallen down a gopher hole. Everything just seems upside down right now."

Ellie couldn't think of an adequate response. Nothing but trite clichés. *It's going to be okay. They'll get through this. Just give it time.* So she didn't say anything, just reached over and slipped her fingers between his.

They sat in silence for the next quarter hour, watching the sunset, both grieving the loss of a friend and hurting for the wife and daughter he left behind. Ellie could feel a resolve hardening within her. A resolve to find out what really did happen to Nick. Tyler suddenly stood up and grabbed his empty bottle by the neck, then whipped it sidearm toward the water. It tumbled through the yard before splashing at the water's edge. "I'll get that in the morning," he said. "But tonight I need to be angry."

Ellie stared into the late evening sky, where heat lightning flashed high over the Gulf's horizon, looking as if heaven itself was shorting out. Just beyond, orange-streaked clouds laced with strands of purple mingled with vibrant and darkening colors against the graying light of dusk.

Like a bruise.

CHAPTER TWELVE

Jet made a mental note to fill his gas tank before making the return trip. He pulled his Nissan Maxima into an oil-slicked parking space and grabbed his phone from the center console before stepping out into an afternoon sun that seemed intent on proving global warming. The drive across the Everglades from Pine Island to Miami had taken nearly three hours. It felt good to finally stretch his long legs. He locked the car and stepped to the sidewalk. Hope House's cinder block walls were painted a bright, fresh yellow that reflected the energetic color scheme found throughout most of West Hialeah. The front yard of the building was landscaped with pebbles in the place of grass, and a bike rack stood just off the wall with a half-dozen bikes cluttered around it. All of them were secured with a lock of some kind.

There were well kept and proud areas of West Hialeah, but the shelter was nestled into a section of town that looked as though not a single taxpayer dollar had been spent on improvements in three decades. Paint was peeling off buildings like old skin. Forsaken telephone poles leaned at dangerous angles, and the sun-bleached asphalt of W 37th was full of neglected potholes and contained more fissures than Mick Jagger's face.

Across the street sat a small wood-framed church, the Iglesia Metodista, whose decrepit marquee sign was missing several letters that at some point in the past had been part of a message inviting all to come for Sunday School at 9am. Doughnuts would be provided. A 'For Sale' sign tilted lazily in the overgrown grass, and an unpainted sheet of plywood was screwed into the door frame to prevent trespassers. All the windows were broken out.

Down from the church was a strip center with narrow shotgun shops: a laundromat, a hair salon, and beyond that a Cuban eatery whose sidewalk sign boasted the best empanadas in Miami. Jet had half a mind to walk down there and try a couple when he was done here. The hole-in-the-wall restaurants always had the best food, provided you didn't get food poisoning.

Jet stepped beneath an elongated awning covering the sidewalk. It led to the double-glass doors at the front. Entire sections of the walkway had been scribbled upon with permanent marker:

I love Hope House - Renaldo
Thank you for helping me read, Mr. Alex - Diego
H H makes me happy - Rita
You saved my life - MC

By Jet's estimation, there were over a hundred of these little notes of gratitude. Perhaps more. He pulled the front door open and stepped inside. The noise level was acute. The din of excited conversation, laughter, and competitive insults echoed off tiled floors and concrete walls. The front area, roughly the size of a tennis court, was entirely open with no walls to section off groups or their activities. Nearly two dozen children were in various stages of play. At the far side of the room, two boys stood at one end of a ping pong table, waiting for a solitary girl on the other side of the net to serve the ball. Next to them, a cluster of children was gathered around a foosball table, loudly cheering for the player of their choice with all the fervor of a crowd at the World Cup finals. A group of pre-adolescent boys was huddled in front of a television clasping Xbox controllers, selecting their next play on Madden.

Aluminum picnic tables lined one wall and terminated at a large opening that led back into a kitchen. There was no receptionist's desk, no counter where you could readily identify yourself and state the purpose of your visit.

A side door led to an outside playground. Sunlight temporarily flooded inside as it opened and Alex Serrano stepped through. Before he could notice the silver-haired man standing amongst a sea of olive-skinned children, a tiny girl with her dark hair in pigtails ran up to Alex, sobbing loudly. He squatted down and embraced her before pulling her back and looking at her forehead like a concerned parent. He spoke softly to her and wiped her tears away. She nodded, brushed at her face, and returned to a small pile of dolls in the corner of the room. Alex smiled at her, his gaze moving around the room until it landed on Jet. A look of surprise and recognition crossed his face. He stood and approached the older man with his hand outstretched. He didn't bother to hide the intrigue in his voice.

"Jet, you came to see us." They shook hands.

"I thought this would be the best place to start. Did you think I wouldn't come?"

"Of course, I hoped you would. But if I am honest, the previous two investigators we hired never bothered."

"I'm sure that was frustrating. I wouldn't have taken the job if I couldn't give it the proper attention."

"Well, I thank you very much." Alex looked around like he was unsure where to start. "I was just about to get some work done in my office. But why don't I show you around first?"

"Thank you."

Alex spent the next ten minutes showing him the kitchen, the playground, and the accompanying courtyard. He introduced Jet to several adults who volunteered at Hope House.

"Was anyone here friends with Juanita?" Jet asked.

Alex scanned the room before answering. "No. I wouldn't say friends. Many of them knew who she was. She was very kind to them." Alex gestured toward the little girl who had been crying just minutes earlier. "Chantal was Juanita's shadow whenever Juanita was here. The detective—Wilson, I believe his last name is—spent a couple of days here speaking with the children and interviewing anyone in the neighborhood who might have known her. But he didn't find anything of substance."

Jet was already privy to that last bit of information. He had spoken with Timothy Wilson yesterday. The detective had worked the case hard for the first week after Juanita's disappearance. But after that, a lack of leads and a pile of new cases diverted his attention. The case hadn't been touched in any substantial way in over five weeks. Mr. Wilson gave him the go-ahead to proceed on the case under the Closure Act.

Jet asked, "Juanita didn't spend time with anyone her age?"

"No. There aren't many older teenagers who come here. Those that do are mostly here for the sake of a younger sibling. Juanita mostly kept to herself. Sometimes she would just walk Junior over here and then come back and pick him up. There was one girl a couple of years younger than her, Olivia. But I think she moved out of state a few months before Juanita disappeared."

"And she never spoke to you about this Jesse guy?"

"No. Not to anyone as far as I know. And she told Junior to stay quiet about it." Alex's disposition suddenly lifted. "Did you see the mural as you came in?"

Jet shook his head.

"Then you must have come in from the other end of 36th. Come with me," he said. "I'll show you what Juanita left for us." He led Jet back out the front doors. He swung left at the end of the front walkway, and Jet followed him around to the side of the building. Alex stopped and extended an arm. "This," he said proudly, "is what she did."

Jet looked across the expanse of the wall to witness older men playing dominoes and a lady behind them frying plantains in a large pan. Further down, the painting showed men engaged in soccer and a teenage boy connecting his bat to a baseball. The shelter's name stood tall in the center with the Cuban and American flags flying over it.

"Incredible," Jet said. "And Juanita did all of this?"

"Every bit of it."

It wasn't simply the images themselves but the detail

in each face: the way one of the men was studying the checkerboard, the joy in the cook's face, the intent of the boy's eye as he made contact with the ball. Juanita had not only detailed the people, she had also captured how they felt as they did it—their humanity. Looking at the mural, studying it, Jet could feel the breadth and heart of a community he could not have related to otherwise. He brought his phone out and took a few pictures.

Across the street, a man who looked to be in his early twenties was sitting on the curb in front of the old church. He was staring intently at Jet. He wore black jeans and an oversized Stray Rats t-shirt, a streetwear brand that was growing in popularity with Miami gangs and troublesome subcultures. Jet ignored him and turned his attention back to Juanita's artwork. Alex stepped up to the wall and ran his fingers down the mural. "The afternoon she finished this was the last time I saw her." He sighed and took a step back. "Thank you, Jet, for coming. This situation is so terrible."

"Certainly," Jet said, and looked down 37th Street. "I'm going to walk the neighborhood for a bit."

"Of course," Alex said. "But please be careful. There are many good people around here but also those who might wonder how much you have in your wallet."

"I don't mind standing out. I just want some answers."

A volunteer appeared from around the corner. The older lady had a pleading look on her face. "Alex, Jose is causing trouble again. I'm sorry, but he won't listen to me."

"Go on," Jet said to Alex. "I'll call you with any more questions." The men said goodbye, and Jet took in the mural for a little longer before crossing the street and slowly making his way further into the neighborhood. The man who had been staring at him stood up from his place on the curb and followed Jet from twenty yards behind. Jet's handgun rested safely in his ankle holster, hidden behind the cuff of his pants leg. At just six-and-a-half inches long and only four inches from the magazine's floor plate to the top of the rear sight, the Glock 26 was the perfect size for a concealed carry while still providing its owner with the stopping force of a 9mm.

Jet passed an empty lot where an abandoned shopping cart was turned upside down and an old carpet, a couch, and a pile of laundry had been discarded. As he strolled past an elementary school, he shot a quick glance over his shoulder to find that the man was gone. Still, he remained alert, passing up a Dollar General and a small grocery store whose front window was advertising a sale on mangoes and shredded beef. He crossed at the next intersection and turned east, keeping his trajectory set toward the motel where Juanita was last seen by her brother.

An elderly lady was walking ahead of him. A large purse hung from her shoulder, and she moved with slow, arthritic movements toward a fruit stand perched in the center of the sidewalk.

The man who had been following Jet appeared just in front of her, in the entrance to an alley. He eyed the lady as she strolled by him. Her attention was set on the stand before her, and she didn't seem to notice the man.

Suddenly, he stepped forward and reached a hand out for the purse. He grabbed the strap tightly in his fingers and pulled. The lady cried out as she struggled against him. Her frail frame was no match, and her purse came loose in his hands. He stepped backward and, after a quick glance back at Jet, bolted down the street. Behind him, the lady had an angry fist pumping high in the air as she yelled frantically at him in Spanish.

Jet immediately drew his weapon and took off after him, stepping off into the street to avoid both the lady and the fruit stand. He couldn't use his gun to get the purse back, but in the event the man was armed, Jet didn't want to be caught off guard.

The man darted around the next corner, disappearing behind an old stucco building. Jet made the turn and, approaching a wide alley at the back of the building, pulled up and stopped.

The young man was on his knees. He was facing Jet, and his fingers were laced behind his head like he was ready to be arrested. He spoke quickly. "Easy, yo. I just want to talk to you." The purse had been dropped at the front of the alley and lay ten feet away.

Jet was in good shape for his age, but the quick sprint left him a little winded. "Why did you have to steal that lady's purse if you just wanted to talk with me?" he asked, glancing over his shoulder to check for any sign of the young man's friends.

"You're not a cop, right?"

Jet told him he was a private investigator.

"You're trying to find that girl, right? Juanita?"

"Why? Do you know something?"

"You good if I stand up now?"

Jet nodded. "Stand over there against the wall." Jet moved further into the alley and swiveled so he could get a better view of the street. He kept his gun trained on the man. "Get to it," he said. "Quickly."

"Yeah, so, this girl, Juanita. She was all right, you

know? Real nice *chica*. And I think I might know who took her."

"You *think*?"

"I'm not all the way for sure."

"I'm listening."

"So this guy, he starts coming around a few months ago and I seen Juanita and her little brother with him a couple times. And I thought he looked like someone I'd seen back in the day. But I couldn't place it, you know? But a couple weeks ago I was rolling in from my job out in Little River and seen a billboard out by the casino of some chick that made me think of Juanita. It wasn't her, you know, but it reminded me of her. She had the same hair and those dark eyes. And then," he snapped his fingers, "I was like, I know where I've seen that guy before."

"Where?" Jet asked.

"I got this cousin up in West Palm Beach, and she got me into this party a couple of years back. A real *burumba*. And that was where I seen him."

Jet, a little skeptical, asked, "How do you remember a random guy from a party from two years ago?"

"Because some fool had too much tequila and started feeling up this guy's girl. So he pulls out a .45 and parks the muzzle in the drunk guy's mouth." He shrugged. "You kinda remember stuff like that."

"And his name is Jesse?"

"I don't know his name. Might be Jesse. But if I was running a game swiping *chicas* off the street, I wouldn't be using my real name. You know what I'm sayin'?"

Jet did know what he was saying. "So where can I find him?"

"I don't know that neither. But I know who probably

does." He motioned toward the gun. "Yo, can you get that outta my face? I'm tryin' to help here."

Jet glanced down the street again and lowered his angle of focus to forty-five degrees so the weapon was now pointing at the man's feet and not his chest. "Go on," he said.

"I don't got his number anymore, but you need to go up to Papi's La Cubana. It's a restaurant in Little Havana and ask for a guy named Saint."

"Saint?"

"Yeah. He's a cook up in there. He was at that party, and he knows everybody on the street. Everybody."

Jet lowered his weapon to his side. "Why are you telling me this?"

"I just want to help, *ese*. Like I said, Juanita was all right. Her little brother too. They've been through a lot like a bunch of us around here."

"The police were in the neighborhood asking questions after Juanita didn't come back. Why didn't you tell them this?" Jet knew why, but he had to ask.

"It's like I told you. I just remembered a couple weeks back." He shook his head. "Besides, I'm not ratting to the *la jura*. Half of them won't listen, and the other half are as crooked as my *abuelo's* teeth. They'd probably try to pin her being gone on me."

"What's your name?"

The young man huffed as though Jet had just made an attempt at humor. "I ain't giving you that, *ese*. You know, I might be crazy for talking to you. But I ain't stupid."

"Fair enough."

The man raised his open hands up to his shoulders. "I'm gonna go now. You cool with that?"

Jet stepped to the side. "Go on."

The man used his chin to indicate toward the purse. "Think you can get that back to the lady? Maybe tell her I'm sorry."

"Sure," Jet said.

The man started a quick trot down the sidewalk before pausing long enough to turn around and say, "I hope you find her and the *bastardos* who took her." Then he was gone.

Still cautious of his surroundings, Jet kneeled down and returned his Glock to his ankle holster. He stood and walked over to the purse. He picked it up and opened it. Inside was a cell phone in a purple case, a small notebook, an orange prescription bottle, a tube of lipstick, and a pink wallet. He withdrew the wallet and unsnapped it. There were several credit cards, thirty-two dollars in cash, and a driver's license for a Valeria Sanchez. He shut the wallet and returned it to the purse, impressed that the young man appeared not to have taken anything.

The fruit stand was back down E 87th Street. He would return the purse and complete the route to the abandoned motel.

Then he was off to Little Havana.

CHAPTER THIRTEEN

ELLIE LOWERED her boat into the canal and waved hello to a couple on the bridge of a passing catamaran. She idled her Bayliner off the cradle and into the center of the canal, then gave it a few more knots. A couple of minutes later she was in Pine Island Sound, the southern waters of which separated Pine Island from Sanibel, which lay just two miles out. She gave the Norma Jean pier a wide berth and passed up York Island and Havelock Key as she turned north.

A half hour later she rode by six charred and blackened pilings that stood out of the water like ancient sentinels. They were all that remained of Quinton Davis's burned down fishing shack. She had nearly died in that fire. Had it not been for a stranger that she never did get the chance to thank, she would have. She continued on and soon approached Mondongo Rocks, a series of sand and oyster bars flanked by luscious red mangroves. An old wooden fishing boat was beached on one of Mondongo's tiny keys. As Ellie's Bayliner moved past it, she easily recalled last summer when she searched the fishing boat's broken stern and discovered gas cans filled with fuel. It was the beginning of a months-long investigation that culminated in the takedown of three local drug operations. Now, as she began a new investigation, this time into the death of a friend, she could feel a latent angst begin to rise, the determination to find out what really happened to Nick after all.

She ran her boat into Gasparilla Sound, continuing north until she entered Cape Haze and drew up into Coral Creek where the coastal vegetation grew closer together. As she curved around the bend, a long dock materialized. It was made of fresh, sturdy boards that shined brightly in the sunlight. Ellie brought her engine down to idle speed as she approached. Drawing near, she tossed out a couple of fenders on her port side. The Bayliner bobbed closer, and Ellie grabbed a dock cleat and tied off the bow before moving to the stern and securing that end of the boat. She cut the engine. Closer to the property, a twenty-one foot Bowrider was resting on a lift beneath the shade of a canvas canopy. Ellie stepped on the gunwale then onto the dock, which terminated on a stilt house bearing an unusual ovoid shape and painted bright white, looking like a gargantuan egg. Two tiny windows in the front seemed to resemble a large pair of eyes, and the entire structure looked like it was better suited for an Angry Birds theme park than a stretch of Florida backwater.

Ellie found Barry Corbin's address online without Jet's help. The property had no road access, and it took a little extra digging to pinpoint an exact location. The only way in or out was the way she had just entered. Her sneakers came off the dock and crunched into a crushed shell walkway, the sun hot on her skin, the air thick with moisture. A narrow set of steps with a rail on just the right side led up to a door on the side of the egg. Ellie squinted through her sunglasses past the pilings that supported the house and saw sparks flying and dying out mid-air. She took the path around the house to where a wide canopy sat, its roof made of clear corrugated plastic. Thin sheets of steel the size of a door were laid out across a long workbench. On a slim wood-top table sat a jigsaw and a grinder, along with several sizes of ball-peen hammers, metal brushes, clamps, and a band saw. On the ground, sitting at the back edge of the structure, were scorpions, sharks, and what looked like a seagull, all made of welded bolts, nuts, and washers.

A tall, stocky man was leaning over a steel pole. One hand was holding a strip of metal with a pair of pliers while the other gripped a welding torch. He had a sizeable midsection and thick arms. He wore blue jeans, a leather welding jacket, and an auto-darkening helmet. Ellie moved further to his right in hopes that he might catch her movement when he paused to resettle the torch.

It worked, and when he looked in her direction, he stopped and just stared, unmoving for several seconds, as though someone had paused him. Just when she was starting to think he had gotten stuck in the position, he stood erect and turned off the oxygen and fuel gas valves before pushing back his helmet. His thick eyebrows lowered as he squinted at her. "Help you?"

"Yes. I'm sorry to intrude." There wasn't much she could offer in the way of banter, so she decided to just get to it. "I wanted to see if I could have a minute of your time to discuss Breakwater."

He frowned deeply, a long furrow settling in between his eyes. "There some kind of problem?" he asked.

"No, sir. I was speaking with Avi Narrano, and he suggested I come see you. Would you have a couple of minutes?"

He set the torch on a sheet of metal, and when he removed his helmet, it revealed a bald head absent of any sunspots. He put the helmet next to the torch then peeled off his jacket, revealing a sleeveless gray t-shirt. "Avi, huh?" He tossed his gloves onto a metal sawhorse. "Well I haven't had anything to do with Breakwater in, well, I guess coming up on three years now." Barry's head tilted to an angle, and he seemed to study Ellie's face like he was trying to assemble a cluster of disconnected thoughts.

Ellie said, "You worked with them for quite a while, didn't you?"

"Nearly twenty years. Twenty good years except for the last one." He took a step toward her, and his eyes narrowed slightly as he continued to assess her. "Do we know each other from somewhere?"

"I don't believe so."

But as the words were still leaving her lips, Barry suddenly brightened and snapped his fingers. "St. James City," he blurted. "You work at The Salty Mangrove." He shook a finger at her. "You're... Ellie, right?"

Ellie instantly felt exposed, which, given the furtive circumstances of her visit, was undesired. She didn't know Barry and didn't know if he could be trusted. But now she could only concede her identity. "Yes, Ellie."

"You're Frank's daughter, aren't you?"

Hearing her father's name spoken caught her emotions off guard. "You knew my dad?"

He chuckled. "Did I know your dad? Sweetie, I played poker with him every Thursday night for nearly a decade. When he wasn't traveling, the six of us were out at Lee Ackerman's place in Cape Coral. As a matter of fact," Barry's expression softened, "he was driving back home from the game the night he died in that god-awful crash."

Ellie suddenly wanted to hug this man.

"With you studying overseas all those years, you and I never got a chance to meet. I hated when your sister told me you couldn't make the funeral. I believe I sent you a sympathy card when you got back home."

And that was when Ellie realized where she had seen Barry's name. It was on the front corner of the envelope; the return address. But on the inside, he hadn't signed it "Barry." No, it was a nickname of sorts. Muddy? Morty? Then she had it. "You're Mutt?"

"In the flesh," he grinned. "I don't really ever get down to St. James City. Most of my time not spent here is out on Boca Grande. But I did see you behind the counter at The Salty Mangrove once. Would have said hello, but I was late getting on a charter, and the bar was slammed.

"Thank you for the card," she said. "I do remember getting it. It meant a lot."

"Your father, he was one of the good guys. I'd be lying if I said I didn't miss him something terrible. We all do."

Ellie couldn't tell Barry the truth concerning her father's car accident that night. So she said the only thing she could. "I miss him too."

"Well, come on," he said. "Let's go inside and talk." Barry led the way out from under the pavilion to the stairs. As she ascended, Ellie wondered why there wasn't a rail on the left. As they neared the landing, a nervous lizard skittered off a step and flung himself off into a cluster of high-standing hibiscus. Barry opened the side door to his home and went in first. Ellie followed behind him and entered a small kitchen that smelled of fresh pineapple. A window unit was pouring in a generous stream of air conditioning that was welcome against her hot skin. Barry wiped a line of sweat from his cheek. "Get you something to drink? It might be January, but someone seems to have forgotten to tell the sun."

"Water would be great. Thank you."

Barry offered for her to take a seat at a tiny table nestled against the wall. He grabbed a cup from the dish rack next to his sink. A filter was attached to the end of the faucet, and he flipped a nozzle and filled the cup before setting it in front of Ellie. "My ice maker quit on me a couple of months back. Haven't gotten around to fixing it yet."

"This is fine. Thank you."

Barry left the kitchen for a moment and disappeared into another room. When he returned, he sat down across from Ellie and slid his hand across the table. When he opened it, Ellie heard a thin metal click on the formica. Looking down she saw a large gold coin. She picked it up. It was a solid gold poker chip. Engraved on it were the words "Life is no different than poker. Go all in." It was followed by the initials F.O.

"Frank gave that to me," Barry said. "In fact, he gave us all one, not a few weeks before he was killed by that idiot truck driver."

The coin was thick and had to be a couple of ounces. Six of these would have cost her father a fair amount. She smiled at the thought. He lived what he taught her and Katie from a young age, that a rich life was synonymous with having good friends. Ellie set the chip down and gently slid it across the table. "I'm glad you have that," she said. "That's quite special."

Barry folded his hands on top of his manatee-sized midsection. Long gray hairs stood out along his shoulders and arms and danced in the flow of the air conditioning. "Now," he said, "you didn't come all the way over here to reminisce about your father. What's your interest in Breakwater?"

Even the good guys could break bad, but Ellie decided that if her father had once trusted this man, then she would too. She spent the next several minutes filling Barry in on Nick, the email, and her brief conversation with Avi. "To be honest," she finished. "I'm just trying to sketch an outline. I don't really know what I'm supposed to be looking for."

"I'm sorry to hear about your friend," Barry said. "I hate to tell you that I don't know anything about the new ownership. They took over after I left."

"How do you mean?"

"If you've talked with Avi, then he may have told you that Breakwater used to be called Garwood Construction. It was never a huge company, but we kept thirty folks or so on the payroll. Beyond that, of course, we had our subs. John—John Garwood—owned it for as long as I was there. He hired me on just a couple of years after he started the company. A good ol' boy, John was. Cared a lot about his employees and treated all of us like family. When he decided to hang up his cleats, he sold it off to David Tolson and, well, that's when things went off the rails. John, you see, had a specific way of doing things. A standard, and it gave the company a certain reputation among suppliers, subs, and customers. David Tolson was a project manager with the company for nearly half the time I was there. Ten years, I guess. Smart guy. Got things done well and on time, if not ahead of schedule. But after he bought the company from John, it went down faster than a sick seagull. Turns out he didn't have the business sense we all thought he had. He's the one who changed the business name to Breakwater. Which was foolish in itself because everyone knew the company by Garwood."

"So he sold the business too?"

"After John retired and left it in Tolson's hands, I stayed around for another year before leaving. He sold it a little while later. Don't know to who."

"What did you do for them?"

"Bean counter." He tapped his head with a forefinger. "I love numbers. They have an inherent beauty, like that of any music, if not more. Problem was, the company's numbers weren't looking so beautiful. The worse they got, the angrier I became."

Ellie took a sip of her water as she vaguely recalled a principle about not upsetting the company accountant. "Angry?" she asked.

"Oh yes. See, when John sold Breakwater to Tolson part of the agreement was that I would get a small stake in the company. That was his way of thanking me for sticking with him over the years. However, the finer print had it so I wasn't able to cash out of my shares until at least three years after the transition. That clause was there to make sure everything remained stable and the company kept its cash flow. But by the next year, there wasn't much left. I'm in the back office working through the numbers, and every week I'm seeing more and more stuff I don't like. We were paying our subs way too much, over-ordering materials that were never used or returned. And no one was playing the part of the bulldog, making sure invoices were paid in a timely manner."

"So you left?"

"So I left," he repeated. "My pops taught me how to make hobby art years ago. So I decided to start doing it for income. I spent too much time behind a desk anyway." Barry tossed his meaty hands. "This is the life I was meant to live."

Barry's home was at least a mile from the nearest person. With no road access and an unsullied view of the sunset every night, there were certainly worse places to live. Ellie asked, "Do you know what happened to the company after that?"

He nodded. "About a year after I bailed, Tolson ended up selling it to someone else. I don't think he got much for it. There wasn't much left. Last I heard he was back to framing houses for a developer up in Jacksonville."

She said, "I couldn't find a website on them. Seems a little unusual for a company serving the general public."

"I suppose. Unless they're serving government contracts or won a large bid of some kind. They may not market to the general public."

She took a sip of her water before continuing. "Avi mentioned that the new ownership asked him to invoice for work he didn't do."

Barry frowned easily at that. "Really? I don't think

Avi is the kind of guy who would do something like that."

"He said he didn't. But other subs he knew were asked to as well. Any ideas why?"

"Well, I can only think of one, really." He hesitated. "You need to understand that I'm not saying this is true, but if they were testing the waters and seeing who was willing to over-invoice, they might have been looking to wash some dead presidents."

"Money laundering?"

"It happens a lot. And in construction, there are a lot of trades, a lot of different kind of work that can be done. Getting subs to invoice for more than they charge and then giving them a little kickback on the side is a creative way to launder dirty money. Did your friend Nick do any work for them?"

"Maybe," she said. "I'm not sure though." And suddenly the lines were starting to fill in. With a dull pencil perhaps, but at least now she had something to work with. Nick was new to the area, having moved to Pine Island only three months ago. If someone from Breakwater had poked him to see if he might be willing to over-invoice them, and if Nick said "no" with enough gusto, if he threatened to out them, there could be the motive.

But then a sickening thought swooped through Ellie's mind like a dark bird dispatching appalling lies. What if Nick was actually working with them? What if he needed a little extra cash of his own and massaged his invoices? And what if something finally went wrong? She pushed the thought away but was troubled that she couldn't rid herself of it altogether.

Barry shook his finger at Ellie. "But you know, it's funny you should bring up Breakwater. I've got a fabricator—Tim Ellis—that I sell most of my welding art to. He offloads it retail from there. But he's got a shop in east Fort Myers, out in the old industrial district. Last week I took some finished pieces over to him." Parenthetically, Barry said, "I've got a truck I keep parked about three miles from here, over at a dock in Placida. That's how I get things to and from here. Whenever I drop my stuff off with Tim, we usually end up sharing a small case of Miller Lite and shooting the breeze for hours. Sometimes I don't leave until ten or eleven. A couple weeks ago I left late again and saw an F-250 pull out of the old fire station. The one they quit using years ago. The truck had the Breakwater logo on its door. Kinda strange."

"Why was that strange?" Ellie asked.

"Because it didn't look like it belonged. There were other cars parked along the curb, and one followed the truck out. They were all black, with dark windows. A couple men were standing around smoking, and they were wearing leather jackets."

"Maybe someone had the work truck on personal time."

"Yeah," Barry said. "Could be, but I looked into the building when I passed, and it looked like a brawl of some kind was just breaking up. I don't know, something just didn't seem right. Can't really explain it."

Ellie stood up and for the first time, really noted the inside of the odd building. She spent a curious childhood going through all the estuaries and coves off Gasparilla Sound and could not recall ever seeing this place. It wasn't something easily forgotten. "Did you build this?" she asked.

Barry let out a spirited laugh that brought him to lean against the table for support. "No, sweetie. I didn't build it. Believe it or not, an old chicken farmer from Pasco County sold off his farm to one of those conglomerates about ten years ago. He moved out here and built this place. Got about four or five years in before he had a stroke and had to move to a nursing home. Can you believe no one wanted to buy it?" He tossed her a wink. "So when I retired this place was going for a steal. I keep meaning to paint it a dark blue or green but just haven't gotten around to it yet. So for now, it's still 'The Egg.' It's not the coolest place to entertain, but as you can imagine, I don't get a lot of folks coming out here. Joe Benson, he's on marine patrol with the Sheriff's Office. He'll stop by every now and then. And then Brenda Tate, she keeps on thinking she'll convince me to leave here and join her over in Punta Gorda." He smirked. "But I'm not going anywhere. Not even for a looker like Brenda Tate."

Barry walked Ellie down to the dock and gave her an open invitation to come back and see him. She left thinking that she would like that very much. As she ran her boat back to St. James City, she did so beneath a small cloud of disappointment. She wasn't sure what she had been hoping to hear from Barry. "Oh, of course, I know who killed your friend. And I can also tell you why." Whoever sent her the email appeared to be somewhat inefficient when it came to leads in an apparent murder investigation. Still, she owed the email a response. After that, seeing as she had no other plans for tonight, Ellie decided to take a drive into Fort Myers and check out the old fire station.

CHAPTER FOURTEEN

The doorbell didn't work. His knuckles tingled as he rapped on the door. He waited a half minute before it flung open and revealed a man in an oversized t-shirt and baggy jeans. Felipe acknowledged him with a quick thrust of his chin. "Benito. Hey."

"Whoa, Felipe! How are you, man? It's been a quick minute." The men drew close and clapped each other on the back. "What are you doing here?"

"I was around. Thought I'd come by. What you been up to these days?"

"Man, just chillin', you know? Come in, come in." Felipe stepped into the small house and followed him back into a dirty kitchen where old dishes were stacked high in the sink and the garbage can was spilling Taco Bell wrappers and used napkins onto the floor. Benito reached into the cabinet and pulled out a plastic food container. He produced a couple of joints and handed one to Felipe. "Just got this stuff last night. They're calling it Purple Tsunami. You had it before?"

"No." They lit up, and Benito led them into a side

room with thick brown carpet and a couple sagging couches. The television was set to Maury, where a panel of women was getting ready to tell their boyfriends that they had been simultaneously dating their fathers.

Both men sat in silence, the drug starting to hit their blood and flood their minds as they watched women in tank tops and men with mullets start to yell at each other. "You really watch this *basura*?" Felipe said slowly.

"Oh, yeah. It's *loco*. They go out and find all the crazies and get them to come on the show. Yesterday, they had on a bunch of people that looked like they were from that movie I watched when I was a kid." He said nothing else as if that cleared everything up.

"What movie?" Felipe finally asked.

"You know, that one with Johnny Depp. Where he plays that creepy guy who makes all the chocolates."

"You mean *Charlie and the Chocolate Factory*?"

"Yeah, that's the one. The little people in that movie. That's what they looked like."

"An Oompa Loompa? You're telling me that they all looked like Oompa Loompas?"

"Yeah. Just like them."

"So they were midgets?"

"I think it's not cool to use that word anymore."

Felipe rolled his now bloodshot eyes. "A little person then?"

"Yeah, yeah. They were all little persons." Benito chuckled. "One of them was all mad because he was saying he identified as a tall person." On the television, two women were now throwing chairs at each other as a boyfriend and a security guard tried to hold them back.

"By the way," Felipe said, "the old one was better."

"What old one?"

"The old *Charlie and the Chocolate Factory*."

"There's an old one? Before the Johnny Depp one?"

"You didn't know that?"

"For real? Is it any good?"

"Better. The Oompa Loompas look really dope in that one."

Maury went to break, and a commercial for a do-it-yourself DNA test appeared on the screen. "So where you working now?" Benito asked. "I'm still down at my brother's car shop."

Felipe took another hit off his joint. He closed his eyes and felt the room fall away from him. He felt lighter now, like he was floating or on top of something that was floating. He couldn't tell which. "I got a good thing going. Been at it for a while now."

"So what is it?"

As it turned out, Purple Tsunami was far more potent than Felipe had anticipated. Maury Povich was now in the living room with them, floating in the air just in front of him. And it was also potent enough to loosen a tongue that, had his mind been unaltered, would have never spoken his next words. "I help some *chicas* get into another line of work."

"Another line of work? You mean like stripping?"

"No. Think about it like this." Felipe put the joint back to his lips, and hazy bursts of smoke escaped his mouth as spoke. "You're rich. I mean, like you could buy your own city kind of rich. But you live in a different country. Maybe Frankfurt or Hong Kong or Rio. But you're in Miami for business and want to have a little fun."

Benito asked, "So you're recruiting hoes? I guess if

you got big money clients, then the girls get paid a lot more than they would at the clubs, huh?"

"No, no. You don't get it." Felipe looked knowingly at Benito. "We don't pay them."

Benito's own circuits were working slower, but his eyes finally lifted in understanding. "Oh. Damn, man." He whistled low. "I'll bet you're makin' the good money. How'd you get into doing that?"

"Doesn't matter. But yeah. Pretty soon I'll be getting my own condo downtown."

"Well, don't forget about me," Benito said. Then he asked: "So like, how do you get the girls? You just grab them up?"

Now Maury was walking on the ceiling and for some reason was no longer wearing a shirt. He was looking at Felipe and giving him a thumb and forefinger circle. "No. They don't like me working it like that. Brings too much attention. I get to know the girls first. Makes it all a lot easier. Then they just come with me." Felipe smiled at Maury and returned the thumb and forefinger circle.

"Boy, you're one of the coldest people I know. Everybody who really knows you is half scared of you I'm pretty sure. Especially since you popped Paula's cousin last year. How are you getting girls to like you and not run from you?"

"It's easy." Felipe jutted his chin toward the television. "It's kinda like those girls on that show. You just have to find one who's lonely and lie to her. The lonely ones want to believe you. They're desperate."

Both men shared a hearty laugh before taking another hit.

. . .

An hour later Maury had been replaced by Judge Judy when Felipe pried himself from the couch cushions and rubbed at his cheeks. He stood up. "I better fly. I got stuff I've gotta do. It's been good hangin' with you."

"Man, you too." Benito came to his feet and slapped his old friend on the back. "You shouldn't wait so long to come by again. Next time, you bring a couple of your girls. We can make it a real party."

"You got any more of that *marimba* I can take with me?" Felipe slipped a hundred-dollar bill from his pocket and put it in his friend's hand.

"You know I do." Benito disappeared around the corner and into the kitchen. He was back a minute later with a baggie half full of weed. Felipe's money was tucked inside. He handed it over. "Keep your money. You and me, we go back too far for that kinda thing."

After giving each other a quick hug, Felipe said goodbye and walked down the front steps to the cracked sidewalk. The neighborhood was familiar. He had grown up here, spending far more time on these streets as a boy than he did at school. He scanned for oncoming traffic and, seeing none, he crossed the street. He spent the next half mile walking at an unhurried pace. Nearly everything he looked at held a memory of some kind. Homes where friends or old girlfriends had grown up—some of them dead now, many of them incarcerated. Storefronts where he had spent hundreds of hours loitering or selling drugs. Nothing had changed over the last few years. Everything still looked the same. Same tired buildings and tired people. The same chain link fences rusted out, pulled up, and cut through. Everything about this neighborhood made him feel tired and depressed.

Everything about it felt like a dead end with no hope of ever getting out.

But he had gotten out, and he didn't regret a single decision that helped him to it.

Felipe turned down Alazon Avenue and stopped in front of a forsaken bus stop. The city had rerouted the bus lines five years ago, and somehow this one had missed inclusion into the edict to pluck up the old ones.

There wasn't much to it. The backdrop was a steel mesh square with a concrete bench set in its center. Both were covered in layers of graffiti, and the bench had a chunk missing from the right side.

He sat down, still feeling the effects of the marijuana, but not so much that his chest couldn't feel the ache. This was where he was headed when he stopped off for the unplanned visit at Benito's. But the dull pang inside him had compelled the diversion. It was also what pressed him to accept the joint and to carry some out with him, even though he'd been clean of everything but cigarettes and alcohol for the last year.

He ran a hand down the top of the bench, remembering it all like it was yesterday. Except that it wasn't yesterday. It was eighteen years ago today. He had been sitting right here in this very spot, his six-year-old hand clasped firmly in his mother's. Felipe remembered her being tired that day. Waking before dawn each morning and juggling three low-paying jobs had produced dark circles beneath her eyes and stolen most of her smiles. Most days he wouldn't even see her before he went to bed. But that day was different. Felipe had begged her for weeks to take him to his cousin's house on the other side of town. She finally relented and took off the first half of the day to escort him there.

He remembered that morning being chilly. A storm had moved in the evening before and left the city damp and cloudy. The bus pulled in and left. When he asked his mother why they didn't get on, she said that it wasn't their bus. The next one would be by in five minutes.

But she only lived another three.

Felipe had been sitting right here with his legs dangling toward the sidewalk, his mother humming a quiet tune, when a dark car drove by and slowed in front of the bus stop. He watched the window roll down and a gun appear in its place. Then the shots came. One after another.

He could remember screaming, falling to the pavement with his hands clasped over his ears. It took an old man grabbing him up and getting him to his feet before realizing that the car was gone, the shooting over.

His mother lay dead at his feet, her body riddled with bullets.

The killers were never caught. The police said it was random. Justice never came for his mother.

Felipe learned something that day. Something the schools never taught him.

The world was cold and heartless. Those around him still worked and lived as if life rewarded the kind, the caring, and the hard working.

But he did not believe that. Life rewarded no one because it did not care. His mother's killers had lived—probably still were alive. She was the one who had died, not them. This place should have been turned into a memorial and a statue or a tomb erected in her memory.

The good die young, and the rich grow old.

If being caring and kind got you gunned down at a

bus stop, then why be good at all? If it was the cruel who survived, why not join them? At least then you weren't waiting around for life to squash you. Why not live with the upper hand?

And so he had. Felipe had joined the darkness with abandon. He was eight when he started with petty theft —bubble gum, a bag of Doritos, Slim Jims. By the time he was twelve, he was slinging drugs with the best of them. Now, it was the girls, a new career twist that served to reinforce his life's philosophy.

Only the strong survive.

He stood up. He wouldn't come here again. A part of him was surprised that he even had. The past was the past. His mother wasn't coming back.

He walked another three blocks along Alazon Avenue and turned south onto Emilio Siboney Drive. A dark gray van was parked on the curb across the street. Every few weeks they repainted it a new color and gave it different wheels. Cruz had even slapped a pink "Save the Tatas" bumper sticker on it. Felipe climbed in, started the engine, and was near to putting it in gear when he remembered the baggie in his pocket. He pulled it out. Cruz had left his cigarette lighter in the center cup holder. Felipe gave a quick glance down the street and, satisfied that there were no police in the near vicinity, he lit up.

And felt himself relax all over again.

CHAPTER FIFTEEN

Several miles southeast of Hialeah, far from the gaudy clamor of South Beach and the pastel-hued elegance of the art deco district, sat the epicenter of Miami's Hispanic culture; Little Havana's Caribbean spirit and Cuban character combined to make it one of the city's most iconic neighborhoods.

At one time, a lower-middle-class Jewish neighborhood, Little Havana materialized in the 1960s when a large concentration of Cuban exiles, fleeing from fallout from Fidel Castro's revolution, settled into the area. In the present, it continued as one of Miami's largest Hispanic districts, rich in Cuban culture, its people well known for their friendliness and hospitality.

Jet stepped off the curb onto Calle Ocho and crossed to the other side. The vibrant street was famous for its restaurants and bakeries, ventanitas, and vibrant street festivals, and busy locals combined with curious tourists to create an atmosphere charged with an energetic hum. He turned at Máximo Gómez Park and entered through its double iron gates. Also known as

Domino Park, Máximo Gómez Park was host to several small, wood-framed pavilions boasting red tile roofs. Beneath each green painted pavilion sat a cluster of tables, each with room to seat four. All the tables were full. Elderly men with leathery skin, distended bellies, and gray beards joked and laughed as they slapped down dominoes, smoked cigars, and chided each other about past losses and old baseball scores. Jet joined the onlookers alongside one of the tables, thinking that playing dominoes outside with several friends wasn't the worst way to pass your retirement years. The game finally ended when a man on Jet's left added his last tile to the layout. The man across from him stood up. He indicated to Jet. "Are you playing?"

Jet held up a hand. "Thank you, but I should be going." A frail, ancient of a man, whom Jet thought could have been friends with Methuselah—if not Methuselah himself—came around the table and delicately placed himself into the empty seat. Jet took his leave of the park and continued down Calle Ocho.

He passed up souvenir shops selling Cuban cigars, key chains, mugs, colorful sundresses, and fedoras and walked by a street vendor who was sitting on a bucket, making grasshoppers and parrots out of thin strips of palm fronds that he skillfully wove together.

At the corner of the next block, Jet stood in the doorway of Papi's La Cubana, a local eatery whose sidewalk sign advertised today's specials on ceviche and yuca frita. Beginning at 4 pm and ending at 6 pm, margaritas would be half price. He went in and was immediately hit with the pleasant smell of fried plantains. The lunch hour was nearing its end, and he stepped aside to allow a group of men in slacks and ties to pass.

The wood-framed ceiling hung low and was painted a dark blue. Potted palms and banana trees were positioned at regular intervals across the bare concrete floor, and across the room, a small wooden stage sat beneath a stained-glass window. Wooden table tops were inlaid with glazed orange, blue, and red tiles, and on the stage were perched a keyboard, a Batá drum, and a set of timbales, ready for whichever band would be playing this evening's entertainment. Energetic Timba music streamed from speakers mounted in the rafters, complemented by hearty laughter coming from a small crowd at the bar.

A young lady in a light blue sundress offered a generous smile as Jet approached the narrow lectern that served as a hostess station. "Just one?" she asked.

"Actually, I'd like to speak with Saint," Jet said. "If he's here today."

The young lady held the smile against the unusual request. "Yes, he is here today. Let me see if he can step away," she said. "Is he expecting you?"

"No. But I only need a couple minutes of his time. My name is Jet."

"One moment," she said, and turned toward the kitchen. While he waited, Jet grabbed a soft peppermint from the bowl, unwrapped it, and popped it in his mouth. It dissolved quickly and was gone entirely by the time the lady returned. She gestured toward the bar. "You can wait over there. He'll be out in a moment."

"Thank you." The television above the bar was showing the first of three away games the Marlins were playing against the Rockies. It kept Jet's attention until a huge man came out of the kitchen. He looked like a Spanish version of a sumo wrestler, as though every part of his body had been overinflated. He went to the end of the bar and assessed Jet.

"I'm Saint. You wanted to talk with me."

"Yes, please."

"You a cop?"

"Private investigator." Jet half-expected the cook to dismiss him and turn back to the kitchen. Instead, he motioned toward an empty table near the stage. They sat, and Saint folded his thick arms—which came close to resembling two legless dachshunds—across his chest.

"What do you need to know?" he asked. Jet introduced himself and spent the next couple of minutes explaining his interest in Juanita as well as the information he received from the young man in Hialeah. When he finished, Saint asked, "And this guy, he didn't give you his name?"

"No. And I can't say that I blame him. Any chance you remember that party?"

Saint scratched at his chin. "I do. I made a lot of money that night."

"How so?"

"Cocaine. I used to deal. Had me a good hustle going. But one day I was helping my *abuelita* and found out that I like to cook. Even better, that people liked my cooking. So now that's what I do. I got tired of looking over my shoulder every five minutes." He shook his head. "Makes you feel old real quick."

Jet asked, "Do you remember this guy being at the party?"

"Yeah. I do."

"What does he look like?" Saint went on to provide the same description Alex had given him—the same one Juanita's little brother had given the detective: tall, broad-shouldered, not skinny, but not overweight either, and possessing average facial features that offered nothing that would distinguish him from the next guy.

"Any idea where I can find him?" Jet was hoping this wasn't where he hit a dead end.

"No. I have no idea." Saint set his elbows on the table and folded his hands. "Now, I'm not saying this man is the same as your Jesse. The same man this guy in Hialeah saw. But the guy who pulled that gun at the party, his name is Felipe."

"Any last name?"

He shook his head. "I just know him by Felipe. He used to work some of the curbs closer to downtown pushing smack."

"He doesn't anymore?"

"Nah. He almost got busted and quit. I'll tell you this though. People like me," he slapped his chest with an open palm, "are hard to find. I'm legit out of the game. Just a cook. But people like Felipe, they always gonna be running some kind of play. If you think he took this girl—or a bunch of girls—then that don't surprise me."

Jet had over thirty years in with the DEA. Saint, he knew, was right. It was rare that a dealer walked away from selling drugs on their own compulsion. It was especially rare if they were making a lot of money at it. Jet had only known one other person to have made such a decision: Samuel Diego. His girlfriend gave birth to a baby boy, and it seemed that was all the motivation he needed. Samuel quit the street, went to college, and, the last Jet had heard, was now the owner of a used tire shop in Estero. Assuming that Saint was telling the truth and that his dope days were over, it was to be commended. "Any idea where I could find him?" Jet asked.

Saint shook his head. "Nah. I made a clean break with my old *plebe*. That's what gets you back in the game at some point. Got to change your friends if you want to change your life." Saint shifted in his chair, and it protested loudly under his weight. Jet thought there was a good chance the man might end up finishing the conversation from the floor. "But you know," Saint said, "I can make some calls after I get off and try to find out. Someone will know what he's up to. Give me your number, and I'll let you know when I find something." Jet recited his number while Saint punched it into his phone. When he was done, Saint used the table to leverage himself off the chair. "You eat lunch?"

"Not yet."

"How about I make you a Cuban sandwich or something? It's on me."

"Sure," he conceded. "Thank you."

Saint motioned toward a waitress. She was chatting with a co-worker near the kitchen door. "Maria will get you something to drink. Give me a few minutes." He started toward the kitchen before pausing to turn back around. "I hope Felipe's your man. I hope you can find that girl."

"Thank you, Saint. Me too."

CHAPTER SIXTEEN

Felipe slipped the keys into the ignition and started up the van. He felt better. The powerful strain of marijuana had been long overdue, and his time at the bus stop had served to reaffirm his cynical view on life.

He pulled into the road and drove until a red light forced him to come to a stop. An elderly gentleman crossed in front of him, and Felipe nodded a curt reply when the man lifted his hand in a gesture of friendliness. The light switched to green, and he eased forward. Save for the occasional car or bus, there was hardly any traffic. Most people on this side of town did not own a vehicle of their own, choosing instead to take advantage of the conveniences afforded to them by public transportation and taxi services like Uber or Lyft.

Up ahead, on his right, he saw two girls with dark hair. The tallest of the pair turned her head and laughed in response to something her friend had said. Her profile was clearly visible, and Felipe recognized her immediately.

He always planned his engagements with care. To

the girls, he would "bump into them" or stop by at the perfect time, when they were on the way to the store or when he knew they would be alone at home. The friend up ahead did not know him; she had never seen him before. That was just the way he liked it. The fewer people who could identify him the better.

Felipe had not scheduled any engagements for today. Had his discernment not been tempered by the marijuana, he would have felt the impulse to drive past quickly or pull a U-turn before she was afforded a chance to recognize him or his van.

But that was not to be the case. His decision-making facilities were temporarily disconnected from the area of his mind that assisted him in making sound judgments.

The girls were wearing short sleeve shirts and black shorts. One of them had a large pink purse thrown over a shoulder. He smiled to himself as he slowed the vehicle and pressed a button on his door that brought down the passenger window. He leaned toward the open window and whistled. "Hey, Ana!" The girls stopped and cautiously assessed the van. "It's me." The sun was bright in the sky, and Ana stepped closer as she squinted into the vehicle. "Jesse!" she said excitedly, "I was just talking about you."

"Were you?"

"Yes. I was telling her how you got me that box of chocolates last week. I miss you," she said. "Where have you been?"

Grooming another girl in Fort Lauderdale and another in Kendall. "My mother has been sick," he replied. "The flu or something. I've had to watch after her."

"I'm sorry. You're good to take care of her."

"She's better now. Who's your friend?"

"Oh, this is Carla." Felipe pulled the van to the sidewalk and left it running as he came around to the other side. Ana reached in and gave him a hug but quickly pulled back. She took a step back and shriveled her nose. "You've been smoking. I thought you said you didn't do that kind of thing?"

"I don't. I was at a friend's house."

"It's on your breath, Jesse."

Alarm bells were started to sound off in the back of his mind, but he did not currently possess the ability to act on them properly. His eyes drooped a little. Benito's stuff was still working at him. That was exactly why he'd quit smoking weed when he took this job. But when Benito had offered him some a couple of hours ago, it hadn't seemed like such a bad idea. Nor did lighting up in the van a few minutes ago. He smiled, but it was overdone and looked unnatural. "Okay," he conceded, "I had a little bit. But it helps me relax, okay? Not a big deal. It's not like I'm hitting the hard stuff."

Ana frowned. "You lied to me?"

"No. I didn't lie to you. Today was the first time in a long time." That much was true. And the irony was that it was probably the only bit of truth he had ever spoken to her.

"I don't like you smoking that stuff, Jesse. My old boyfriend did it, and he wasn't any good." This received a huff of agreement from her friend, who was looking at him with grating suspicion. He decided immediately that he didn't like her. And he didn't like the way Ana had responded to him enjoying a little smoke.

An idea suddenly burst through the haze like a rising sun on a foggy morning. The metal cylinder containing the knockout gas was still in the van. He hadn't taken it out since they last used it last week. The gas mask was under his seat. The look of betrayal and disgust on Ana's face was beginning to annoy him. Her voice was suddenly whiny, and, while her looks were striking, he was tired of her. The thought of spending a few more weeks grooming her now seemed about as fun as hanging out at the old bus stop.

He could end this. Right now.

He looked afresh at Ana's friend. She wasn't bad either. A little on the plump side. But some men preferred that. He turned to the van and opened the side door, then gestured with his hand. "How about I take you both to dinner? Where do you want to go?"

"Really?" Ana perked up, seeming to forget all about the last minute of conversation. She bit down on her bottom lip and peered up at him with large, pleading eyes. "Could you take us somewhere downtown?"

"Sure I can. Get on in."

"Okay!" Much to Felipe's delight, Ana stepped toward the van. She ducked her head and had just set her foot on the inside step when her friend grabbed her shirt and pulled her back. "What are you doing?" Ana snapped.

Her friend was shaking her head. "I don't want to go anywhere with him."

"But it's Jesse. You know him. I've told you about him."

The friend's face was severe now, and she looked Felipe directly in the eyes as she spoke. "I don't like him. Something isn't right."

"What are you talking about, Carla?" Ana reached out and ran the tips of her fingers down Felipe's forearm. "He's fine."

Felipe made a quick glance down both ends of the empty street. Ana's fingers were still resting on his skin when he chose to act. He reached for her, grabbing her by the shoulders and thrusting her toward the open door of the van. She wasn't expecting the sudden act of violence, and she went easily, tumbling onto the cracked vinyl of the front rear seat. She yelled out in a confused medley of both pain and anger, but Felipe paid her no attention. He had already turned his attention to her friend.

Carla's eyes were wide with fear, and Felipe could see the panicked indecision in them as she wavered between defending herself against him or trying to save her friend. He didn't wait. He reached out and snatched her by the hair. Carla cried out, and as he pulled her toward the curb, she shot a foot out, catching him just below the kneecap. A burst of heat exploded inside his leg, and he released his grip on her hair. But, much to his surprise, the pain subsided as quickly as it came, allowing him to regain his focus.

Carla had taken advantage of the tiny window of time to slip behind Felipe. She was at the door of the van now, reaching through as she screamed at her friend to grab her hand.

She was right where Felipe wanted her to be.

He shoved Carla with both hands, and she fell forward. Her face smacked into the floor of the van, and Ana screamed as Felipe grabbed Carla's feet, which were still floundering outside of the door, and tried to push her the rest of the way in.

Felipe had been grooming Ana for nearly two months now. All along she had displayed the textbook qualities that revealed her as the perfect girl for him to choose. She was naïve, lonely, and with no family to speak of, alarm bells wouldn't sound too loudly when she turned up missing.

Felipe was tall, his hands strong, and under normal circumstances, the girls would have been no match for him. But these were not normal circumstances. The second joint he had relished not thirty minutes before made his movements sloppy and languid, and he was slow to notice Ana leaning back on the seat before she propelled the heel of her boot into Felipe's face while he continued his struggle with Carla. The sudden force to his face made him stagger back away from the van, and it gave the girls just enough time to scramble back out to the sidewalk.

Carla opened her hand and slashed haphazardly at Felipe's face. Her nails caught the flesh at the top of his cheek, and as she pulled down, they raked away the top layer of skin. She followed it up with an angry foot to his groin.

It was in that moment, as his loins took the brunt of the kick, that Felipe realized he had acted rashly. He bent forward, and his eyes bulged in his skull as the pain took over and he tried to breathe through it.

Ana finally found her lungs and pealed off a ragged shriek of a scream, one sharp, elongated note of terror that brought two ladies out of a hair salon at the far end of the street. Carla grabbed Ana's hand and pulled her away from her wannabe kidnapper. They turned and fled down the street as though they had just flipped to the wrong page in a choose-your-own-adventure novel, only this wasn't a story about ant people or being lost in the Amazon. No, this was real life, where real men with fake names tried to draw you into their wicked webs.

Felipe watched helplessly after them as he hobbled back to the van. He slammed the side door and, as a middle-aged lady in curlers pointed toward him, he went around to the driver's side and slid in behind the steering wheel.

As he put the van in gear and sped away, he glanced in the rearview mirror and watched as the girls disappeared around a corner. He hit the steering wheel and cursed loudly. All the work, the dozens of hours he spent trying to win Ana over, they had all been in vain.

The girls would tell the authorities. There were at least two other witnesses to his crippled attempt at an abduction. They would tell the authorities too.

He couldn't come back here. He would have to forget about Ana and continue his focus on the other girls in his sinister pipeline.

Felipe could feel the pulsating rhythm of his heartbeat, and his chest rose and fell as he tried to catch his breath. The pain around his groin was beginning to ease, and the rush of adrenaline was like a sudden breeze that served to clear some of the lingering haze from his mind.

The light at the next intersection turned red, and he slowed to a stop behind an Altima. Other cars began to slow as well, and they gathered around him. He suddenly felt as though the entire world was looking at him, that they were privy to his kidnapping attempt and were, at this moment, calling it in to the police. Even the red light up ahead looked like an ominous, all-seeing eye intent on discovering his secrets. He flipped on his turn signal. When the light switched to green and the space widened between the other vehicles, he changed lanes and turned left. He would take the long route home.

Felipe sighed and tried to forget about the last several minutes. He glanced over at the baggie of marijuana that was still resting on the seat next to him and almost reached for it. But he didn't, choosing instead to roll down his window and let in a humid breeze that was freshened by the ocean beyond.

It was time to paint the van again.

CHAPTER SEVENTEEN

When Ellie was a little girl, her mother took her two small daughters to a bygone but still functional fire station nestled on the edge of Fort Myers's industrial district. In the late 1920s, just before the Great Depression began its grand sweep across the country, the city built the narrow station into the corner of a two-story red brick building that had been home to a munitions factory during the first World War. The building's wooden bi-fold doors were a glossy dark green, and two archways were wide enough for the fire engines to pass through. The old building was nothing if not charming.

Katrina O'Conner had grown up in a bleak and harsh Cold War Russia where happiness, if it was to be had, was found in the little things. Ellie remembered her mother peering inside the red fire engines and watching a fire drill and a demonstration on the fireman's pole, all the while appearing as enchanted and captivated as her daughters.

She died three months later undergoing an emergency appendectomy, leaving two little girls to face a strident world without her. In the years since, Ellie had stacked up three decades' worth of memories, all absent of her mother. Even so, it had become her experience that a daughter's longing for her mother never fully subsided. Her absence, while no longer at the forefront and all-consuming, remained ambient, and, like the air, it covered everything.

It was ten-thirty in the evening. Ellie had spent the last hour observing the old building from a darkened doorway further down the street, away from the revealing glow of a crescent moon. At some point in recent years, when the industrial district began a slow migration into North Fort Myers, the city decided to relocate the fire station a mile west, off Tice Street. Whoever purchased the old building from the city had since swapped the green doors with plain metal ones, and one of the two arches intended for fire truck access was now fully bricked in, as were the windows. The second vehicular entrance, while still in use, was bricked in at the top, an industrial roller door finishing out the lower portion. The street number was hand-painted above the door, but there was no sign to designate which business, if any, worked out of the location.

The entire area felt like a modern-day ghost town, and there were no dark cars parked along the edge of the curb or men in leather jackets smoking outside. Ellie had seen no one, heard nothing. Only two trucks and one car had lumbered by, and the latter, Ellie was fairly certain, had been lost. The streets were empty, their lighting intermittent and poor, setting the deserted intersection into a dingy afterglow.

So far, she saw no indication that anyone was inside. A thin sliver of light shone through the side edge of the roller door, but the door had yet to go up; no one had gone in or come out. Coming here had been a gamble to begin with; she knew there was but the smallest of chances that anything would come of it. It seemed that her final option before reaching a dead end was to ask Jet to look up the name of the building's new owner. An online search performed a few hours ago had yielded nothing on Breakwater's ownership either. Jet would need to help with that too.

Ten-thirty gave way to eleven o'clock, and Ellie was considering heading back to her truck when a pair of headlights appeared at the far end of the street. They drew closer, and the vehicle began to slow. It was a white van, and much to Ellie's satisfaction, the roller door rumbled up, and the van drove in.

Ellie was wearing blue jeans and a dark hoodie over a gray tank top. The hood was already up, but she tucked her hands into her pockets and started to walk. A sheen of yellow light emanated from the open doorway, and she heard the hollow thud of a vehicle door slamming shut inside. She was thirty feet from the entrance when the van reappeared, turned out, and went back down the street before turning at the second intersection and disappearing altogether. Ellie quickened her pace, hoping to get a glimpse inside, but the door rumbled back to life and shuddered down before she had the chance.

She paused at the entrance and set her ear to the door. The light inside was still on, but she heard nothing and was unable to determine whether there was anyone inside. A new set of headlights emerged down the street, and she was forced to start walking again. She drew up at the end of the block and waited. The vehicle turned before it reached her, and Ellie was about to go back when, from a rooftop across the street, a brief glint of reflective light suddenly activated her defensive instincts. She slipped around the corner and set her back to the wall.

The building directly across from the old fire station had been home to a fiberglass factory for nearly six decades before getting bought out by a conglomerate that uprooted the operation to New England. Now the massive structure was nothing but an empty shell. Along the entire perimeter, the top edge was lined with rows of casement windows, some broken, all of them dusty and opaque from years of neglect.

Someone was on its roof.

Ellie cautiously peered around the corner and looked up. She could just make out the head of a darkened figure over the roof's parapet wall.

The glint of light told her they had a lens, and whether it belonged to a rifle scope or a camera, she was unable to say. Whatever the case, they certainly weren't there for her; she didn't tell anyone she was coming here, and she had already exposed herself by walking down the street and pressing her ear to the door.

She stayed out of sight and jogged down the street, away from the factory and fire station. After putting two blocks behind her and turning south again, she finally made her way to the back side of the old factory, still a block away from where she had been two minutes earlier. Staying close to the wall, Ellie quietly tested steel doors along the perimeter until she found one that opened to her. She stepped inside.

She waited while her eyes adjusted to the darkness and gathered in what little light pierced through the upper row of windows. A wide, empty floor was open before her, punctuated only by steel support columns that rose like naked sentries in the musty air. Working on the assumption that whoever was on the roof might have a lookout below, Ellie stepped into the shadow of the outer wall and quietly worked her way to the other end, where she finally made out the skeleton of a staircase zig-zagging up the wall.

She padded quietly across the concrete while scanning the floor and the staircase for another figure. Seeing nothing alarming, she placed a foot on the bottom rung and slowly set her weight into it. It was solid. She moved up to the next step, careful of the speed at which she advanced. The last thing she wanted was for a temperamental step to belie her presence with a raucous squeak.

Finally arriving at the top landing, she moved to the far end where three more steps led to the roof hatch directly above. Her orientation informed her that when she opened the hatch, she would be facing whoever was on the roof, assuming they were still there and hadn't altered their position. She set her fingertips against the metal and held her breath as she pressed upward.

The figure—clearly a man by his countenance: tall, strong legs, and wide shoulders—was stationed at a four-foot parapet not five yards in front of her. He was wearing blue jeans and a black long-sleeved t-shirt; a dark ball cap sat atop his head. He was on a knee, looking over the wall. Ellie couldn't see what he was looking through, but she relaxed as she saw that his body positioning did not speak to a rifle or a gun. His shoulders were too straight, and whatever was clasped in his hands was too close to his face.

She continued observing from her concealed position and soon heard a series of muffled clicks. The man stepped back, and when he shifted around, the moonlight's silvery glow caught him along his cheek.

It was Jet.

CHAPTER EIGHTEEN

During the three-hour ride across the Everglades, Felipe smoked half a pack of cigarettes and emptied all the tequila from his tall flask. He felt good now, as the double-duty buzz produced by both the alcohol and the nicotine surfed through his bloodstream. He closed his eyes and leaned his head back against the headrest, glad that he didn't have to drive to their destination.

He couldn't remember his driver's name or where he had seen him before. But his white pants and shirt, stained with half a dozen colors of paint, gave away his skill set. As did the paint cans in the back of the van. During the last half an hour, neither had spoken a word.

The driver took the next exit off the highway and slowed at a stop sign. He turned right and continued down an empty road that led to a cluster of buildings in the distance. The area was familiar to Felipe; he had been here many times before. More than he would like to recall. The van completed a final turn, slowed, and pulled through the vehicle entrance. The high ceiling of the old building was fifty feet above. The scars along the upper perimeter of the wall could still be seen from where the second floor had been secured decades before. But it was gone now. Other than a half wall near the back, the place was a hollow shell.

Felipe hadn't been here in a couple of weeks, not since Cruz decided to use an alternate location for their staging area. But he was surprised to see that it had been emptied so quickly. A few panels of sheetrock lay against the bare bricks of the outer wall. All the shelves, previously filled with equipment and supplies, save for a few paint cans, were empty too.

Felipe got out of the van and noticed his driver was still buckled, his hand on the gear shift. "You getting out?" he asked.

The man replied in Spanish. "No. You're getting a ride back with someone else." He put the van in reverse and backed toward the shelving before changing gears and exiting out the way he had come in. The door shut behind him automatically.

A metal staircase hugged the interior wall and led up to a windowed office. The light was on. Cruz's Tundra was parked near the base of the stairs, and next to it, spread out across the concrete, were two large, gray tarps. Felipe walked across the tarps and made his way to a heavy door in the center of the half wall. He opened it and peered inside the rear space. The mattresses were gone. There were a couple of folding chairs, a small table, and a toilet at the far end, where a yellow janitor's bucket sat next to the wall. Felipe thought he smelled a faint hint of bleach. A steel mesh door was still bolted into the brick wall, covering the back door.

Felipe shut the door and waited. He was beginning

to grow impatient. Cruz had a way of making him wait. He didn't like it. He had just started toward the stairs when the office light went out and Cruz appeared above him, and his heavy footsteps created a thin echo as he descended. "Cruz," Felipe said, letting his irritation fall away, "you've got the place looking good. I can hardly recognize it."

Cruz stepped onto the tarps and stopped in the center. Felipe followed him, and, as Cruz turned to him, he noticed that the muscular man was wearing a scowl. "Felipe, what's your role in this operation?"

The question surprised him. "I find the girls. I get them to trust me."

"And what is my role?"

"What is this? I know what you do."

Cruz suddenly smiled. But it was an irritated smile as though he were speaking with a toddler. "Yes. But I want you to remind me. What's my role in this operation?

"You do a bunch of stuff. With me, you tell me when you're ready for them and come help me get them."

"When I brought you in on this, I did it because you and me, we go way back. You slung a lot of dope on the street, and I knew you were up for this job. And you've done good. Very good, in fact. But tell me, what else did I ask you to do?"

Felipe gave a weak shrug. "Nothing. That's all."

Cruz rubbed at his chin as he nodded. "See, I don't think it is. Because it sounds to me like you're also running your mouth, telling people what it is you do."

"What? No, I don't."

"Benito Salazar's brother says differently."

An icy sensation, like a slowly melting snowball,

worked its way down Felipe's neck as he recalled his THC-induced confession to Benito the other day. A slip he knew he never should have made.

"And if that wasn't bad enough, you decided to try and grab up not just one, but two girls. In the daylight. Without my authorization. The only reason there isn't a warrant out for you is because my guy on the inside stopped the girls' report from going anywhere."

"Okay," Felipe snapped. "I get it. I screwed up. It won't hap—"

"Please tell me you weren't about to tell me it won't happen again. That would just be too...obvious."

Felipe turned his hands up. "What do you want me to say? I'm sorry. Half the girls you've got is because of me. Just lay off."

"Do you realize how many moving parts there are to our organization? If one piece slips out of line, it risks the exposure of everyone else. I vouched for you when I brought you on. If you screw up, Mr. Zedillo will hold me responsible."

"You think I don't know that?"

"I think you do know that. Very well, in fact. And that's exactly why your actions concern me. On top of that, there's a private investigator looking for one of the girls. Somehow he's learned your real name."

"What? That's not possible."

"And yet it is. People have been talking. It seems they have no allegiance to you."

"Who? I'll go shut them up myself."

"No. Mr. Zedillo believes you have become a problem."

"You told Zedillo? Why would you do that?"

"Because, Felipe. You're a liability. A problem. And

you of all people know what we do with problems." Cruz reached behind him and tugged a revolver from the seam of his jeans. He thumbed back the exposed hammer and pointed it at Felipe.

And now Felipe was silently cursing Maury Povich; although he knew this wasn't Maury's fault. It was that damn Purple Hurricane or Purple Haze or whatever it was that Benito had given him. "Oh, come on." He huffed boldly. "Intimidating me isn't gonna work. I can fix this. Let me talk with Zedillo. Now get that gun out of my face before I—"

Cruz pressed the trigger, and Felipe's right eye disappeared as his head swung back and hit the ground with a sickening crunch on the back end of the discharge's echo. His body now lay sprawled unevenly across the tarp, and his right leg twitched as blood pooled around his head like a hellish halo.

Cruz shot him again.

CHAPTER NINETEEN

ELLIE RETREATED two steps and silently lowered the access hatch. Withdrawing her phone, she typed out a message to Jet, hit "send," and waited.

She knew Jet kept a concealed carry wherever he went. The last thing she wanted was to frighten him and give him a reason to reach for it. The hatch door creaked above her and disappeared as it swung away. Jet's face appeared in its place. He extended his hand and helped her the rest of the way up. When both her feet were on the roof, he spoke in a charged whisper. "What are you doing here?"

She indicated toward his camera. "What are *you* doing here? I'm scouting the place across the street."

"What, the old fire station?"

"Yes."

"So am I."

They stared quizzically at each other, their features shadowed in the moon's muted light.

"That was you listening by the entrance a couple minutes ago?" Jet asked.

"Yes."

"Why?" Jet asked.

"Someone told me that—" Ellie was interrupted by the distinct sound of a gunshot coming from across the street. She and Jet exchanged knowing, concerned glances, and she followed him back to the parapet, where they peered across the street as another shot pulsed through the air. Then the night was silent again.

"Stay up here," she said. "You have the camera. I'm going down there." She returned to the hatch.

"No, Ellie. Just let me—"

But she was already gone.

* * *

As soon as her feet left the stairs and touched the concrete, Ellie ran across the dusty floor and exited the same door she had entered through just minutes earlier. She turned north and ran down the sidewalk, pulling up as she neared the corner. She peered around to get a glimpse of the fire station. The roller door was still down, and there were no windows to offer the possibility of a peek inside.

She crossed the street and took the sidewalk down the length of the old brick building, hurrying around to the rear. She cut down the narrow alley and found a freshly painted metal door set into the brickwork. When she set her hand on the doorknob and tried it, she wasn't surprised to find it locked. Ellie returned to the front corner and looked up to the roofline of the factory where Jet's camera lens winked against the moonlight.

Under normal circumstances, Ellie would have already called in the shots. But this was not an ordinary circumstance. She was looking for who killed her friend. She didn't know which of Jet's cases had led him here, and she was anxious to find out, but she wanted answers of her own before she went out and blew the whistle to the authorities.

Someone was still inside the building. A gun didn't go off by itself. Certainly not twice. To Ellie's trained ear, the report sounded like a revolver. At some point, whoever was inside would have to leave.

Her truck was parked a quarter mile away, in an empty dirt lot on Staley Avenue. She left her spot on the corner and jogged to it with a hundred questions pulsing through her mind. She arrived at her truck, got in, and as she started it up, her phone rang. It was Jet, still whispering. "Where did you go?"

"To get my truck."

His next words charged her with adrenaline. "Someone just left. A black Tundra."

Ellie accelerated into the street and floored the pedal. "Which direction?"

"Ellie, I need to call in those shots. Someone could be hurt."

"Did you get a picture of the license plate?"

"No. I couldn't get a good angle on the rear of the car."

"Which direction?" she repeated.

"East down McCallister."

Ellie eased off the gas and took her next left. "Give me a window before you call it in," she said. Her fingers gripped the phone tightly while she waited for his reply.

When he spoke again, a heavy reluctance filled his voice. "All right. Just be careful."

* * *

Ellie found the red glow of the Tundra's taillights just before it turned left at a green light and disappeared from view once again. She followed it onto Franklin Street and kept her Silverado trailing behind at a speed that wouldn't attract attention. Over the next few minutes, the ragged commercial buildings thinned out and disappeared altogether as they put the city further behind them and continued into the rural darkness of east Fort Myers. Ellie trailed behind at a steady distance of a hundred yards and watched as the car turned north, taking Orange River Boulevard until it became Louise Street just beyond the overpass of Florida State Highway 80. Another half a mile and Louise Street became Maynard Street at a sharp bend, and the Tundra's taillights disappeared once again, this time around a thick cluster of towering oaks.

The Orange River was one of the Caloosahatchee River's many tributaries, and the road snaked unevenly as it traced the river's banks before once again straightening out and transitioning from asphalt to hard-packed dirt. River reeds and oaks lined the road, and campsites opened on the left, nearly all of them vacant. Ellie observed as the Tundra turned into a campsite. She maintained the posted speed limit of fifteen miles-per-hour, driving past the other truck and fighting off the urge to turn and look out her window.

She parked five campsites further down and got out. The air was cooler here by the river, and a lingering breeze stirred the reeds and grasses near the river bank. Each campsite was an open clearing and separated by its neighbor by several yards of natural undergrowth. Ellie quietly slipped past the campsites. The third one she came to was occupied, but, with it being near to midnight, it appeared that everyone had already turned in for the night. A late-model Suburban was parked on the edge of the lot, and dying coals issued a weak and fading glow in the center of the fire ring. Nearer to the water, a large gray tent was zipped up.

Ellie passed on, finally coming to the edge of the campsite where the Tundra had turned in a minute earlier. Her cover was a thick copse of sword fern, coonie, and river reeds, and she looked on as the truck, still on, sat idle. The driver still had their foot on the brake, and the lights illuminated the front curtain of Ellie's cover, basking it in a soft red glow.

Five minutes slipped by. Ellie was starting to hope they wouldn't just drive off again when the familiar sound of an outboard engine caught her ear. Squatting, she peered through the stalks of reeds and saw the white hull of a boat ghost through the darkness and slip up the river bank like a beached whale. The Tundra's engine shut down, and the brake lights went out when the front door opened. The driver stepped out and shut the door before walking around to the side facing the bank. The truck was a crew cab, and when he opened the rear door, the dim light from the interior escaped into the night and touched his face, giving Ellie her first glimpse of him.

A strong chin and flat cheekbones went nearly unnoticed beneath a bulbous and twisted nose that, in some strange way, resembled a broken light bulb. His dark hair was cut back behind his ears, and his t-shirt was filled out by a large stomach and protruding muscles. The boat engine was silenced, and its operator jumped down to the muddy grass and approached the truck. The men greeted each other, spoke a few words Ellie couldn't make out, and the truck's driver reached into the back seat, grabbed something with both hands, and heaved it toward himself. He backed up as he repeated the action and the side of a large white ice chest appeared. The other man reached into the cab, presumably to grab the chest's other handle, and with a final, laborious tug, the chest slipped out of the truck and was lowered to the ground with a heavy thud. The man with the odd nose opened the front passenger door and rifled through the contents of the glove box while the other bent over the ice chest and lifted the lid.

"Ai yai yai," he exclaimed. "Felipe, man. Sorry, bro." The truck's driver slammed the glove box, stood up, then shut the passenger door. "What'd he do, Cruz?" the other man asked.

"He got sloppy. Now help me with him." The lid of the chest thumped shut, and he leaned over and grabbed the handle closest to him. His associate heaved up on the other end, and they walked the ice chest down to the riverbank like a couple of committed party-goers. Once on the boat, the Tundra beeped, and its lights flashed as it received instruction from the key fob. Ellie continued to watch, and one of the men pushed the boat off the grassy embankment and backed it into the water before treading in and slipping back on board. The engine started up, and the boat and its passengers were quickly absorbed by the darkness as it ran up river with whatever was left of Felipe.

Ellie came out of hiding and checked the Tundra's doors for good measure. They were locked and the men gone, which meant that unless she wanted to wake the folks a couple of campsites away and borrow some marshmallows for roasting, there was no more to be done here.

But that didn't mean there was nothing left to do.

For Ellie, the night was just getting started.

CHAPTER TWENTY

THERE WAS a twenty-four-hour Walgreens on the corner of State Road 80 and State Road 31. Ellie went in and selected items from cosmetics, body care, and a small shelf containing popular cooking ingredients. She took her purchases to the counter, paid, and called Jet as soon as she was back on the road. His voice came through her truck's speakers via a Bluetooth connection.

"Ellie, where are you?" he asked.

"On my way back."

"Where did the car end up?"

"An empty lot off Orange River. Someone was waiting for him." Ellie relayed what she had seen: the cooler, its transfer to the boat, and both men disappearing down the river.

"Did you get a good look at the driver?"

"Enough of one to recognize him if I saw him again. The other guy called him Cruz. I did get the license plate number. You want to write it down?"

He told her to wait, and when he gave her the go-ahead, she recited it before repeating it back once more. She asked him if he was going to call it in.

"Ellie, I was at that location tonight trying to find Juanita, the girl who went missing in Miami. For all I know those shots could have been for her. It could have been her in that cooler."

"It wasn't her."

"How do you know?"

"When the other guy opened the lid, he called the guy in the cooler 'Felipe.'" When Jet did not reply and the call stayed silent, she gave a verbal prod. "Jet?"

"I'm here. Felipe was my lead. You're telling me he's dead?"

"Unless they had a dog in that cooler with the same name, then yes. I guess they killed him tonight. Right under our noses." She exited the highway and turned left at the stop sign. "I need to know if you plan on calling it in," she said again. "It would be a big help to me if you waited." What concerned Ellie the most was that the email had been clear that going to the police was not safe. It could have been a ruse, or there could be something to it. She just didn't know yet.

Jet was a PI, which meant that he held such a license from the state of Florida. It also meant that he had to play by the rules.

Ellie, however, did not.

"Why?" he asked.

"I'm looking into something. Let me call you when I'm done if it's not too late. Then we can compare notes."

"Do you want me to come with you?"

"I need to go this alone."

"Ellie?"

"Yes?"

"I trust you," he said. "I'm not calling it in."

She knew he made the decision on the fringes of his conscience. "Thanks, Jet."

"Just call me when you're done. I'll be up."

Five minutes later, she found herself in the same parking space on Staley Avenue she'd left less than an hour before. She grabbed the Walgreens bag and stepped out into the deserted silence. The bed of her truck contained a crossover toolbox, and she flipped the latch and opened the lid. After selecting a couple of tools and pulling out a canvas backpack, she shut the toolbox and went around to the back of the truck. She lowered the tailgate and set everything down before dumping out the contents of the shopping bag. Above her, a tired sodium light was perched high on a creosote-covered telephone pole that was leaning at a disconcerting angle. Its light was meager and dim, but it was enough for Ellie to work in.

She slipped a bobby pin from its cardboard sleeve and used a pair of wire cutters to remove the rubber tip on the straight end and then set a crimp at the tip. She tucked it into a pocket and grabbed another bobby pin, then pinched it an inch below the center loop, and bent it into a ninety-degree angle. She tucked that one in her pocket, too, and stuffed the remaining items into the backpack before shouldering it, shutting the tailgate, and retracing her path back to the old fire station.

She arrived three minutes later beneath an eerie darkness brought on suddenly by thick, portentous clouds that shrouded the back alley in a darkness near that of an abandoned coal mine. Not wanting to risk the betraying beam of her flashlight, she felt along the doorway like a blind vagrant seeking shelter. When the lock finally settled beneath her fingertips, she plucked the bent bobby pin from her pocket and crouched before the door.

It was one of the greater ironies of modernity that the world could lay claim to private aerospace companies, smartphones, and driverless cars, while billions of people across an enlightened globe continued to secure their valuables and protect their loved ones behind Civil War-era technology, easily bypassed after three minutes spent in front of the proper YouTube video. It was not a petty fact that nearly ninety percent off all door locks, from Buenos Aires to Toronto, from Beijing to Cape Cod, all utilized the ubiquitous and infirmed pin tumbler lock, which, as it turned out, made keys, rather than a necessity, only an easy convenience which served to lull the mind into a false sense of security.

It was just such a lock that now held Ellie's attention. The mechanism was simple: inside the plug—the space where the key entered—were several vertical holes, each containing a driver pin and a key pin, with the latter under spring-driven pressure. The pins were there to block the plug from rotating and freeing the lock; they were responsible for keeping a lock locked. To properly pick a pin tumbler, all one had to do was set the driver pins up out of the plug by gently pressing each one into the top of their respective holes. Once the pins were out of the way, the lock would be compromised, and the plug would be free to rotate.

The bent bobby pin would serve as a tension wrench. Ellie inserted it into the bottom of the keyway and applied a small amount of rotational torque. Her second bobby pin would serve as the actual pick, and

Ellie brought it out and inserted it above the tension wrench. While keeping outward pressure on the wrench she raked the pick back and forth, probing the driver pins until she found one that bound up and separated from the key pin beneath it.

In less than a minute, all the pins were set, and when Ellie applied extra pressure to the tension wrench, the plug rotated fully, and the bolt slid away from the door.

Ellie pressed gently on the door, and it moved inward a half inch. Earlier, when she was observing the building from the street out front, there had been a thin crack of light coming from the side of the roller door. But it was dark inside now. So dark, in fact, that Ellie couldn't see her eyelashes, much less her nose.

Gently and cautiously, she pushed the door back. It hadn't moved three inches when it hit something with a muted thump and stopped. Ellie slipped her hand behind the door, and her fingers fell onto a cold and rigid surface. It was another door—a steel mesh door by the feel of it—but it responded to an easy push and swung silently into the darkness. After opening the outer door enough to step in, Ellie moved lightly across the threshold. She was hit by the heavy scent of bleach as she drew the outer door shut and brought out a flashlight from the bag. She turned it on, unsure of what the light might reveal.

Fifteen feet in front of her stood an unpainted wall reaching halfway to the ceiling high above. There was an open door in the center of it. It was a back room of sorts. A few folding chairs sat around a small table, and a toilet with no privacy barrier was positioned at the far end. She turned her light to the door she entered through. On the inside, the steel mesh door was mounted flush to the floor and the wall, as if to ensure no access through the rear exit.

Ellie stepped through the door in the center of the wall and came into the main area. Metal-framed shelves lined the exterior wall to her left, all of them empty save for a few paint cans. Several panels of sheetrock were leaning against the wall, and a yellow janitor's bucket sat near the roller door, its mop handle leaning out like a broken reed. An empty container of Clorox was turned over beside it. Her light revealed a flight of metal steps leading to a windowed area at the top. She hurried to the stairs and was careful not to touch the railing as she made her way up to the room.

It was a small office. Save for an empty desk and chair against the right wall, the room was vacant. Ellie was beginning to think she'd found this place a little too late. They had cleared out. She stepped to the desk and slipped her fingers beneath her hoodie before opening the drawers one by one. They were empty too. No leftover papers or forgotten folders. Not even a rogue pen or a stray memo.

Ellie pulled out the chair and set her bag on it, then stood the end of the flashlight on the desk so the light reflected off the ceiling and covered the room. She unzipped the middle pocket of the backpack and removed several items before placing them on the floor and taking a knee.

The desk was dark wood. Ellie opened the bottle of talcum powder and sprinkled a light dusting along the top edge. Then she selected the large makeup brush and gently flicked the outer bristles over the powder in a circular, back-and-forth motion. Near the front right corner, she found what she was looking for. She set the brush down and brought out the roll of transparent packing tape, then tore off a strip before leaning over and blowing out a gentle puff of air. With steady hands, she laid the tape over the fingerprint and pressed gently. She peeled it up and held it to the light. Other than an area near the bottom where the powder was over-distributed, the ridges and curves of the print were clearly visible. She cautiously laid it across the floor and tore off another strip of tape, placing it over the exposed side of the first strip. The print was now encased in tape. She put it in her bag.

Crime scene technicians used fingerprint dust that contained a mixture of elements: ferric oxide, rosin, and lampblack, as well as inorganic chemicals such as bismuth, lead, and cadmium. But when such powder was not accessible, white talcum powder could be used to dust on dark surfaces, and cocoa powder on lighter, non-porous surfaces. When applied properly against a clear print, they got the job done.

Moving quickly, Ellie dusted the arms of the chair, the light switch, and the door handle. A partial print showed itself on the switch plate, but Ellie wasn't able to pull it off before it smudged off on the tape.

After checking the office window, she left the room and dusted portions of the handrail, then went to the back room and checked the table, the chairs, and the toilet's lid and flush valve. The handrail presented nothing, and the back room was spotless, as though it had been carefully and thoughtfully cleaned. As though evidence had been intentionally cleared away.

Hurrying back upstairs, Ellie pulled out a pack of baby wipes and a dishcloth that she hadn't bothered to strip the tags from. Using the wipes, she cleaned away the powder and brought in the cloth behind them to draw away any leftover residue.

She was done now. She zipped up the bag and, after taking a final look around and turning off her light, exited the same way she had come in, using the bobby pins to lock the door behind her.

CHAPTER TWENTY-ONE

IT WAS NEARLY one in the morning when Ellie walked in the twenty-four-hour Starbucks in Cape Coral, and her senses were quickly mauled by the trenchant smell of over-brewed coffee. Jet was in the back, nestled into a plush leather chair, and he waved her over. She took the chair across from him and laid the backpack at her feet.

"Do you have as many questions as I do?" he asked.

"Maybe more."

"So how did we end up in the same place tonight?"

Ellie didn't know, but she spent the next five minutes relaying her conversations with Avi and Barry and how something the latter had said had brought her to the old fire station.

"So this Breakwater," Jet said, "Avi said they might be inflating invoices?"

"Yeah."

"Sounds like money laundering."

"That's what Barry said. But what about you? You said you were looking for the girl? Juanita, right?"

"Yeah. She went missing in Miami a couple months

ago." Jet went on to tell her about his time in Miami yesterday: Alex giving him the tour of the shelter, the young man who told him about Felipe, and stopping off at Papi's La Cubana to see Saint. "Saint called me this afternoon. Someone he knows said Felipe was doing some work out of that old fire station. That he was usually there at night. He didn't know anything more than that, but I thought it was worth following up on."

"And you think that guy in the ice chest tonight is the one who took the girls?" Ellie asked.

"I don't know. Honestly, I feel like I'm walking with one eye open. I'm not exactly sure what I'm looking for."

"Me neither," she agreed.

"Ellie, the only reason I'm not telling the authorities what we saw tonight is because I don't want to scare the wrong people off if they think someone is getting close. If Felipe really was this Jesse, the guy who took Juanita, then him getting killed is the least of my worries." Jet sighed at that point. "Except that it means my one lead just got fed to the fish and I'll be spending a lot of late nights up on that rooftop with my camera. It would have been nice if I could have gotten a glimpse inside."

That was when the corners of Ellie's mouth turned into a suggestive smile. Jet had spent enough time working alongside her at the DEA to know that when she smiled like that, and when it was accompanied by that easy twinkle in her eye, she was about to say something he was going to like. "What?" he asked, studying her. "Wait. Is that what you were doing? You went back there?"

Ellie reached down, unzipped her bag, and handed him the double strip of tape.

"What is this?"

"There was an office inside. That's a print from the desk."

"You're kidding me." And now it was his turn to smile. "How did you get in? I tried a back door in the alley after you took off. It was locked."

She gave a coy shrug of response.

"You broke in?"

"I wouldn't say that. I didn't break anything."

Jet turned the strip of tape over, examining it. "So that's what you were doing while I was just sitting here? You were in there getting this?"

"I was."

He shook his head, unbelieving.

"What's your turnaround time on finding out who that print belongs to?"

"Tomorrow afternoon at the latest. I'll have to take it in and get someone to scan it."

"Have you run the plates yet?"

"No. The state doesn't want any PI's on this new directive having wireless VPN access. I can only access that database from my office. I'll run them in the morning and let you know as soon as I get something back." He had a leather satchel sitting on the floor next to his chair, and he was careful as he slipped the tape inside. "What all did they have inside that building?"

"Not much. But it looked like whatever they had going on, they're on the way out. The office upstairs was completely empty, as was nearly everything else. I could be reaching, but there was a back section that could have been a perfect place to keep a kidnapped girl. Or several."

Jet's posture noticeably straightened. "How so?"

Ellie explained the table, the toilet, and the steel mesh door secured over the rear entrance. "If someone stayed to guard a girl, or girls, from somewhere inside, there would be no way for them to escape. That said, the mesh door could have served another purpose a long time ago, and the back area could have been a break room that accommodated awkward trips to the restroom."

"Maybe," Jet mused, and Ellie could see the sprockets turning behind his eyes.

"Also," she said, "they cleaned the whole downstairs with bleach. The back area too."

"You're kidding." They both knew that strong applications of bleach killed DNA, making it impossible to use skin or fluid samples in lab tests.

Ellie asked, "Did you look up who the building is registered to?"

"Yeah. It belongs to a Sandstone Holdings. I couldn't find anything else on them, and based on what we both saw tonight, I'd be willing to bet it's a shell company. What about who sent you that email? Have you heard back from them?"

"No, but I only replied back before dinner time and basically said that I went and saw Avi and asked what they want to know. I didn't say anything about Barry or where I was going tonight."

"Smart girl." He drummed his fingers on the chair's armrest while they both worked silently to gather loose streams of information into a cohesive picture.

Ellie finally asked, "It is a given that whoever took Juanita is trafficking her?"

"Yes. I haven't been given a reason to think otherwise."

"So do you think they're taking the money they get from that operation and are using Breakwater to launder it?"

Jet folded his hands and set his knuckles under his chin. "Maybe. Maybe," he said again, this time with a little more certainty. "That could make sense. Let me see what else I can find on Breakwater."

And suddenly it dawned on Ellie that not only had her investigation merged with Jet's but that at the end of this serpentine trail of unenlightened inquiry might be a scared and hurting young lady. A couple of days ago, when Ellie was at Jet's office, he showed her a picture of Juanita. But at the time, Ellie was processing the unnerving idea that Nick may have been murdered. "Do you have that picture of her on you?"

"I do," he said, and unzipped the side pocket of his satchel. He plucked it out and leaned forward, handed it over.

Juanita's black hair was shiny, and well-defined cheekbones accentuated a slender face. She was beautiful. But her smile was artificial, prosaic, as if it had been manufactured in the moment strictly to appease the incessant demands of an over-eager photographer—*"say cheese! say cheese!"* And her eyes, like the entrances to twin tunnels bored in the center of a cold mountain, were dark and absent of mirth. A beautiful girl holding a bad deck of cards.

Ellie studied the photo. "Juanita," she mused, "where are you, sweetheart?"

CHAPTER TWENTY-TWO

She would never get used to stepping out of the shower and still feeling dirty. No amount of soap or scrubbing could clean her skin which crawled with what men had done to her. What she had to do to them. But that wasn't the worst of it. It wasn't so much that her skin—every inch and pore—felt dirty. It was that she felt filthy on the inside. Somehow her very soul had become contaminated, like a used rag, absorbing people's scum.

Juanita toweled off and dressed into cotton leggings and an oversized t-shirt.

There were eight girls in all, each with her own room decorated in what Juanita could only guess was like a very expensive hotel suite. A large bed with silk sheets and a thick bedspread lay against the back wall. Noticeably missing was anything that could be used as a weapon. No candelabras, no glass-top table that could be smashed, no bedside lamps; the lamps were mounted into the wall above the nightstand. Each girl had her own clothes dresser filled with plain, comfortable clothing.

Each of the eight bedrooms was windowless and successively ran the length of a single hallway that terminated at an elevator. On the other end was a communal bathroom and, beyond that, a large community room with several couches, a small kitchenette, and a flat-screen television with access to Netflix and Hulu. The kitchenette was stocked with flimsy plastic utensils, a microwave, and a refrigerator. A pantry contained basics such as oatmeal, dry cereal, and crackers. There were no windows there either. No sunlight at all, leaving all of them to wonder just where they were.

Other than the exploits they were forced to engage in, they had been treated well enough. Decent food, comfortable clothing. Juanita was no fool—not like she had been when she had trusted Jesse. She knew they were treated this way because of the type of clients they serviced. If the girls were kept comfortable, the clients would sense it.

They were put to work only on the weekends, and that, only one night of the two. Once every seven days. The clients were paying extra for a "fresh" girl, and this is where they came to get it.

Fresh girl. That's how one of the men referred to her one night. The bald one with the fat neck and double chin and those evil, beady eyes. The clients were promised a girl who had been untouched for the last week, and which one did they want tonight?

All the men who entered her room were well dressed —nice suits, fancy shoes, perfectly combed hair, and smelling like cigar smoke—as though they had just come from an important business meeting. And each one, without exception, spoke with thick, accented English. Juanita didn't know her countries very well, but she didn't think that any of them were citizens of the United States. Some had blonde hair and sharp jawlines, some slanted, oriental eyes, and one of them spoke only Spanish. But all of them, without exception, carried themselves with an air of dignity that would have been comical were it not so repulsive.

The clients would step into the room with a sickly smile on their faces and a thick key card in their hands. Several of the girls had peeked their heads out of their doorways after the men left their rooms. They would see the card being scanned near the elevator and the doors open. From there, they didn't know if the elevator went up or down. The elevator shaft made no sound. The doors slid shut...and that was it.

No one knew just what day it was. There were clocks in each room. But this was only so they could keep track of the time on the one night of the week when it was necessary for them to do so. The man with the strange looking nose—one of the girls had nicknamed him "Pig Nose"— would come down and restock their toiletries and food. He would tell them, in the event they didn't know, that tonight the clients would arrive. Nine o'clock. Be dressed. Be ready.

They hadn't started their new lives at this location. After waving goodbye to her brother and waking from her gas-induced nap in the van, Juanita had found herself in an old building with brick walls and a bare, concrete floor. Several mattresses lay side-by-side on one end, a table and open toilet on the other.

On their third day, Jesse had shown up, and every few nights thereafter. He would always come at night. He told the girls how sorry he was and how much he cared for each one of them. He told them that he was in trouble, that he had been forced to take them, and that if they didn't help him, some bad men were going to kill his family.

The lie that had been so glaringly obvious to Juanita, the other girls bought hook, line, and sinker. The entire fishing rod, too, for that matter. She tried to convince them that none of it was true, that Jesse was an evil man, but they all, every one of them, said they loved him and would do what he needed.

They stayed at the first location for what seemed to Juanita about two weeks. Then they gathered up the girls, fastened dark hoods over their eyes, and brought them here—wherever *here* was. Since their arrival, Pig Nose had been the only captor they had seen. He also had a key card, although that didn't matter much. They were all too scared of him to plan anything too crazy. Jesse hadn't even come by to see them since they were brought here. The conviction that the girls needed to help him was, for some of them, finally beginning to wane.

So talk of escape never went farther than a short-lived talk about hitting him on the back of the head and running to the elevator. But then what? No one knew what lay beyond that. By counting the number of clients she had seen, Juanita concluded she had been at this new place for ten weeks. Twelve weeks since she got into the van and watched her brother disappear from view. Twelve weeks since this cold waking nightmare began.

Looking back now, she should have known it was too good to be true. And deep down, maybe she had. But she'd wanted to believe that things could change for her and Junior, that someone could actually have their best interest in mind. Sometimes hope could make you see.

But sometimes it was just as guilty of blinding you, keeping you from seeing the glaring truth right in front of you.

Juanita discovered a pattern early on. None of the girls here had any family to speak of. Juanita had her *tía*. But she didn't care about her and Junior. She was in love with a needle. Other than Alex at Hope House, there had been no one else to show any interest in their lives.

Juanita left her room and walked down the hall to the community room. A couple of girls were at the table playing a card game. Cami was sitting on the couch picking mindlessly at a loose thread. Juanita settled into the other end. "Hi, Cami."

Cami didn't look up. "Hi."

Juanita could see that the other girl's eyes were puffy. She had been crying. Not an unusual sight for this group of girls. They had all cried, some of them still every day.

"What are you thinking, Cami?" They all learned early on not to ask each other what was wrong. There was only one glaring and mocking answer to that question.

Cami huffed, and another tear jostled loose and sped down her cheek. She didn't wipe it away. "Vivian," she said, and that was all.

Juanita bit down on her bottom lip and nodded. "I know," she said softly.

Last week, Vivian reached her breaking point. She was here, in the common area, watching Survivor, when she quietly stood up and walked down the hall to her bedroom. Minutes later, they heard a varying cadence of screams issuing from her room, and everyone ran to investigate. Vivian was standing on her bed in front of a large hole in the wall, screaming angrily at it. Jagged chunks of sheetrock lay strewn across the bedspread, around her feet, and on the plush carpet below. She had shattered a nightstand drawer and used a large piece of splintered wood to create a hole in the sheetrock. Then she pried away chunks of the wall, exposing what was behind it, hoping for a way of escape. They had all discussed it before, wondering if perhaps, behind the sheetrock, there might lay a brick wall or wooden siding that could be broken through and torn away.

But what Vivian discovered sent most everyone into an emotional tailspin. Behind the sheetrock, past the steel-stud framing and the insulation, was a thick wall of smooth gray concrete, cool to the touch. They were hemmed in exactly as they had feared all along. The only way out was through the elevator. They were captives in a concrete box.

That realization—that they could never escape—was the final haunting.

There were no cameras in their rooms. Juanita assumed it was because there was an agreement with the clients. A camera was, however, perched high in the corner above the elevator, offering whoever was on the other end a view of the entire length of the hallway. Another two cameras were mounted in opposing corners of the common room ceiling.

They must have seen the girls flock into Vivian's room. For not a minute passed before Pig Nose flung the door to her room open, his eyes flaring wide in hot anger as he took in the damage done and the intent behind it. He immediately ordered all the girls except Vivian out of the room, and as they returned to the common area, they listened while he berated her and his fists punctuated his anger as he repeatedly slammed them into her body.

Vivian was taken away, up in the elevator, a couple of hours later. Everyone knew that they would never see her again, that she was probably not even alive. The wall in her room was repaired, given a fresh coat of paint, and two days later a new girl was introduced in her place, a clear testament that the girls were as valuable as a roll of toilet paper.

The taunting certainty that there truly was no escape, along with the knowledge of what their captors were willing to do should they step out of line, was unnerving. That, coupled with the reality of what they had to do each weekend, had covered Cami in a fresh blanket of darkness that she had yet to shake. Juanita was beginning to doubt she ever would.

"What do you think they did to her?" Cami asked.

"I don't know," Juanita answered quietly.

"She dreamed of owning her own restaurant one day. She used to cook for her grandfather before he died."

Juanita nearly smiled. Vivian would hog the television most days, streaming cooking shows until a small revolution formed among the girls for the remote to be handed off. "She would have been great at it," Juanita said. She wanted to add, "maybe she will be one day," but she couldn't do that to Cami.

The sound of a strong sniff came from behind them. Juanita turned and saw Sandra hunched over a line of white powder. She held a small straw to her nose and sniffed again, then pulled away and shook her head. She looked over at Juanita and smiled happily. A cocaine smile—one that stretched across the pain deep within.

After the first client, Juanita felt herself begin to unplug from reality. She tried the cocaine as a means to cope. It was, after all, why their captors furnished it. Before coming here, Juanita had never experimented with drugs. Not even a cigarette. But after that first night with the first man, after realizing just what kind of nightmare she had fallen into, the cocaine quickly became a trusted friend. The only one she had left, it seemed. When she was suddenly thrown in a world where the only reason she was allowed to live was to please others with her body, drugs became a potent grace.

But two weeks ago, she quit the stuff. The cocaine helped to mask the pain but somehow left her feeling even more out of control. And she couldn't think clearly when she felt like that. She wasn't sure why thinking clearly was more important than keeping the pain at bay; she couldn't explain to herself why the cocaine should go untouched.

The reason, however, was simple.

Somewhere, in the back of her mind, grew sprouting seeds of revolt.

CHAPTER TWENTY-THREE

Young children did not possess the ability to discern when their parents should be left alone to sleep in or how to mind sensitive areas of the body that had played a leading role in their existence.

Blake Duprey was thinking something along those lines microseconds after his four-year-old daughter woke him up by base jumping off his bedroom dresser and landing most of her forty pounds below his waist.

"Emma...baby. You...you can't do that. Okay?"

"Okay, Daddy!" And now she was jumping on the bed like it was her private trampoline. "Hurry up! I want to go to IHOP!"

Jillian, Blake's wife of nine years, rolled away from the ruckus and tucked back into the sheets. Blake made a groggy effort at sitting up, but his groin was still in AFib and he winced as he leaned against the headboard. "Oh, honey. I can't this morning." The fog from two people sharing nearly three bottles of wine clung to his brain and muddled his thoughts. He tried to focus on his daughter but couldn't get his eyes above half mast.

"Whhhat??" the little girl exclaimed. "But we always go to IHOP on Saturday mornings!"

"I know, honey, but I have to go into work for a little bit. We'll pick back up next weekend. I promise." A shrill cry came from down the hall. Blake nudged his wife's shoulder. "Baby's up. I've got to go."

Jillian groaned like she was allergic to sunlight and threw the sheets off of her. She slowly slid her feet to the floor and shuffled out of the room.

Emma jumped off the bed and walked over to her father. "But what am I going to do for breakfast now?" she asked.

"Ask Mommy. Cereal probably." His daughter dipped her chin and gave him a chastising look that made him a little sorry for her future husband. "I won't be gone long, okay? Just a couple of hours."

"Can we go when you get back?"

He stood up and scratched at his lower back. "Maybe. Let me check with your mother."

"Okay!" she said. "I'll go ask her." Then she was gone.

Blake looked over at his bedside clock. It was just after seven. He had foolishly agreed to a meeting this morning at eight. His pre-wine logic had told him that eight o'clock was a good time because, when it ended, it still left him the rest of the day to hit the golf course. Fighting back the urge to call and reschedule, he staggered into the bathroom and stared at himself in the mirror, then turned on the cold water and splashed a couple handfuls in his face.

. . .

He was in the car twenty minutes later, having consumed only three Excedrin and two glasses of water for breakfast. A travel mug full of coffee sat in the cup holder between the seats. Jillian had fixed it for him, but he had yet to touch it. Coffee never helped his hangovers; he didn't really even like the taste of it to begin with. Mostly what he needed right now was a liver purge. He felt woozy and thought that he might still be a little drunk.

He pointed his Ford F-250 north onto Florida State Road 31 and rode it for twelve miles. He was in the country now, passing the occasional house and the ever-present farm. After weaving through Arcadia, he turned off south of Brownville where a stone monument sign was flanked with lavish patterns of purple and yellow pansies, blue lilies, and areca palms. The sign read "Palm Rivers" and formed the entrance to a stone paved driveway that was flanked with royal palms and led visitors to an expensive cream-colored stucco building with a brown tiled roof. In front of the building's porte-cochère stood a fountain of three nude women clasping earthen pitchers. The location served as a quiet and isolated event venue for weddings, graduations, birthdays parties, and quinceañeras.

Blake navigated around the fountain and pulled in beneath the porte-cochère. When he stepped out onto the stone, a wide yawn escaped him, and he complemented it by spreading his arms and trying to stretch the tired from his body.

It was quiet out here, away from the hum of Interstate 75 and the smaller cities that hugged the Gulf Coast. Two scrub jays were perched on the fountain, slipping quiet chirps into the cool morning air, while in the distance a loose gathering of black cows had formed along a fence line.

The building's entrance had two heavy wooden doors rising ten feet above the threshold. Blake pulled on a brass handle and stepped inside, where the rotunda's domed ceiling was frescoed with a stunning replica of the magnificent Minoan leaping bull, the original of which was still on display in the Heraklion Archaeological Museum in Crete.

The interior was everything one would expect from a venue catering to those with refined tastes and high expectations. The theme was Greco-Roman, infused with a modern flare. Diamond-cut marble floors lay in alternating colors of white and sapphire blue. The front hallway was wide with Murano glass chandeliers hanging from its coffered ceiling and life-size marble statues of Greek gods and goddesses lining its floors. The hallway led guests away from the rotunda down to a carpeted lounge at the end where it split off in two directions. To the right, where, save for a few busts resting on freestanding columns, it became an empty corridor that led to the bathrooms and another door at the end. To the left, it brought guests into the ornate ballroom, where dinner and dances were hosted and parties lasted well into the night.

Blake took a right when he came to the lounge and made his way to the open door at the end. He stepped inside. The style of the room was in stark contrast to the rest of the building. A visitor might think he had stepped back in time, and to old London, not Rome or Greece. Wood-paneled walls and exposed wooden rafters set the room in a dark ambiance. Built-in bookcases were filled with vanity books, vases, and picture frames inlaid with black and white photos from an earlier age. A red-felted card table took precedence in the center of the room, and eight Shattuck wood chairs surrounded it, their seats and armrests adorned in oxblood satin. An old pedestal desk sat opposite the doorway, at the other end of the room, where a bank of flat-screen security monitors sat on top of it. Seeing no one in the room, Blake returned to the lounge and took a seat at the empty bar. He waited.

A sliding glass door at the back of the lounge provided access to the pool area. A shadow stretched across the glass just before the door slid back and Victor Cruz stepped through. He shut it and went around the bar, then poured himself a glass of water. "You been here long?" he asked Blake.

"Couple minutes."

"You want something to drink?"

"Water, please." His head was still spinning.

Cruz snatched another glass from a shelf behind him. He filled it from the tap and placed it on the bar. "How's the family?" he asked.

"Good. Jillian wants me to take her up to Coeur d'Alene next month. Might do that for a couple days."

"Coeur d'Alene...that's where, Oregon?"

"Idaho."

Cruz watched as Blake drained his glass in one swift motion. "You look like you could have used a little more sleep," he said.

"Yeah, well. You have the paperwork?"

"I do. Be right back." Cruz left the lounge and

entered the office at the end of the hall. He returned a minute later and settled into the bar chair next to Blake. He slid a file folder across the polished granite. For now, they were the only two people on the property, so Cruz spoke freely. "These are the new ones. With the extra seven percent added."

Blake picked it up and flipped through the invoices. He scanned the numbers, nodding his approval. "This is better. Tell them this needs to be the standard going forward. I can't keep up with what you're giving me if they don't bill at this rate."

"I told them."

"So you fixed the other problem?" Blake asked. "I haven't heard of it being an issue any longer."

"It's done. Clean and easy. The cops think he fell off the balcony. Looked like a suicide. Nothing more to say."

Blake waved the file at Cruz. "How about you don't go leaving this on job sites anymore?"

"How about you forget about it? I fixed it. We move on."

"We good? I owe Emma breakfast."

"No," Cruz said. "Mr. Zedillo, he wants a meeting with you and me in person."

Blake blinked. "In person? Why?"

"You think he told me?"

Blake set an elbow on the bar and rubbed at his tired face. "He makes me nervous," he said through his fingers. "Doesn't he make you nervous?"

"Not really. As long as we keep our end of the deal. He seems like a fair man.

Blake sat back up and released a heavy sigh. "Yeah, I

guess so. At least I get to see Emma grow up. If it weren't for him, she would have been sixteen before I got out. Has Abby let you see Nino yet?"

"No," was all he said, and then he stood up. He doubted he would ever be allowed a relationship with his son, and that wasn't something he wanted to think about. So he changed the subject. "I finished cleaning out the old location in Fort Myers."

"Where will the new one be?" Blake asked.

"I don't know."

Blake's phone rang in his pocket. It was a FaceTime call. Emma was holding the phone under her face, and he could see up her nostrils. "Daddy," she whispered. "Are you almost done, Daddy? Mommy said you and me could still go to IHOP if you get home soon. But that we have to *hurrrry* because I have gymnastics."

Blake grinned mildly. Gymnastics always came out "jim-nasses." "Sure, honey. Why don't you—" But he was interrupted by a scream of childish delight as the phone was dropped to the floor, and he heard Emma running off to tell her mother that breakfast was back on. He called out for her to come back to the phone but was answered by a shiny black nose quickly followed by a dog's muzzle as his German Shepherd sniffed loudly at the phone.

"Hey Rowdy...I'm going to hang up now. Okay?" Blake disconnected and leaned back in his chair. He blew a long puff of air from his cheeks and ran a hand through his hair. "I'd better go," he said. "Apparently pancakes are in my future." He stood and thanked Cruz for the invoices. "You'll let me know the when and where for our meeting with Mr. Zedillo?"

"I will." Cruz noted the concern in Blake's eyes. "Relax, he likes you. He likes both of us."

Blake nodded but did not appear convinced. The men said their goodbyes, and Blake stopped at the restroom on his way out.

Cruz returned to the office down the hall.

CHAPTER TWENTY-FOUR

Reticle's gunsmithing shop was at the back of the main building that held the offices, restrooms, and store. The shop was lit by halogens hanging from thin chains screwed into the ceiling. Several wood-top tables filled the room, along with a mini-milling machine, belt sander, bolted table-top vice, a grinder, and a gunsmithing lathe that sat against the rear wall. A line of gun racks ran along the opposing wall, full of weapons in the queue to be cleaned or modified.

Tyler sat on a stool, cleaning a customer's bolt-action rifle. He sprayed some solvent on a brush and picked up the bolt he had detached from the gun. He ran the brush across in short strokes.

Tyler had been fascinated by guns of every caliber and type since he was a young boy. He loved their elegance, mechanical simplicity, and the refinement of skill that was necessary to use them well. He even loved the smell of the lubricants and the cleaning solvents, much in the same way his father used to appreciate the smell of carburetor cleaner or fresh cut wheat or Dairy

Queen on a Friday night. And there was something about the way a grip felt solid in your hand, or the smooth sound of the action when properly oiled, and the crisp snap of a trigger release.

A Liberty safe was bolted to the floor on the other side of the room, and it was filled with his own private collection. In a world of throwaway plastics, where possessions were easily discarded and replaced by a simple and quick online order, old guns, like classic cars or worn-out boats, had a story to tell.

He set down the brush and grabbed a clean cloth, then ran it over the bolt, drawing away old powder and brass fouling. When that was done, he set the cloth down and picked up a cleaning rod. He attached a cleaning patch, sprayed on some solvent, and slid it down the breach end of the barrel, slowly working it back and forth.

Footsteps echoed down the cinder-block hallway, and a young man of about twenty appeared in the doorway. It was Ben Underwood, Tyler's newest hire.

"Hey, Tyler?" he asked. "Where's the Coon Punch?"

For the better part of the last year, Tyler had invested tens of thousands of his own money and dozens of hours with a gunsmith in Cape Coral and a first-class fabricator in Sarasota. The collaboration had finally resulted in a solid rifle that he simply referred to as the Coon Punch.

The rifle utilized the barrel and bolt from the AR-15, and Tyler had reduced the overall weight of the gun by employing polymer for the lower receiver in the place of steel. The recoil impulse was still a little stronger than he liked, but it was lighter and quicker than most anything in the carbine family.

He was still testing gas plug diameters, vent locations, and rail mount lengths, but overall he was pleased with the weapon's handling and performance and had recently made it available for members of his gun range to rent.

"Not sure. Why?" Tyler asked. He slid the cleaning rod out of the barrel, discarded the dirty patch, and slipped off the patch holder.

"Mr. Bennington just put in a reservation for it online, and I don't see it in the rack."

Tyler rubbed the back of his neck as he recalled where he'd left the gun. "I've got it at my place," he said, frustrated. "I took it on my hunting trip last weekend. Forgot to bring it back in. When's the reservation?"

"Noon."

Tyler noted the time displayed on the wall clock. It was ten after ten in the morning. The simplest course would be to call Mr. Bennington and ask him to reschedule for another day or ask him to consider a different weapon for his time at the range today. But Tyler had founded Reticle on a commitment that members should get the best possible experience. It was one of the reasons the range had seen such rapid success in the wider community. Ted Bennington was a former Green Beret and responsible for referring most of Tyler's earliest members.

"I'll just run back home and get it," he said, and Ben watched him reach across the table and grab the proper size bore brush. Tyler screwed it to the tip of the cleaning rod, sprayed on some solvent, and sent it down the barrel.

"You sure?" Ben said. "I can call him and see if he's

good to use the Widowmaker instead. They're nearly the same."

Tyler stopped the rod mid-push and looked at Ben as though he had just been informed that Justin Bieber and George Strait were equals. "They're not nearly the same. One is a Romanian piece of crap, and the other was built by me."

"Sorry, Tyler."

"Just don't ever put a gun your boss designed in the same category with a Cold War knock-off. Ever."

Ben smiled apprehensively. "Got it."

Tyler pulled the cleaning rod out of the barrel and snatched off the dirty cleaning patch. He tossed it in the garbage can beneath the table and came off the stool as he wiped his hands on a clean rag. "I'll be back in forty-five." He grabbed his keys from a nail on the wall and motioned toward the rifle he had been working on. "See if Frank has some time to finish cleaning this girl, will you? I don't want to leave her naked and laid out across the table like she is now."

Ben sent an eyebrow toward the ceiling.

"And get your mind out of the gutter."

FIVE MINUTES LATER, Tyler was in his F-150, heading north on Burnt Store Road while belting out *Chattahoochee* along with Alan Jackson and unexpectedly recalling the dozens of times he and Nick had sung it together during their high school years. Back then, being from West Texas, they didn't know where the Chattahoochee was or if it was even a real river. But it didn't matter; the song spoke to them because it spoke of easy times and heartfelt living.

Tyler turned off Acapulco Road onto his pea-pebble driveway and followed it around until the thick vegetation gave way to his wide and open yard. A white heron was standing idly in the marsh behind his house and stared him down as he parked in his usual spot on the side of the house. Leaving his truck door open, he took his front steps two at a time, his boot heels clomping loudly on pine boards.

He unlocked the front door, and as he stepped inside, he looked across the room and saw that the back door was open, along with a man wearing a dark hoodie and loose-fitting blue jeans who was quickly making his way toward the steps at the end of the back porch.

Tyler bolted across the floor and yelled for him to stop, but it only quickened the intruder's pace, who arrived at the top of the steps, leveraged off the handrails, and took them three and four at a time. Tyler shot out the back door and began his descent just as the man pushed off the final step and started across the back yard.

Seconds later, Tyler's boots were in the grass. He raced after the intruder, who had already shot into the underbrush and disappeared. Tyler followed him into where the feral hogs had chased Citrus a couple of days earlier. Negotiating trunks of palmettos, pines, and withering cypress, skirting cabbage palms and ficus, he gained, finally reaching out and grabbing at the man's shoulder just as the latter's foot snagged on a tree root and forced him into the trunk of a cypress. He stumbled awkwardly, and like a drunkard, fell forward, his face planting hard into a layer of old leaves.

Tyler drew up, panting as he stood over the man. He

set a hand on the back of the man's shoulder and flipped him around. He froze.

The man looked up at him, his face a contorted mess of hot pain from whacking the tree. "Hey...Tyler."

Tyler's eyes were suddenly the diameter of a couple of all-you-can-eat dinner plates.

"What the hell?"

* * *

THE DISHES SANG a discordant harmony as they clattered into the sink. Ellie rinsed them under the faucet before refilling her coffee and returning to the kitchen table where Tiffany was sitting, her hands wrapped around a cooling mug, her face still reflecting the harsh grief of the last twelve days. Chloe had spent last night with Tiffany and Kayla, and the three of them had come over to Ellie's for breakfast.

Ellie woke tired from a late night with Jet, but the coffee and conversation had quickly swept the sleepiness away. The girls had helped Ellie lay the cinnamon rolls out on the tray and ice them when they came out of the oven. Tiffany spent the time sitting alone at the edge of the canal with her legs dangling toward the water, lost in thought. She returned to the kitchen table when Ellie finished frying bacon and eggs, and when breakfast was over, the girls tore down the short hallway to Ellie's guest room where she kept a few plastic bins full of toys and dolls.

The ladies were alone now for the first time all morning. Ellie knew better than to ask a grieving person how they were doing. "What can I do for you?" she asked.

"Just this," she said. "It's good for me to be here." Tiffany picked thoughtlessly at the corner of her empty placemat. "I know I said that I was thinking about moving back to Texas. But I'm not sure. This place, this island, it's...healing somehow."

Ellie could relate entirely. She had been raised on Pine Island, and raised by it. And when her career with the CIA had finally reached the end of its last lap, when she was finished traversing the globe as an elite operative with TEAM 99 and as an undercover agent in Afghanistan, there was only one place on this pale blue planet she wanted to be.

To her, there was nowhere else.

And she had found healing of her own. That was what good people, ocean air, and slow living could do for a person. There was something about the tangy scent of salt water, the piercing cry of a seagull, and the dry rustling of palm fronds that all worked into some kind of medicinal harmony to mend the soul.

"Is Kayla talking about Nick?" Ellie asked.

"Not really. She can't seem to grasp that he just didn't leave for a while. Nick's gone on work trips before. When he came out here to find us a house and make construction contacts, he was gone for nearly two weeks. To Kayla, the only difference between then and now is that he hasn't FaceTimed with her, hasn't called and spoken with her. I'm not sure I know how to explain to a child 'not coming back.'"

Ellie thought back to when her own mother had passed. She remembered her father setting her on his knee and explaining that she had died. She recalled how he had said that it meant she wasn't coming back, that Ellie wouldn't see her again, and how her mother didn't want to leave, but that she would always love Ellie. Ellie hadn't known what to make of that at the time, and it took years to work it all out in her heart. Thinking back on it now, she realized that when the permanence of her mother's absence finally did take root, it did not occur in a single moment of comprehension; it was not like a light abruptly being flipped on. Rather, it was more like the way the sun comes up in the morning, touching only a portion of the earth at first, but eventually rising high and bright into the noonday sky, dispelling all shadow.

"She'll understand in time," Ellie replied. "She doesn't need to grasp it all right now."

"Thank you," Tiffany said. She took a sip of her coffee, and Ellie noticed something else behind her eyes. *Fretting*, she thought.

"But there's something else bothering you."

Tiffany flashed a quick, uneasy smile before letting it fade as quickly as it came. "Okay," she said. "This might sound a little paranoid, but I think someone might be watching my house."

Ellie felt her insides tense and forced herself to maintain an easy expression. She hadn't said a word to Tiffany about the email, hadn't told her about the investigation that stemmed from it. "What makes you think that?"

"Well, you know how dark it gets on the island at night. I'm probably imagining things since I'm not used to being alone without Nick. But I was locking up a few nights ago and peeked out the front window. Kayla's bike was laying behind my car, so I went out and put it in the garage. On my way back in, I looked across the street and could have sworn I saw someone standing at the edge of the treeline."

"You didn't get a good look?"

"No. It was the outline of a figure. Could have been a bush, I guess, but then I saw it last night too. In a different spot this time."

And suddenly Ellie was thinking it was time to take the email to the authorities. If someone killed Nick, then it wouldn't be a far stretch to think they might have a good reason to go after his family too. "Why don't you and Kayla stay here for a few nights?"

Tiffany waved her off. "Thanks. I'm sure I'm just imagining things. It's not like someone tried to break in or grab me while I was outside."

Ellie decided this was a good time to ask. "Do you know if Nick did any work with a construction company called Breakwater?"

"No. Not that he said anything to me about. Why?"

"No reason, really." She drained the rest of her coffee and frowned. "It's too quiet," she said.

And it was. There hadn't been a peep from the back of the house in several minutes—never a good thing when small children were in the general vicinity. Tiffany was rising from her chair when the bathroom door opened and the scurry of little feet sounded from the hallway. Chloe and Kayla materialized and stopped near the table. Tiffany gasped and followed it with a mournful groan. Ellie sighed.

The girls were clutching a handful of Crayola markers; all the caps were missing. Their eyelids, cheeks, foreheads, and lips were a haphazard mess of squiggly lines and blotchy ink representing nearly every color of the rainbow. The hackles on Citrus's back stood up, and he circled the girls with a low growl. Ellie hushed him, then curled her pointer finger toward Chloe. She made a cautious approach, and her aunt placed a hand on her small shoulder and spoke softly. "Chloe. Honey. Let's just use the markers on paper from now on. Maybe not your face anymore. Okay?" The girl nodded, disappointed. Ellie didn't have any children of her own, but she wasn't about to ask a six-year-old what she was thinking. "Were you just being silly?" she asked.

"No. We were trying to look like Lady Gaga."

"Were you now?" Ellie's gaze met Tiffany's, and they both gritted their teeth to hold oncoming laughter.

Tiffany turned to her daughter. "How do you even know who that is?"

"Emery, my friend at school, showed me on her phone. She likes Lady Gaga."

"Well, I don't," Tiffany said sternly, and then muttered, "I can't believe six-year-olds have their own phones."

"You don't think we look pretty?" Kayla asked.

"Yes," Ellie said enthusiastically. "You look completely amazing. But," she returned her attention to Chloe, "your mama has beach pictures planned for you tomorrow. Could you maybe go try to clean it off so I don't get in trouble with my sister? Can you do that for me?"

"Okay! Come on, Kayla!" And they were off again. Five seconds later, the water was running in the bathroom with muted giggles flowing down the hallway.

THEY LEFT AN HOUR LATER, and after Ellie loaded the dishwasher and started some laundry, she brought her laptop to the table and opened it up.

She hadn't heard from Jet yet and was growing

steadily anxious to get something back on the license plate and fingerprint. After coming off the events of last night, just waiting around wasn't in her wheelhouse. She navigated to her browser and started a fresh search for Breakwater Construction, while Tiffany's suggestion that someone might be watching her house had a red caution flag flapping in the back of her mind.

Her phone lay on the kitchen counter. It rang, and she stood and grabbed it up. It was Tyler. She slid her finger along the glass and set it to her ear. "Hey," she said. "I miss you."

His voice was strained, heavy. "Ellie, can you come over to my place?"

It was the middle of a workday. Tyler was never at home before six on a workday. He didn't even go home for lunch. "Sure," she said. "What's wrong?"

"Nothing's wrong." His tone contradicted his words. "But I need to you to come over."

She slapped her laptop shut. "I'll leave now," she said.

"Thanks."

They hung up, and she grabbed her keys from a hook by the coffee maker while addressing her dog. "I'm going over to Tyler's." Citrus's ears stood up. He catapulted to his feet like he'd been hit with a taser and ran to the door leading into the garage. His tail fanned the air around him while he stood there excitedly, his chin up, waiting for Ellie to open the door for him.

"No," she said. "No, you have to stay here."

The dog lowered his head. The expression in his eyes swiftly changed from excited animal to entitled human teenager.

"Sorry," she said flatly.

He gave a yip of protest and stood up on his back legs, pawing gently at her leg with a forepaw. "Nope," she said. "That's not going to work this time. When I get back, I'll take you on a run. Deal?" Citrus huffed and trotted to his bed in the corner of the kitchen. He nestled in with his back to Ellie. "You're acting like an adolescent girl," she said. "You know that, right?"

Citrus didn't move but uttered a temperamental snort: a dog's version of giving someone the bird. Ellie rolled her eyes and stepped into the garage.

Citrus waited for the door to shut before giving a final bark. The last word.

* * *

A THREE-CAR ACCIDENT on Burnt Shore Road put Ellie back fifteen minutes. She stirred nervously while waiting for the car in front of her to start moving again. Something was wrong, she knew. It was strange enough for Tyler to ask her to come, but more disconcerting was that he wouldn't tell her what was wrong over the phone. The accident finally cleared, and she pressed her El Camino's accelerator a little lower, and the world's coolest vehicle shot down the road faster than the speed limit allowed.

SHE TOOK Tyler's front steps two at a time, and as soon as she arrived on his front porch, the door swung open, and Tyler stepped to the side as she went in. She looked in his face, currently a conflation of concern and relief. "Are you all right?" she asked. He shut the door and used his chin to point silently to a spot behind her.

A man was sitting on the couch. The back of his head visible above the top edge of the cushion. Ellie looked cautiously back at Tyler, but he encouraged her forward with an affirming nod.

As she moved slowly toward the couch, the man stood up and turned around.

Ellie gasped and took a step backward.

It was Nick Barlow.

CHAPTER TWENTY-FIVE

Ellie clasped a hand over her mouth and stood at the edge of Tyler's living room, staring at a ghost. She studied his face, her mind working furiously to reconcile what her eyes were seeing. The person standing before her looked closer to a homeless man than the friend she had had breakfast with less than two weeks ago. He was unshaven, his hair was greasy, and dark hollows had taken up residence beneath scared and weary eyes. He had lost weight. She took a cautious step forward. "Nick?"

"Hi, Ellie." He came around the couch and embraced her. She smelled a foul odor of unwashed sweat. When Nick released her, he took a step backward. "Sorry, haven't showered in a while."

"Me and Tiffany," Ellie said, "we identified your body. How...how are you...here? How are you alive?" She had a sudden vision of Harold Wilson, the old Miami-Dade medical examiner, being a secret master at Photoshop. The person they identified was clearly Nick. There had been no doubt about it.

Nick's face suddenly grew darker, the easy mirth from reuniting with friends dissolving before a heavy wave of sadness. "The body you and Tiff identified..." He trailed off before trying again. "That was my brother."

"Your brother?"

"Yes," he said quietly. "Nate." His jaw tensed as he forced willing tears to remain behind his eyes.

Tyler extended a hand toward the couch. "You guys have a seat. Nick's already told me some of this."

Ellie turned to him. "You knew?" she asked. "All this time?"

"Of course I didn't know. I came home to grab a gun, and he was running out my back door."

Nick nodded toward a small desk on the far wall. "I was replying to your email. Tyler's never here during the day."

"You?" Ellie said. "It was *you* emailing me?"

"Yeah."

"Wait," Tyler said. "What email?"

Ellie quickly explained, and after he fussed at her for not telling him earlier, he paused. "Hold on a second," he said to Nick. "How'd you get on my computer? It's got a password."

"Tyler," Nick chided. "Your password is 'password.'"

Ellie raised her brows to Tyler. "You're joking, right?"

"It's got a capital 'P,'" he said defensively.

Ellie turned back to Nick. "Your brother—what...happened?"

Nick's expression took on a dazed appearance, and he stared vacantly at the coffee table. "The night before we all had breakfast at The Perfect Cup, I was wrapping up some work on a job site—a new country club out in Lehigh Acres. The framing was nearly complete, and I was running some wiring. I ended up working late, so it was dark by the time I loaded my tools into my truck. Halfway home I remembered that I'd left a drill and went back to get it. I had to use my flashlight to find it and was about to start back to the truck when I saw a file folder sitting on a stack of lumber. So I thumb through it, and at first glance, it just looks like a stack of invoices billed to some company called Breakwater."

At the mention of Breakwater, Ellie listened intently, trying to piece together what Nick was saying with what she and Jet had discussed the night before, and all the while feeling like she was in some kind of spiteful dream, that she would wake up at any second to Citrus wanting her to let him outside.

"The first invoice seemed pretty high for the work they were billing for. So I flip to the next one. It was from a different subcontractor but the same thing. Unusually high amount. And they were all like that. I didn't think too much about it. I'm new to Florida, so I just assumed that I wasn't completely up on costs. None of it was billing for electrical, which is really all I know. But right as I was closing it, a slip of paper fell out. I picked it up and saw where someone had scribbled a note that all the attached invoices needed to add an additional seven percent."

Tyler said, "So they were already over-billing, and someone wanted them to charge even more?"

"Yeah. Exactly. Then I heard a vehicle pull up through the rear entrance and a couple doors slamming shut. At this point, I was the only other one out there. I started making my way to the front, and just as I was about to step off the foundation, a flashlight beam caught me, and they called out. One of them hung back in the dark, but my light caught enough that I could see he was a cop. The other guy, he comes up to me, looks at the folder tucked under my arm and casually says, 'Oh, my invoices. You found them.'

"I hand them over, and he asks what I'm doing here so late. I told him about my drill. Then he goes, 'Did you, uh, look through my paperwork here?'

"I told him 'no, not yet.'" Nick paused and scratched earnestly at the back of his head, the way a man does who hasn't showered in a couple weeks. "I think if it had been a couple hours earlier, I could have pulled off a good poker face, but he just stared at me in this blank way that made my insides shiver. And then he thanks me, and I could hear the two of them whispering as I walked away."

"Did you get a good look at the cop?" Ellie asked.

Nick shook his head.

"Are sure it wasn't just a security guard?"

"I'm sure. He had a holstered weapon, a badge, and the nameplate on his chest shimmered in my light." Nick released a deep sigh before continuing. "When I got back in my truck, the guy walked out to me, waving for me to wait. I rolled down my window, and I saw him looking hard at my license plate like he was memorizing it. Then he gets right up at my door, nearly puts his face inside, and says real calmly, 'You sure you didn't see anything?'"

Tyler started shaking his head. "I would've busted his nose right there."

"I almost did," Nick countered, "but I kept thinking about that cop. So this guy goes, 'It wouldn't be a problem if you did look through them. But I would need to know about it.' So I told him to get the hell away from my truck and tore out of there."

"Why didn't you just go to the police after that?" Tyler asked.

"And tell them what? I had enough sense to know these guys were up to no good, but that was it. What really bothered me was knowing he got a look at my plate. Like he wanted to find out who I was."

"But how did your brother factor in?" Ellie asked.

Nick gave a slight shake of his head, and his shoulders settled into a defeated slump. "Stupid bad luck," he said. "I hadn't seen Nate in...eleven years, I guess. I'd just finished teaching a breakout session at the convention center for this electrical association I'm a part of. I was heading toward the exhibit hall when I see my brother about to walk right past me. We recognized each other at the same time and just stopped and stared." Nick scratched at his head again like a feral dog and then continued. "The condensed version is that he was thinking of starting a consulting business for construction companies, and he was at the convention to make industry contacts."

"He lived in Miami?" Tyler asked.

"No. Somewhere up in Ohio. He was flying back that night, so we made plans for him to meet me up at my hotel room after the convention closed for the day, and we'd decide where to have dinner from there."

"Did you tell Tiffany you saw him?" Ellie asked.

"No. The last time we saw Nate, he said some pretty terrible stuff about Tiff right to her face. I wanted to see how things went first and just tell her in person when I got home." Nick paused long enough to ask for something to drink. Tyler went to the fridge and brought out a beer. He popped the top and handed it over. "Thanks." Nick closed his eyes, took a long pull, and after draining half the bottle and wiping his mouth on the back of his hand, he continued.

"When Nate got to my room, we ended up just talking there for about an hour. I finally went downstairs to grab us something to eat. He's always struggled with migraines and wanted to rest until he had to leave. But I got down to the hotel restaurant and realized I'd forgotten my wallet on the dresser. When the elevator opened on my floor, I stepped out and saw the guy from the night before—the one who asked me about the folder. He was past my room walking toward the stairwell."

"Did he see you?" Ellie asked.

"No. And at first I thought it was just a coincidence until I got back in the room. My brother wasn't in there. The balcony door was open, and I heard a commotion from outside." Nick's head lowered on his next words. "That's when I saw him on the sidewalk, when I realized the man had come for me."

Ellie reached out and placed her hand on top of his. "I'm so sorry, Nick." She stood up and went to the window, looked out over the marsh. "Your brother looked a lot like you," she finally said. "It even fooled Tiff."

"I hate that she had to do that," he said. "But yeah, we should look alike. We're twins."

"Twins?" Ellie repeated, and turned to Tyler. "You didn't tell me Nick's brother was his twin."

"Didn't think about it. Would it have mattered?"

"I guess not." He was quiet for a while, the stress of

the last couple weeks and the trauma of losing his brother clearly evident in his face. "I still don't even know what I'm looking for. That's why I emailed you. I didn't want to put you in harm's way, so I just tried to set you on an indirect trail that might turn something up." He looked up at her. "I'm sorry."

"Don't be sorry," she said. "It worked."

Nick looked up. "What do you mean?"

Ellie explained how Avi had directed her to Barry Lourdes, what Barry had told her, and where it led her from there. She explained how Jet was looking into the disappearance of a girl who had been kidnapped in Miami and how his investigation had crossed with hers just last night. She left out the details surrounding Felipe's apparent demise.

Tyler listened to her with growing anxiety appearance on his face. "I think you both just need to go to the police," he said. "Nick can identify the guy who killed his brother."

"But I can't," Nick said. "I didn't actually see him do it. Plus, the other guy who was with him when I picked up my drill was a cop. I'm not going to risk them finding out I'm still alive and possibly put my family in danger."

A piece to all this didn't seem to fit. "But when Nate fell he was wearing your tie," Ellie said.

"Wasn't mine. It was orange though."

"He didn't have a wallet or phone on him?" Tyler asked.

"It was in his carry-on, which I think is all he had. As soon as I connected what happened, I just reacted. I grabbed his bag and left all my stuff in the room. I knew they had come for me, so I thought I would let them think that for as long as I could. I was pretty sure someone would find out it wasn't me. But they haven't yet, I guess."

"No one has come looking for him?" Ellie asked. "Was he married?"

"No," Nick said. "And he was out of a job. Like I said, he was over there considering a new career, and I don't know that he had a lot of friends." Nick paused long enough to take a long sip of his beer before continuing. "He'd checked out of his hotel and was heading to the airport after we were done eating. I'm guessing that other than not catching his flight, no one's even missed him yet."

Ellie cringed at Nick's last sentence. To live in a world where no one missed you. It was a gloomy narrative to ponder. "You've been watching your house at night," she said. "Tiffany said she saw someone."

"Yeah," he said. "I miss them."

"We need to tell Tiff," Tyler said. "She's going to flip."

"No," Nick said firmly.

"What? Why?"

"I need answers first. Until I know who tried to kill me and why, everything stays the same. I don't want to give Tiff a reason to act differently or decide to go to the cops anyway."

"All right," Tyler sighed. "Then you stay here with me. What's the plan then if you're not going to the police?

"I'll handle that," Ellie said. "Nick, what did the guy who took the invoices look like?"

"He was a normal height, but he had strong arms and a decent belly. One of his eyes wasn't right either. It looked dead...white, just no color at all. And his nose, it's huge. Like a damaged avocado or something."

Ellie kept a poker face while sirens sounded off in her head. Nick had just described the same man she saw last night, the man who had apparently killed Felipe. The guy who came in on the boat had called him Cruz.

Nick let out another sigh and shook his empty bottle. "Could I get another beer?"

Tyler stood up again and looked back at Nick. "Hey, you didn't come in here and take my hat did you?"

"No, I know better than that." Then Nick, seemingly for the first time today, really looked at Tyler. "Dude," he said, "what's wrong with your hair?"

Tyler's jaw tightened. He shook his head. "Get your own damn beer."

CHAPTER TWENTY-SIX

It was not one of nature's requirements that stern and ruthless men should possess towering physical statures. The history books record Stalin as coming in at less than five-and-a-half feet tall. Napoleon too. Leaders who valued false conceptions of victory and treasured their own visions of power over the lives of individuals beneath their care. For these men, people merely existed to serve their own narcissistic ends.

Miguel Zedillo, standing at five feet, three inches, was just such a man. And had poor Felipe still been alive, had he been afforded a chance to meet him in person, he may have caught himself thinking for a brief moment about Oompa Loompas. Zedillo was short and slender. A pinky, not a thumb. His hair was nearly white, his ruddy skin starting to crease along his forehead and around his mouth like old leather.

On paper, factoring in his legitimate businesses and investments, the man was worth nearly sixty million dollars, most of it earned in the Mexican telecommunications industry over the last decade. But through business conducted in the shadows—some might even say in the sewers—his net worth was four times that amount.

Blake Duprey had met the man only twice before, and both times he walked away feeling as if, during some point during their conversation, Zedillo had come to a silent decision to get rid of him. That by the end of the day he would be in a dozen pieces at the bottom of a gator-infested swamp. But so far he had been wrong.

He stood silently next to Cruz as they rode the private elevator to the top floor of Miami's Mandarin Hotel. The car finally slowed, and as the doors slid open, they were silently greeted by one of Zedillo's private security guards. The sound of a well-played piano drifted from around the corner. Lifting an arm, the guard directed them where to go.

A baby grand took up the center of the marble floor, and their boss sat on the piano's bench, running expert fingers across the keys. Cruz didn't know Bach from Barney, but Blake had accompanied his accounting major in college with a minor in music. He recognized the song: Mozart's Piano Concerto No. 21. They waited off to the side, Cruz beginning to shift on his feet, Blake entranced by the older man's ability.

When Zedillo finished the piece, he gracefully removed his hands from the keys and placed them in his lap. Not bothering to look at his guests, he said, "My father was a concert pianist in Mexico. He was, unfortunately, also given over to gambling." A red Solo cup was sitting on the piano. Zedillo picked it up and spat in his tobacco juice. "Perhaps not the worst thing in the world," Zedillo continued. "But he struggled to pay his debts. His bookie had a reputation for being a patient man, but he finally grew weary enough to break both of my father's index fingers. He snapped them like two dry twigs." He frowned and shook his head. "A shame." When he finally looked at his guests, the frown had been replaced by an artificial smile.

"Blake," he said. "How are you?"

Zedillo's bushy gray eyebrows were perched above cold, gray eyes that Blake was fairly certain had x-ray capabilities. When Miguel Zedillo looked you in the eye and smiled that mellow, disarming smile, you thought he was reading your thoughts, as though the purposes and intents of your heart had just been spread out before the all-seeing eye of Sauron.

Which was precisely how Blake thought of Miguel Zedillo: a Mexican Sauron. Only much smaller.

"I'm good, sir," Blake replied. But he didn't feel good. Sweat had popped up along the back of his neck, and he was starting to feel a little lightheaded.

Zedillo stood and took the Solo cup with him into the next room while he worked the tobacco from the inside of his lip and discarded it into the cup. He stopped at a mini bar and used a set of tongs to toss a couple of ice cubes into a glass before pouring himself a generous serving of rum from a decanter. Without offering anything to his guests, he put his back to them and walked to the window, which looked over downtown Miami and Key Biscayne. "I'm sure you are both wondering why I asked you here," he said without turning around.

Not knowing what else to say or how to say it, Cruz simply replied, "Yes, sir."

"Yes. Of course, you are. Well, I'm shutting down Breakwater," he said blandly.

Cruz glanced quickly at Blake, who had just turned

a sickly shade of white, as though he had just been handed his execution date. And to his own embarrassment and horror, Blake discovered that his next words did not come out smoothly like he thought they would. Somewhere between his brain and his mouth something shorted out. "Shu-shutting it down, sir?"

They were expendable. They both knew that. Zedillo had made far more on them than he had ever spent on the lawyer who ensured their drastically reduced sentences. And Zedillo had a reputation for those in his employment to go missing suddenly, never to turn up again. Men like Felipe.

"You'll wonder why, of course." And without waiting for a reply, he said, "If I don't change things often, the wrong people will catch wind. And I can't have that."

Blake was surprised to discover that he had located a spoonful of courage. He swallowed hard. "Mr. Zedillo, sir. I just got things to where they're running smoothly. I finally have subcontractors who are doing everything that I ask. And no one suspects in the least what we're doing."

Zedillo nearly laughed. "Blake, you went to prison. Remind me why?"

Blake's lips were dry. He tried wetting them and said, "Well, sir, because I embezzled some money from my uncle's company."

"Indeed. And I needed a good accountant." He turned suddenly and stepped forward, placed a hand on Blake's shoulder. It was small and light and felt as though a bird had perched there. "And that was why I made sure that you and I could come to a deal. How is your daughter, Blake?"

"She's great, sir."

Zedillo smiled that fake, serpentine smile again. When he removed his hand, Blake felt like a boulder had just slid from his shoulder. "But you got caught, Blake. Let me make the business decisions."

"Yes, sir."

"You both have done very well," Zedillo said. "And you'll be compensated well. Blake, someone will come to see you the first of next week and help you shut everything down in a way that is satisfactory to me." He turned his attention to Cruz. "You will continue as usual. I will let you know where we will be funneling the cash instead."

And it was a lot of cash. Eight clients, all foreigners in the U.S. on business, paying ten thousand dollars for three hours each Saturday night. Eighty thousand a weekend, over five million a year. Cruz knew Zedillo had many such operations around the globe. Miami was just one.

"Of course," Cruz replied.

Zedillo took a sip of his drink and nodded thoughtfully. "I have postponed my return trip to Mexico City. I will be on your side of the state this weekend," he said. "Please ensure there is a place for me at the card table."

The request took Cruz off guard. He hesitated.

"Will that be a problem, Victor?"

"No, sir. No, of course not."

"Good." Zedillo smiled that easy, plastic smile again, but this time his eyes were elsewhere. His interest in his present company had come to an end. He turned to the window and looked back over the cityscape. "Thank you both for coming."

Blake glanced uncertainly at Cruz, like a pauper

who was unsure if it was all right to leave the presence of the king. Cruz nodded toward the elevator before saying, "Thank you, Mr. Zedillo."

As they rode the elevator back down, Blake wiped his sweaty palms down the front of his pants. He looked over at Cruz. "He wants to play cards? Has he done that before?"

"No. He hasn't."

"Don't you think that's a little strange?"

"He owns the place. I guess that means he can do whatever he wants."

"Yeah," Blake said. "I guess it does."

CHAPTER TWENTY-SEVEN

"That's incredible." Jet shook his head as he leaned back in his desk chair and tossed an ankle over a knee. Ellie had spent the last ten minutes relaying the events of her morning: the revelation that Nick was actually alive and the details of what had really happened. "And Nick is certain it was a police officer he saw?" he asked.

"He swears by it. I asked him again just before I left."

"Well, that keeps things complicated, doesn't it?"

"Did you get anything on the Tundra's license plate?"

"I did. It's registered to a Victor Cruz. Which matches what you said the other guy called him last night. Unfortunately, the address on the truck's registration points to a defunct trailer park in Immokalee that was bought up and torn down by a condo developer a few months ago."

"What about Cruz's background?" she asked.

"Nothing recent. He spent two years in jail for beating the pulp out of someone and breaking his back.

He got out last year but no work history or known addresses.

"He only got two years for a violent assault?"

"Yeah. A little strange, isn't it? And I thought about calling his parole officer. But guess what?"

"He doesn't have one."

"He doesn't have one," Jet echoed. "Cruz commits second degree assault, is charged with third degree assault, and is out in less than three years with no parole."

"And what about the fingerprint?"

"The print belongs to a Blake Duprey. That name mean anything to you?"

"No."

"Well, I had to peel back a few layers of paperwork, but Mr. Duprey is *El Presidente* of Breakwater Construction."

And finally the dots were connecting, a clearer picture beginning to emerge. "What's Blake's background?"

"Oddly similar to Victor Cruz," Jet said. "He was an accountant for a financial services group and wound up in prison for embezzlement. Got nine months for it."

"Nine months? That's it?"

"Yep."

"And no parole," Ellie guessed out loud.

"Correct."

"So we can probably assume that they aren't the decision makers," Ellie said. "If someone helped them shorten their prison terms, it would have to be someone with deep pockets and a big influence."

Jet stood up and went to the coffee maker, started brewing another cup. "Here's how I see it," he said.

"Victor Cruz was in possession of dubious invoices from Breakwater. Nick accidentally comes across them, and they tried to tie off that loose end by throwing him over a balcony and making it look like suicide. Cruz is also connected to Felipe, who was involved with grabbing girls off the street and forcing them into the sex trade. The money made from that is laundered through Breakwater. Sound right?"

"It fits," she said. As she worked to piece everything together, she could feel the ache of Nick's death begin to melt away. But she was no less anxious to find justice for his brother and for the trauma the Barlow family had experienced. Even more, she wanted to find Juanita. She wanted to find all those responsible for taking her and using her.

Ellie had started this investigation on her own, but she and Jet were in this together now. In spite of her persistent reluctance to accept his request to join his agency, something had successfully conspired to make a team out of them. "So how do you see us moving forward?" she asked, and then unenthusiastically added, "We probably have enough to take this to the authorities."

"I think we have plenty here that I could take it to my friends at the FBI," he said. "But what concerns me is that assuming Juanita is still alive, we have no idea where she is. I don't think Cruz or Blake know we're on to them. If I take it to the FBI, there's a small but legitimate chance a bad cop could catch wind of it. Other than what you saw with Felipe, and what Nick saw, we have nothing concrete to give them. We don't have any invoices. No smoking gun."

"Yeah," Ellie said. "So let's find her."

Jet grabbed his coffee and returned to his desk. He snatched up a Post-it Note and handed it to Ellie. "I can't find any work history for Cruz since he got out. But he has a young son by an ex-girlfriend. Best I can tell, she broke up with him after he went to prison. That's her address. Might be worth a shot to pay her a visit. She may know where he frequents or lives."

"Great. What are you going to do?"

"I was thinking I'd set a camera on the roof of that old fiberglass factory where we bumped into each other. I want to see if I can catch anyone else coming or going. And I'm going to see what else I can dig up on Blake too."

Ellie stood and studied the address in her hand. "Sounds good," she said, and felt a determined resolve hardening within her. "Let's find her."

CHAPTER TWENTY-EIGHT

THE APARTMENT BUILDING was Section 8, part of a large cluster of tumble-down edifices that took up most of the block. The landscaping, however—St. Augustine grass, azalea bushes, and date palms—was well maintained. The stairwells were open-air, and Ellie took a flight to the second floor. She located apartment 203 at the end of the corridor where a clay flower pot, filled with artificial yellow roses, sat next to a purple doormat. Ellie's knock was followed by the voice of a small boy calling out to his mother inside the apartment.

The door chain rattled, and the door opened a few inches, a young lady's face appearing on the other side. "Yeah?"

"Hi, are you Abby?" A small boy with a pudgy stomach materialized beneath the lady's legs.

"Yeah." She looked suspiciously at Ellie, who quickly noted the hardened, embittered expression of someone who had clearly been hurt one too many times.

"I'm sorry to interrupt," Ellie said. "I was hoping I could get a minute to ask you about Victor Cruz."

On hearing Victor's name, Abby tensed and looked down at the boy between her legs. "Nino," she said urgently, "go watch TV."

His little head was tipped backward, and he didn't take his eyes off of Ellie. "I don't want to. Who is Victor?"

"Nino!" She stepped back and grabbed him by the arm, drilled her eyes into his until Ellie thought lasers might shoot out and turn him to ash. "Go watch TV. *Now.*"

The boy laughed like he enjoyed being the one in control and then vanished around the corner. Abby took a final glance toward him and stepped out of the apartment, pulling the door closed behind her. "Victor is his father," she said quietly. "He doesn't know that."

"I'm sorry," Ellie said. "I didn't mean—"

"It's fine. What do you want? Did he get arrested again?"

"No. Nothing like that. But I was wondering, when was the last time you saw him?" And before Abby could ask, she added, "I'm with a collection agency. We haven't been able to reach Victor."

Abby rolled her eyes. "What, he owes you money?"

"Possibly. Frankly, it could be a misunderstanding. That's what we're trying to clear up. We just fell under new management, and they've been going through old paperwork. We can't see where an old debt was paid, and my records had you down as a past connection."

"Past connection," Abby repeated scornfully. "I guess that's what I am now." She crossed her arms across her chest. "Well, I don't know where he is."

"Do you know of any places he likes to hang out? Any old friends?"

"I wouldn't know what he does these days. If you really need to find him, he used to spend a lot of time at the Ugly Pelican. It's in Cape Coral. Someone there should know where you can find him."

"Thank you," Ellie said. "And thank you for your time."

Abby uncrossed her arms and grabbed the door handle. "Please don't mention anything about me if you go over there. I don't want Victor coming over here and asking me about this."

"Of course." Ellie took the stairs back down and returned to her truck, hoping they had just gotten that much closer to the man who might know where they had taken Juanita.

CHAPTER TWENTY-NINE

Her breathing was a quiet rhythm now, her chest rising and falling in a gentle cadence.

A stark contrast from five minutes ago.

Juanita stroked Almeda's forehead a final time and slowly stood up, rising from her sitting position on the edge of the mattress. She walked to the bedroom door and, taking a final look at Almeda, quietly opened it before stepping into the hallway and shutting it behind her.

She closed her eyes and set a hand on the wall to steady herself against the onslaught of sadness and hot anger that bloomed full force within her. She drew in a deep breath before continuing down the hallway and entering the common room.

The concerned eyes of six other girls fixated on her.

"How is she?" Cami asked.

"Asleep."

Cami nodded soberly. Her eyes were wide, fearful and uncertain. "Do you think they know? No one came down here."

"Maybe they don't care," Juanita said. "Or maybe they weren't watching." But Cami's question only echoed one that Juanita had had for some time now. Was someone always watching what the cameras were sending back? It seemed that they were not. Or someone had simply fallen asleep at the controls.

"Will she be okay?"

"Yes. She'll feel better when she wakes up."

Over the last couple of days, Almeda had entered a gradual slide away from reality. Everyone saw it in her eyes. Or rather, what wasn't in her eyes. Almeda started looking at everything with a mechanical stare, blinking or smiling at the appropriate time like someone had pressed a button on a remote control. A few hours ago, she curled in the fetal position on the couch and began to cry. The tears came quietly and slowly at first—thin trickles of water slipping down her face. But the tears quickly escalated into sobs and then, like someone had broken a levy, she entered a full-on panic attack, her body heaving in great terrified gasps and sobs. She was inconsolable, and like a scared, wild animal, unresponsive to their pleas for her to calm down.

It took her two hours to come off it. Gradually, like someone had slipped her a Vicodin and it was slowly unfurling inside her, she calmed, her screams diminishing into soft whimpers and finally, nothing at all. The girls waited for her eyes to close and her breathing to stabilize before carrying Almeda to her bed.

Cami filled a cup with water from the tap and handed it to Juanita. "Here," she said.

"Thank you." Juanita had it down in three gulps and handed the cup back. She suddenly felt very tired herself. "I think I'm going to go lie down." She returned to her room and lay on her bed, staring at the ceiling, feeling like an elephant was sitting on her chest. In moments like this, when she felt like she couldn't do this anymore, when she felt like she would rather be dead than be here, Juanita would think of her brother.

She wondered where he was and if he was happy. Several weeks ago, Juanita came to terms with the knowledge that she would never see Junior again. By now he would be in a foster home, and she could only hope that they were caring well for him. So many foster children were just a means to another paycheck for the adults, additional cash to be spent on themselves—new clothes, food, or nights on the town. Many times the children left under their care were neglected, if not downright abused. Juanita met plenty of girls and boys at Hope House with those kinds of stories. Juanita knew there were good foster parents. But she had never met any.

Junior would have told someone—Alex most likely—that Juanita had not returned as promised. She knew Alex would have gone to the police. But there was no one else who would care that she was gone. Junior wasn't old enough to make a loud enough noise, one that might keep the authorities sufficiently motivated to keep looking for her.

Cami had a little sister and an elderly grandmother. But both of them were still back in Cuba. The remaining girls had no one. They understood now that they had been selected in part because no one would come looking for them. The world did not miss them because it didn't remember that they existed in the first place.

And that was half the nightmare. That they had

come to America to live a new life, and this is how it was going to end.

Not two years ago, she, Junior, and their mother were living in the Mexican State of San Luis Potosí, on the outskirts of the city of Matehuala, where generations of their family had called home.

But the drug lords steadily overtook the region, making it unsafe to even walk to school. At night you would hear the sound of gunfire; during the day you would see the *capos* ride through town in their Mercedes, caring nothing for whoever had been gunned down the night before so they could enjoy lives of luxury. Their mother finally persuaded a relative already in the U.S. to pay the $25,000 it would take to get the three of them across the border.

They were some of the lucky ones who managed to make it across without being betrayed or getting caught by Border Patrol. They knew as they got on the bus to Florida that they were fortunate. They were in America now where they would be safe. Juanita and Junior started school, began learning English, and were happy. Until their mother got sick with cancer and died. That was, for Juanita, when the happiness ended.

And now Junior was living with someone who did not know him or love him the way Juanita did. That, above anything else, was what made her feel crazy. She was stuck here with no way out.

That elevator at the end of the hall taunted them. It was the only way out, and it did not open without a key card.

They wouldn't keep Juanita forever. They wouldn't keep any of the girls forever. Eventually, they would each be replaced. Discarded like a rancid piece of garbage.

And the great haunting, of course, was when? Next week, next month. Next year?

Juanita had no way of knowing. But she couldn't do this anymore. She would no longer be the means to fulfill someone else's twisted and misaligned fantasies. She was worth more than that. If she knew anything at all, if her mother had taught her anything, it was that.

And it was in that moment, as she stared at the ceiling, thinking of her brother and weighing her worth on the scales of her mind, that Juanita decided that she was done with all this. She was done with being a prisoner.

Somehow, someway, she was going to escape.

Or die trying.

CHAPTER THIRTY

How in the world someone could stay at IHOP for nearly two hours was beyond Jet's comprehension. Especially on a Friday afternoon when there was no wait, and they weren't busy. Blake Duprey had gone in with his daughter a little after 2pm and had yet to reappear. Jet was now in full-regret mode, wishing he had just gone in soon after them and gotten a table of his own at the opposite end of the restaurant. But now he didn't want to chance passing them on their way out. So he waited, listening to a Spotify playlist that included ZZ Top, Van Halen, and AC/DC.

He drove by Blake's house soon after lunch and parked his Maxima four lots further down in front of an undeveloped lot. The house was well-to-do for someone who had recently been released from prison. Two stories, a flagstone driveway, and well-kept Bermuda grass in a neighborhood with homes starting at half a million dollars. It even had a white picket fence. Soon after, the front opened, and a small girl in bright pink shorts and blonde pigtails flew down the steps and ran to the F-150 parked in the driveway. She was followed by her father, who helped her buckle before getting in and taking them out of the neighborhood.

Jet had been in law enforcement long enough that nothing surprised him anymore. He was not struck by the consideration that a man with a pretty wife, a four-year-old daughter, and a baby boy could be laundering money for an organization that trafficked young girls.

His phone rang, replacing David Lee Roth's vocals with a generic tone.

"Hey, Ellie."

"Jet, what are you doing?"

"Staring at IHOP."

"Staring at IHOP? What's that mean?"

"Exactly how it sounds. I've been sitting here for two hours waiting for Blake Duprey to come out with his daughter. How long does it take to sit down and have a meal with your tiny daughter?"

"Are you at the one on North Cleveland?"

"I am."

On the other end of the line, Jet heard Ellie snicker. It was a first; he had never heard her snicker before. "Jet, that location has all-you-can-eat pancakes on Fridays. Chloe begs my sister to take her there every Friday when she picks her up from school."

"All-you-can-eat?" He sounded like a forlorn time management expert. "That explains a lot."

Ellie asked, "Did you get those cameras set up on the rooftop last night?"

"I did. Nothing so far. They may have cleared out for good. Did you find anything else on Cruz?"

Ellie relayed her brief conversation with Abby. "She

said Cruz used to spend time at a bar called the Ugly Pelican. You know it?"

"Yes. We staked it out a couple years back looking for a local dealer. It's heavy on the Hispanic, light on the Caucasian. Not sure that's the best place for you to go asking questions."

"I can handle myself," she said.

"That I don't doubt. I think what I'm saying is that if a pretty white lady comes walking in, you'll get every eye on you for the entire length of your stay. It might not be the easiest scenario for you to stay low key."

"So you want to take it?"

"I'll stop in with my best Spanish accent. I'll blend right in."

Ellie laughed. "All right, it's all yours. Will you go tonight?"

"No. My granddaughter has a varsity softball tournament this weekend. It starts tonight and runs through most of tomorrow. I'll swing by tomorrow night. With it being a Saturday, it should be busy. Might give me a better chance to score some info."

"Okay," she said. "I'll be out tomorrow night, so leave me a message and let me know if you get anything."

"Where are you going?" he asked.

"I've got a gala for cancer research. It's Major's brainchild, and I'm his date."

"Well, have a good time. And try to take your mind off all this. It will be here when you get back."

They hung up, and David Lee Roth returned, singing about dancing the night away while Jet stared out his windshield, wondering just how many pancakes a four-year-old could eat.

CHAPTER THIRTY-ONE

THE CAN of hairspray hissed as she pressed the nozzle and held it away from her body. She heard her front door open and Major announce his arrival. "One second!" Ellie set the can down and, after taking a final look at her hair, escaped the fumes and exited the bathroom. Major was standing in the center of the living room flipping through a copy of Field & Stream that he'd lifted from her coffee table. When he looked up and his eyes fell on his niece, he halted.

Her blonde hair was gathered above her neck in an elegant chignon, set off by a pair of diamond drop earrings that had once belonged to her mother. Dark eyeshadow colored her eyelids, and the perfect shade of red adorned her lips. Her backless dress was royal blue, loose skirts flowing freely below her waist, accompanied by a side slit. Matching high heels gave her five-foot-seven frame another three inches.

"Ellie," Major said. "You're the explicit definition of a lady." He stepped up and placed a gentle kiss on her cheek. "It's nights like this I wish your father were still with us."

"Me too," she said softly, and then nothing else.

The front door opened for the second time in as many minutes, and Tyler's head popped in past the door frame. He stepped in and shut the door, stopping his greeting to Major short as soon as he saw Ellie. He stood straighter and stared at her, then said in a voice full of astonishment, "I want to cat-call you right now, but I'm trying to be more grown—"

He cat-called her.

Ellie smiled. Tyler stepped to her, his eyes bright. "Really," he said. "You look...gorgeous."

Ellie wasn't the blushing type. But she could nearly feel one coming on. "Thank you." She leaned in and kissed him gently, leaving a hint of lipstick on his lips. He didn't seem to mind.

Tyler held a thin, narrow box in his hand, one that might fit a pencil or a letter opener. He removed the lid and gently lifted something from it. Ellie's eyes widened as he held up a tennis bracelet. It threw a thousand spangles of light across the room.

She started to speak but was held back by his hand encircling her wrist like it was gathering up a baby bird. "You've got that internal beauty," he said. "I wanted you to have some on the outside too." He winked at her, and she laughed as the clasp clicked into place.

Tyler stepped back, and Major gave him a gentrified nod, an older man silently informing the younger that he had done well. From behind Ellie, Citrus offered his consent with a sharp yip of approval. Ellie examined the bracelet. "Thank you. It's beautiful."

"You ready?" Major asked.

"Yes." She grabbed her clutch from the kitchen table. "Let's go."

Tyler turned to Major and spoke to him like a protective father. "Don't keep her out past midnight," he said.

"Tyler," Major said, "I held this lady in my arms not five minutes after she was born."

"Bring her back whenever you want."

"There you go."

Ellie said goodbye to her dog, and the three of them went out the front door. Tyler's F-150 was parked behind a burgundy Jaguar XJ. "Major," Ellie said. "Did you just buy a Jag?" For as long as she could remember, Major had always driven a Jeep.

"I couldn't see taking my niece out for a nice date in a Wrangler. So I asked Carlos if I could borrow one of his cars." Major opened the door for her, and Ellie blew Tyler a quick kiss before hiking up the bottoms of her skirt and getting in. Major shut her door and went around to the driver's side, and when he started the Jag, the Beatles continued singing "Penny Lane." Ellie was examining her new bracelet. Behind them, Tyler's truck growled to life.

"He's a good man," Major said as he checked the rearview mirror. "But you really should tell him to get a haircut."

* * *

THE GALA WAS at the Ritz-Carlton in Sarasota, nearly two hours north of St. James City. The luxury hotel was perched on the edge of the water and offered sweeping views of Sarasota Bay and Longboat Key. Carlos

Hernández's call to friends, associates, and philanthropists was happily answered by over one hundred attendees, all gathered in tuxedos and fine dresses to spend an evening fighting pediatric cancer.

The evening commenced outside, near the pool, where guests ordered drinks at a tiki hut and mingled as the sun began its descent into the Gulf of Mexico, while a DJ kept the atmosphere charged with the relaxing and familiar voices of Jimmy Buffett, Jack Johnson, and Don Henley.

Ellie and Major stood in an outdoor lounge holding their drinks while Major discussed his favorite debuts from last year's Miami boat show with the president of Navsec, the state's largest manufacturer of monofilament fishing line. Ellie was about to offer her opinion on the 226 Cayman, Robalo's newest addition to its bay boat line, when a deep voice came from behind them. "Ellie, where did you find your date?"

She turned to see Carlos towering over her, and she thought her head might tip off her shoulders as she craned it to look him in the eye. "I found him panhandling in St. James City. The adventurer in me decided to invite him along."

Carlos looked Major over and grinned. "Well, he cleaned up well."

Major said, "I like your Jag, Carlos. I might not give it back."

"It's a fine machine, isn't it?" Carlos excused himself and navigated clusters of guests as he walked over to the DJ. He grabbed a mic, and the music faded as he thanked everyone for coming and invited them inside for dinner.

Ellie and Major placed their empty drink glasses on

a server's tray and took their seats at a table near the front with Carlos, his wife, and a couple who ran a cancer research foundation based in Lee County. As the servers brought their food course by course, Ken Gambini, a local comedian who had just signed on a three-part comedy special with Netflix, kept everyone in stitches with a flawless routine highlighting water births, airline food, and glitter, which he claimed was one of the ten plagues of Egypt, his authority on the matter stemming from the fact that he had four young girls.

As the meal came to an end, Carlos excused himself from the table and stepped behind a podium on the stage. After a few light-hearted jokes of his own, Carlos turned to the topic of the evening, discussing recent statistics relating to childhood cancer and a personal account of his own grandchild winning her battle with leukemia. Everyone here, he summarized, had a responsibility to continue making the world a better place for current and future generations.

He finished by introducing Major, without whom the night's event would not have taken place. Major joined him on the stage, and the men exchanged hugs before Major took his place behind the microphone. He thanked Carlos for the introduction and began: "I'm just a small business owner from a big island that generally gets overshadowed by Sanibel. But we like being Florida's best-kept secret." Major had taken a piece of paper with him to the podium—a prepared script of what he wanted to say. Now, he folded it and placed it inside his jacket pocket. A frown started to creep over his features, but he overcame it with a forced smile. "Nearly fifteen years ago, the daughter of one of my best friends died of cancer. One day she was playing with friends in her front yard, and the next a doctor was talking to her father about chemo and cell counts and bone marrow transplants."

Major went on to discuss cutting edge treatments that were often held back due to a lack of funding. "Cancer affects us all in some way. If it hasn't touched us directly, it's touched someone we know and love. And kids..." Major paused and took a deep breath before continuing. "Kids shouldn't have to deal with cancer. They should be playing baseball, worrying about ballet recitals, and dreaming of college and changing the world."

Major swallowed hard, overwhelmed by a cause he cared deeply about. Ellie suddenly wished she were up there with him, holding his hand, giving it a reassuring squeeze. But she stayed in her seat, trying to keep willing tears behind her eyes. She knew Major would never fully get over what happened to little Katrina, or the poor choices her father, Quinton Davis, would end up making years later.

Major finished a few minutes later and returned to his table with loud applause, and as the evening drew to a close, the guests drifted back outside, enjoying a fresh round of drinks and lively conversation in the cool evening air.

While Major fell to chatting with a group of people Ellie didn't know, she returned to the tiki hut and ordered a vodka cranberry. Behind her, someone lightly cleared his throat, and when she turned around, she immediately placed the olive-skinned man standing before her. His hair was pulled back into a ponytail, and, like all the other men who were present, he wore a tux.

"Hello," he said. "Am I correct in thinking I saw you on Pine Island last week?"

"Yes," she smiled. "You were leaving Jet's office."

"Yes." He extended his hand. "I'm Alex." They shook as she introduced herself. "Are you a client of his as well?" he asked.

"No. Just a friend." Ellie quelled a desire to tell Alex about her involvement in helping find Juanita. She didn't want to violate any unspoken privacy agreements Jet tried to maintain with his clients. So instead she said, "Is Jet investigating something for you?"

Much of the cheer drained from Alex's face. "Yes. I run a day shelter for children in West Hialeah. A few months ago, one of the girls in the neighborhood went missing. Jet, I am hoping, can help find her. So far the police have not been too persistent."

"I'm sorry," she said. "If anyone can find her, it would be Jet." The bartender extended her drink across the bar. She took a sip before asking, "Do you know anyone here tonight?"

Alex was holding a glass of his own, half full of ice and amber liquid. He took a sip and nodded, "Yes. Carlos, actually. He grew up in West Hialeah and is one of our most generous supporters. He asked me to come so he could introduce me to some individuals he thought might be willing to donate to the shelter. He's actually the one who's offered to pay for the work Jet is doing."

They heard Alex's name called from the other side of the pool. Carlos was waving him over. "Excuse me," he said. "It was a pleasure to meet you."

After Alex left, Ellie walked over to the railing that looked out over the dark waters of Sarasota Bay. Palm fronds rustled dryly above her as a gentle breeze blew across the water, and she closed her eyes, remembering so easily why she loved the Gulf Coast.

She could hear Jet's advice not to think about Juanita tonight, but now she was finding that it wasn't so easy. Not after meeting Alex, and not after hearing that it was Carlos who was funding the investigation. An impatient angst grew hotter inside her. At this late hour, Tiffany would be at home, Kayla tucked in and asleep, both still grieving a husband and a father who was not actually dead. Ellie disagreed with Nick's decision not to tell his family. But she understood it. And Nick's brother was dead, ostensibly murdered by Victor Cruz.

And then there was Juanita.

When Ellie was a little girl, her father ingrained a simple philosophy into her, one that still woke with her each morning: *Do for one what you wish you could do for everyone.* Ellie couldn't help every victim of sex trafficking. But she could help *one*. She could rescue *one*.

Victor Cruz was the key, Ellie knew, and she was going to wake up tomorrow morning and not rest until she found him, until he or someone he knew led her to Juanita.

The ice rattled in her glass as she drained the rest of her drink. After taking a final look at the bay, she returned to the bar and went to find Major.

CHAPTER THIRTY-TWO

The Ugly Pelican sat off Kismet Parkway in north Cape Coral, nestled between a boat repair shop and a defunct bowling alley. It was your basic stucco structure, windowless, painted a searing yellow that served as a backdrop for a sorry mural of a pelican. A truly ugly pelican. Jet couldn't tell if the artist was just that bad or if, given the name of the bar, the eyes were intentionally made to resemble charred golf balls and the beak a melting spoon. Regardless, as he made his way across the dirt parking lot, he thought Juanita could have painted an ugly pelican with at least a little more charm.

The inside was dark, lit by tired bulbs that set the room in a dim and hazy yellow glow. Speakers above the bar poured out Latin Trap that fought with dozens of conversations for auditory dominance.

As Jet made his way to the bar, he fielded surprised and cordial smiles, double-takes, and a few cautious frowns. He was right on target with what he had told Ellie: he was the only Caucasian in the joint, and he stood out like, well, the only Caucasian in the joint.

The bartender looked to be in her late twenties. Her right arm was covered in a sleeve of tattoos, and her hair, shaved at the sides, was dyed blonde. A black tank top was cut off and revealed a pierced belly button. "Help you?" she asked.

He had to raise his voice to be heard. "I'm looking for a Victor Cruz. You know him?"

She spread her hands on the bar top and leaned in, a piece of gum snapping in her teeth. "Why?"

"He owes an old debt. Has he been here lately?"

"What, you like a bondsman or something?"

"No. I'm not a bondsman." He tried again. "Has he been here lately?"

"I haven't seen him." Her interest in the topic was thin to begin with; now it receded altogether. "You want a drink or what?"

"Sure. I'll take a Red Stripe."

"We don't have Red Stripe."

"Okay...a Miller Lite then."

She handed him a bottle. He paid, and as he looked around for an empty table, he spotted only one: a two-seater on the far wall. He went to it and sat down. This wasn't a biker bar and wasn't filled with sour-faced people who wanted him out. He didn't expect to be harangued or interrogated. But two things would happen. The bartender would tell someone, and word would get around, with someone finally approaching Jet to see what his interest was in Cruz. That, or a curious regular would stop by and inquire what a cream-skinned, gray-haired anomaly was doing there alone.

He took out his phone and brought up Instagram, started scanning posts. Social media was a new thing for him. He finally opted in when his grandchildren started using it to showcase their lives. As grandchildren went, they were surprisingly good at bringing their grandparents into their lives, often texting or calling just to say hi or to share a recent experience. But Jet didn't want to miss anything—the goofy faces, the excursions with friends, the laughter with smaller siblings—so he jumped across a generation or two and signed up for an account.

He was nearly finished scanning through the pictures from the softball tournament when someone approached his table and greeted him. Jet looked up to see a mustachioed police officer, smiling and clutching a half drunk bottle of water. The officer wore an amused smile. "I see a white man sitting alone in a place like this, and I think that either his date is running late or his car broke down and he came in here to wait for a ride."

"Neither," Jet smiled back. "I was just looking for someone."

"You doing okay? No one's given you any problems?"

"No problems."

"This can be a trouble spot on the weekends, so we try to keep an eye on it. Who are you looking for?"

"A man named Victor Cruz. Trying to collect on an old debt."

Thoughtful, the officer shook his head. "Haven't heard of him." He looked toward the bar and waved his hand. "Hugo is the owner. He might know."

But alarm bells were already sounding off in Jet's head, screaming incessantly and blocking out the music, the loud babble, and the last part of what the officer had said. He forced himself to remain calm, and he took another pull off his beer.

The officer had betrayed his words by the subtle shift

of an eye, a momentary flash of recognition at the mention of Victor's name that he was unable to repress, leading Jet to suddenly recall what Ellie told him about Nick: Cruz was with a police officer the night Nick found the invoices. He could think of no other reason for the officer to lie; it was the only thing that made sense. Jet glanced casually at his nameplate: "L. Gomez." His shoulder patch had him with the Fort Myers P.D.

Hugo, a hefty man with nondescript features, approached the table. Jet stood up, and Officer Gomez nodded toward him. "He's looking for a Victor Cruz. Has he been in lately?"

Hugo lied even worse. He blinked at Jet with wide, bright eyes, the way a child will when he has a mouthful of Skittles and his mother asks him if he's seen the Skittles. Gomez noticed this and nervously cleared his throat. "What do you think, Hugo?"

The bar's owner swallowed hard. "No—I mean, not in months. He doesn't really come in anymore. Why?"

"Just trying to collect on a debt," Jet said.

"Oh. What kind?"

"Unfortunately, that's private. Do you think anyone else here might know where I can find him?"

"No. No, they won't know." His smile was forced, and even in the low lighting, it revealed crooked teeth, leaning like unkempt tombstones.

Jet finished his beer and set the empty bottle on the table. "Well, I appreciate the both of you trying to help." He shook each man's hand.

"Sorry I couldn't be more help," Hugo said.

Officer Gomez asked: "You want to leave your number or anything? Hugo can call you if he turns up."

"That's all right." He thanked them again and returned to his car.

He smiled as he pulled out of the parking lot and turned back onto Kismet Parkway. His visit to the Ugly Pelican went far better than he'd expected.

He didn't get a lead on Cruz, but what he did find was far better.

CHAPTER THIRTY-THREE

THE AIR in the windowless room was hazy with the smoke from half a dozen cigars. Cruz sat at his desk in the corner, bored, alternating his gaze between the monitors and his phone, which currently displayed the most recent NBA rankings. He would have liked to have gone to the Heat's game tonight. They were playing the Celtics, and man, did he love his Celtics.

He set his phone on the desk and looked across the room where eight men, Miguel Zedillo among them, sat around the card table playing poker, drinking spirits, and talking international business.

Cruz paid them no mind. Their interests did not align with his. He would never broker overseas deals or manage acquisitions. He belonged to Zedillo, owed him nine more years, and that meant right now he was most concerned with finding a replacement for Felipe.

Which was proving more difficult than he imagined when he kicked Felipe into the next life. Felipe had a style, a charm that easily put people at ease. Tito Sanchez had a similar way with the ladies, and Cruz had already pegged him for Felipe's replacement. But yesterday Tito got in a bad car wreck, and the doctors weren't even sure he was going to make it. So Cruz had to start his search all over again. Zedillo wanted to expand, and they couldn't do that without more girls.

The card game ended, and Zedillo waved Cruz over to the table. Zedillo held out an empty can of chewing tobacco. He spat into a cup. "Have someone get me another before I leave this evening."

Cruz took it and examined the label: Copenhagen Long Cut. "Yes, sir. I'll have it for you."

Zedillo looked around the table and pushed his chair back as he came to his feet. "Gentlemen," he said, "are we ready for the evening to begin?"

* * *

Major loosened his bow tie and settled into his seat, turning the Jag onto Bayfront Drive and following it around Burns Square. "Major," Ellie said, "that was a great evening. You helped a lot of kids, a lot of families tonight."

His lively demeanor cooled as he seemed to look back to a past Ellie couldn't follow him into. "I only wish I had thought of that years ago," he said quietly.

The comment took her off guard. It lacked confidence and hinted at regret, both uncharacteristic of Major. "But you did it tonight. And that counts. Other than doing something like selling drugs, you'd have been hard-pressed to get your hands on the kind of money you raised tonight."

He remained thoughtful as he turned south onto Route 41. "I suppose so."

Ellie heard a short buzz come from her clutch. She opened it and withdrew her phone. The screen was glowing with a new email from Jet. She opened it, seeing just two addresses with no accompanying explanation. "You mind if I make a quick call?" she asked.

"Not at all." The light ahead turned red, and Major brought the Jag to a stop. Ellie dialed Jet, noting the time on the dashboard clock: ten forty-three.

"Ellie, I didn't mean for you to call me tonight," Jet answered.

"We're on our way back. What are the addresses?"

"I thought I'd try digging up locations associated with Breakwater. Since they're a construction company, I started thinking that maybe they outfitted a place for the girls. And if not that, then since that old fire station seems out of play now, maybe another one of their properties is a base of operation. I still can't find an office for them."

It made perfect sense, and Ellie couldn't believe she hadn't thought of it herself. "Did you go by the bar?" she asked.

"I did. I didn't get anything on Victor, but there's a decent chance that I may have found the cop Nick was talking about."

Ellie's fingers clutched tightly around the phone. "What?"

"He was at the bar. But I'm still digging around on him. I know a couple of officers in the Fort Myers PD, but I'll have to wait until tomorrow to get in touch with them."

"You still want to meet tomorrow and regroup?" she asked.

"Yes. We've got church in the morning. I'll text you after that."

After they hung up, Ellie slipped her phone back into her clutch. Earlier in the evening, she had spent the ride up to Sarasota telling Major about her investigation, something she had yet to broadcast to anyone. She told him about the email, Breakwater, and how her path merged with Jet's. She told him about Juanita's kidnapping, and that Nick was alive, staying at Tyler's house until they found some resolution. Major said nothing until she was finished, but the entire time his fingers incrementally squeezed the steering wheel harder and harder.

Now, as Major accelerated down Route 41, he looked over at his niece. She was pensive, staring out of the window. "What was that about?" he asked.

"Jet's connected a couple addresses that could be potential properties where the girls are being kept. It's a long shot, but they're up in this area."

He didn't hesitate. "Tell me where to go."

CHAPTER THIRTY-FOUR

WHEN HE WALKED through the door, Juanita felt a paradoxical wave of relief. He wasn't like some others, tall or fat, men who looked like they had eaten a small cow before they opened her door. This man was small—short and slim. He shut the door behind him and smiled at her with all the lust of a depraved demon. He was older, and his bushy gray eyebrows were perched above cold, gray eyes. She stood next to the bed and waited for him to come to her.

She set her hand over his belt buckle and began to unfasten it as he kissed her neck. Revulsion erupted inside her as the belt cleared the loopholes of his pants and she pulled it away from his body. She folded it and snapped it with authority. "Turn around," she said. Zedillo gave her an understanding smile and did what she said. "Now get on your knees." He said something vulgar that made her skin crawl, chuckled, and then got down on his knees.

Juanita's hands were trembling now. She hated this man, all the men previous, and all those responsible for bringing and keeping her here. She hated them all for what they had made her do. And for what she was about to do. Because tonight she was done. Tonight was the night she said, no more. She was taking her dignity back.

Her next action could not be undone. It would, she knew, most likely fail. They wouldn't tolerate such a rebellion, and she would be dead within the next five minutes.

But it was worth the risk. There was no doubt in her mind about that. Her compulsion to get out of this place was undergirded by a vision of her brother's tender face. Wherever Junior was, he wasn't with family. He needed her. She needed him.

Juanita brought in a deep, quiet breath and steadied her hands. She told the client to close his eyes, and she threaded the end of the belt back into the buckle. He chuckled again as she lifted the loop and slipped it down over his head.

She dropped it to his neck and, with a single swift motion, pulled with all her might.

CHAPTER THIRTY-FIVE

The Jaguar's headlights cut a piercing path through the darkness. Ellie was watching the maps application on her phone. "Up here," she said, and Major eased off the gas. "Take a left at the light." They turned onto a rutted dirt road and moved slowly as the tires picked up small rocks and pebbles and threw them into the undercarriage. Major didn't verbalize a desire to return the car in the same condition he'd borrowed it, but Ellie knew he was thinking it. His jaw was set tight, and he seemed to flinch with every knock and ping.

On their left, a field was hemmed off from the road by a three wire barb fence, and to their right was a forest that had yet to be disturbed by human development. As they drove on, Ellie could feel nervous anticipation growing inside her. She wasn't entirely sure what she was hoping to find, or what might serve to inform her that they had discovered the right location. But her experience told her she would know when she saw it.

If she saw it.

A half mile later, the mouth of a dirt driveway materialized and cut in through the trees. Ellie told Major to turn in. The road looked like it had recently been cleared. Bright, freshly cut tree stumps lined both sides of the lane, and piles of branches, bushes, and wild vines were stacked high. Major brought the car to a stop as the headlights illuminated the lot before them, which was naked save for a stack of rebar and PVC piping. Large mounds of dirt filled the back of the lot and sat up against the treeline. "Looks like they're just getting to work on the foundation," Major said.

Ellie already had her phone out, and she punched in the address for the next location. Major cautiously negotiated the luxury car off the lot and back to the main road. "Next one is five miles south," Ellie said.

Outside, more forests and farmland set the night into a dark sheet of black. Even the stars were dismissed by a recent band of cloud cover. Up ahead, a small section of earth glowed bright and grew larger and more obnoxious the closer they got. It was a Sunoco, one of the few reminders that they hadn't driven into a pre-modern past. Their eyes didn't have time to adjust to the light, and they squinted as they passed and sped back into the darkness.

"It infuriates me," Major said, "that anyone would descend to trafficking women and girls."

"Me too. It's beyond sick. Turn here."

They took a narrow paved road until it dead-ended at a wide metal building a half mile later. It was dark, with no illumination coming from any exterior lighting. A small window in the front was dark as well. There were no cars. With no way to conceal their presence, Ellie told Major to just drive up. "Give me a second." She stepped into the night as Major cautioned her to be careful. There was no door of any kind at the front, so she walked to the side of the building, where she found a metal door. She tried the handle and was surprised to find the door opened to her. Inside it was dark and still, perfectly quiet. Her senses were on high alert as she felt for a light switch just inside the door. Her fingers found one, and she flipped it on. Halogens blinked on across a bare concrete floor. There was nothing here. No equipment, boxes, or desks. Not even a mousetrap. She walked across the floor, but there was nothing abnormal, nothing to indicate that she was standing in anything more than a vacant building. She went back out and shut the door behind her then walked the perimeter of the building to ensure she hadn't missed anything. Disappointed, she returned to the car and got in.

"Anything?" Major asked.

"No. I found an unlocked door. The place is empty."

"Any other locations?"

She shook her head. "Thanks for trying."

He swung the Jag around and sighed. "I'm sorry, kiddo."

FIVE MINUTES LATER, the lights of the Sunoco station glowed before them again. Major took his foot off the gas. "I'm going to grab a drink for the way back." He turned into a parking space at the front. "You want anything?"

"I'm good. Thanks."

While Ellie waited, she replied to Jet's email, letting him know the locations were a bust. Then she replied to a text from her sister, who was curious to know how the gala went before setting her phone down and closing her eyes. She took in a deep breath.

Her mind was racing now. Jet was on to something, pulling the addresses associated with Breakwater. Ellie suddenly wished it were tomorrow. She wanted to hear more about the cop Jet may have connected with Victor Cruz. She wanted to do the next thing, to follow the string, to pull it, and see if anything unraveled.

They were getting close. So close, in fact, that she felt as though she could reach out and touch it. Ellie drummed her fingers on the tops of her legs and tried to think, reviewing every detail, every association to find something they could have missed. But nothing clicked; nothing slipped into place.

Finally, she opened her eyes, and as they adjusted to the bright glow of the lights, she froze.

Standing in line, directly in front of Major, was Victor Cruz.

CHAPTER THIRTY-SIX

It was late, he was tired, and the dim lights over the highway created a steady pulse of rhythmic light that acted the part of a silent lullaby. Looking at the clock on his dash, he knew that a stop for coffee would be in order if he was going to make the drive back home tonight. The evening was encroaching on midnight, which meant completing the trip to Miami would put him back home in the early hours of the morning.

His phone was sitting in a dock that was clipped to an air vent. It rang, and Cruz's name appeared on the display. He swiped to answer it, then tapped the speaker icon. "Yes?"

"Where are you?" Cruz asked.

He heard a vehicle door slam on the other end of the call. He looked out the windshield at the passing sign perched over the highway. The white reflective lettering read back "Daniels Parkway." "South Fort Myers," he said. "Why?"

"Gomez just called. Said some guy was poking around for me at the Ugly Pelican. When he left, Gomez got his plate and ran it. It's that PI. You need to end this. And I mean right now. He's getting too close."

He sighed, took his time replying. "Okay. I will."

"If you don't make it look like an accident, they'll search his case files. Don't give them a reason to look into what he was working on."

"That won't be a problem. Anything else?"

"I think that's enough."

He hung up and sighed once more. Leaning over, he checked to ensure his weapon was in the glove box, and then he took the next exit, setting a course for Pine Island. And Jet's house.

CHAPTER THIRTY-SEVEN

THE ATTENDANT HANDED Cruz his receipt, and he came out of the store with what looked like a can of chewing tobacco. He stopped in front of a newspaper stand, and after tapping at his cell phone, he set it to his ear.

The car keys were with Major, and Ellie couldn't roll down her window. She set her fingers on the door handle and pulled slowly until the lock popped and the door opened a crack. Cruz started walking to the Tundra parked right next to Ellie. As he came around to the driver's side, all Ellie heard him say was, "Where are you?" before he got in and slammed the door shut.

Within seconds the Tundra's engine roared to life, three hundred and eighty horses growling unashamedly into the quiet country air. Cruz quickly backed out of the parking space before switching gears and tearing out of the gas station.

Ellie's palms suddenly felt sweaty. Inside, the attendant answered a phone call and was standing idle while Major waited patiently. Ellie darted from the car and went inside, her heels clicking against the linoleum as she came up behind Major. She took him by the elbow. "Hey, we need to go."

Major turned and saw the urgency in her eyes. "What's wrong?"

"I'll tell you outside." Major abandoned his drink and followed Ellie back out the door. "That man who checked out in front of you. He's the one who tried to kill Nick. He just left."

They got back in the car, and Major started it up. "Which way did he go?"

CHAPTER THIRTY-EIGHT

Juanita looked down on the man's body with terrified eyes. He lay in a loose pile at her feet, dead, his face blue and swollen, his leathery skin glistening with sweat like a glove that had just been oiled. She stepped back and clasped her hands over her mouth as the adrenaline started a full retreat and the realization of what she had just done began to set in. Tears clouded her vision, and a dreadful weight descended across her chest, making it impossible to breathe. She slid her hands off her mouth and sat down on the bed. She felt dizzy and her throat was starting to constrict; her heart raced violently and her hands, still trembling, felt cold. She lay back on the pillow and stared motionless at the ceiling, trying in vain to calm herself.

She had a sudden recollection of the panic attack Almeda experienced the other day, and the understanding that she was now on the threshold of one herself spread over her like a heavy, dark blanket, threatening to suffocate her and bring her to the same fate as the man on the floor. She wanted to cry out, to utter a cathartic scream that might purge some of the terror that had savagely crawled inside her. She focused on her breathing, taking each breath in measured stride and forcing herself to regulate the pace at which she brought air into her lungs and released it again. The room started spinning, stretching out like a piece of taffy. When it started to wobble, Juanita closed her eyes and tried to think of Junior.

He came to her easily, mercifully, like a healing vision of the ocean on a cool summer night. She could feel Junior's small hand in hers, see his trusting smile looking up at her, hear his laughter as she tickled him before tucking him into bed.

Her breathing began to calm, her muscles relax, and she slowly slipped into a dark and calming place somewhere between wakefulness and sleep.

She didn't know how much time had passed when she finally sat up. Something told her it was much longer than she would have wanted. But she felt better, calmer —not good, but no longer fully out of control. Taking a slow shuddering breath, she slowly returned her feet to the floor while trying to ignore the dead man's body that lay silently, chillingly, in the center of the room.

She moved to the dresser and drew out a pair of leggings and a t-shirt. She changed quickly and grabbed a hair tie from the nightstand drawer. She slung her hair into a ponytail. The next step would be the worst of all. She had to get the card from the man's pocket. As she forced herself to look at him, she saw that his face had turned a sickly hue of gray and the skin along his hands was a marbled patchwork of discolored splotches.

She swallowed hard against a parched throat and, willing the nausea and revulsion to stay down, made a timid approach. He was lying on his side. Juanita turned her face away as she reached a hand into his pocket and felt for the thick plastic card he came in with. Without it, there was no hope of even an attempt at escape.

The pocket was empty. Juanita quickly snatched her hand back. The man was dead; she knew that. But visions of him suddenly blinking and coming to his feet haunted her imagination. Holding her breath, she forced herself to grab his shoulders, heaving him over onto his stomach. She kneeled down and searched through his other pocket. Her fingers grabbed onto the card's hard plastic, and she snatched it out, stepping clear of him like a scared cat.

Juanita went to the door and listened. She heard nothing. There was nothing left but to walk out of the room, down the hall, and scan the card at the elevator. That was as far as the plan went. What would she see when the elevator doors opened? A room full of her captors? They would surely have guns, and there would be nowhere for her to run. Would she even get that far? The camera in the hall would give her away the moment she stepped from the room.

It didn't matter. She couldn't turn back now.

The panic had passed, but her heart was still beating rapidly as if screaming at her, an old friend telling her not to go. But the dead body behind her and her brother before her compelled her to wrap her fingers around the door handle and, with a final deep breath, yank it open.

She ran. Hard. Her room was the fifth from the elevator. Arriving at the end of the hall, she slapped the key card against the reader and waited for the metal door to open.

Nothing happened. She set it flush to the reader and slid it around in wild, frantic strokes, silently pleading for it to work. But still, nothing happened. Now her fingers were trembling again and her palms slick with sweat. The card slipped from her hand like a traitorous guide and fell to the carpet, and as she leaned down to retrieve it, she could feel the eye of the camera above her, staring down on her like an evil spy eager to tell her secrets.

She examined the card. On one side, imprinted in black ink was the number "5," corresponding to her room number. She flipped it over. The other side was blank. Quickly, she tried setting the blank side to the reader.

The diode flashed green, and the elevator door slid open, as though congratulating her on completing the first step of an inescapable maze. Juanita slipped inside, examining the inside panel as she waited for the door to slide shut.

There was nothing there.

Every elevator she had ever been in was equipped with seemingly standard features. This elevator had none of those. The stainless steel panel was absent of any floor, call, or alarm buttons. It was no surprise that the alarm button was missing, but there were no buttons at all.

The door slid shut.

It didn't move; it didn't go up or down. Juanita stood in the silence not knowing what to do, and a sickening feeling started deep in her chest and rose up into a constricted throat. What if the elevator could only be operated by whoever was watching on the camera?

She looked up. Not long ago she had seen a movie—with Jesse of all people—where a man crawled up through the roof of the elevator and into the shaft. But there were no handrails inside the elevator, and Juanita couldn't see a way to reach the ceiling, much less scurry up through it.

She wanted to scream. She wanted to cry out, to hurl insults at an unjust universe with a fresh anger that was thicker than rage. She looked down at the card in her hand, and in a final act of desperation, she slapped it on the smooth steel panel and rubbed it around with a fast, jerking movement that signaled the return of her panic.

Behind her, she heard a faint click.

She turned and listened, and then she noticed that one of the side panels had a small gap at the edge. It hadn't been there a moment earlier. She set the flats of her hands against it and pressed. It was heavy, but it gave way and swung out into a dimly lit void.

She half expected to hear a malevolent chuckle or slow clap of sarcastic praise. But there was nothing—only the sound of her own breathing. As her eyes adjusted to the low lighting, she could make out a flight of carpeted steps that led up.

The elevator was a ruse. Nothing but a deceitful facade.

Juanita stepped from the elevator, her heart still thumping in a desperate revolt.

She started up the stairs.

CHAPTER THIRTY-NINE

THEY DROVE for nearly fifteen minutes, keeping a reasonable distance between them and the Tundra. They followed it east on State Road 72 before heading north on State Road 17 for several minutes before Cruz's brake lights finally lit up as he reduced his speed. He turned into a long stone driveway that was cut down the center by a grassy median and lined on either side with royal palms. Major turned in, and Ellie noted the name on the monument sign: Palm Rivers. Up ahead, Cruz parked beneath a porte-cochère and tossed his keys to a valet before going inside.

Just before the driveway curved around a large fountain, a break in the median gave incoming visitors access to a parking lot already filled with dozens of cars.

"Are you going in?" Major asked.

"Yes. Pull up to the front."

"I'll go with you."

"No," she said. "I don't know what he's doing here. If he leaves suddenly, I'll need you to be ready."

"I like my idea better," he said, but he pulled around

the fountain anyway and stopped at the front. He set a hand on Ellie's arm. "Be careful, kiddo."

A valet stood to the side, waiting for the Jag's driver to open his door. Ellie stepped out and turned to him. "We'll just be a minute," she said. He nodded politely and went back to his station. Major pulled the car away from the porte-cochère and drew it up along the curb, out of the way.

Off to the side, a floor sign read: "Welcome Gutierrez party. Happy 21st Lisa." A doorman held open a tall wood door for Ellie, and she thanked him as she stepped across the threshold into a rotunda whose ceiling was frescoed with a leaping bull.

The decor was impressive, if not unexpected, the floor set in diamond-cut marble and laid in alternating colors of white and sapphire blue. Ornate chandeliers hung from a coffered ceiling, and life-size marble statues of ancient gods and goddesses lined the hallway which ended at a carpeted lounge filled with guests. It was closing in on midnight, but the heavy beat of modern dance music and sounds of alcohol-assisted laughter reverberated loudly through the building.

The hall split off into two directions. The entrance to a large ballroom was on the left, where guests were still mingling around tables already cleared of their dishes. Ellie glanced to her right and caught a glimpse of Cruz just as he disappeared behind a door at the far end. Halfway down the hall, a purple rope was draped across several chromed stanchions, where a sign read: "Private Party Only."

The skin on the back of Ellie's neck began to tingle, and a cold sensation tracked down both her arms, terminated in her fingertips. It was a physiological reaction, prompted by a trusted intuition she had honed over a decade with the CIA.

It wasn't simply that Cruz was attending a private party. It was also the guard, dressed in a suit, standing in front of the door. To an ordinary person, he would appear to be a well-dressed bouncer, redirecting people away from the private party and back to Lisa's birthday celebration. But Ellie noted something more. It was slight, barely noticeable; but it was there. The man was wearing a shoulder harness beneath his suit jacket. It was the way his left arm hung at his side, accommodating the weapon tucked beneath it. Under normal circumstances, Ellie could have conceived of the need for armed security if perhaps there were a foreign dignitary or a wealthy CEO behind that door. But it seemed highly unlikely, considering an ex-con, tied to human trafficking, had been allowed to just walk right in.

Ellie pulled her gaze away from the guard and turned left, entering the ballroom. The remaining guests were gathered in small groups, chatting away, and a middle-aged man smiled at her, his eyes strolling over her body and lingering longer than would be deemed appropriate. But she simply smiled back and made her way to an open door at the back of the room. It led to a staff corridor where bright fluorescent lighting poured out of a room at the other end.

She entered the kitchen and found it empty. A commercial dishwasher was venting steam, and clean dishes were stacked on a long counter. The kitchen staff had already gone home, leaving the bartender and servers at the lounge to close out the evening. At the other end of the room, a man was pushing a yellow mop bucket, but Ellie moved around a row of stainless steel cabinets before he could notice her.

She found the cooking knives in the third drawer and selected one. It was an eight-inch boning knife that tapered near the tip. She rummaged through several more drawers until she found a roll of aluminum foil. She tore off a strip, returned the foil to the drawer, and worked what she had around the base of the knife, crimping it and squeezing it tightly. Then she reached back over her shoulder, pulled the collar of her dress away from the back of her neck, and brought the knife around. She slid the blade into the fabric, piercing it until the newly formed hilt of the knife stopped the blade's descent and only the handle came to rest outside of her dress, which now acted the part of an impromptu sheath. The cold, bare metal now rested in the narrow space between her shoulder blades. It felt comfortable there, like an old friend she hadn't missed until this very moment.

Moving quickly and careful of her movements, Ellie started plucking bobby pins from her hair, and thick blonde locks cascaded to her chest and past her shoulders. She spread her fingers and fluffed her hair until it lay evenly around her.

She tossed the bobby pins in the trash receptacle on her way out of the kitchen and then retraced her steps through the ballroom before coming back out to the front and stopping near the lounge.

The guard was still at the other end of the hall, looking bored but alert. Ellie slipped around the rope barrier, and he straightened as she approached. He took a step forward and held up a hand. "I'm sorry, ma'am. This area is closed off. I believe your party is in the main ballroom and over at the lounge." He extended a hand, gesturing behind her.

She lifted her chin and her eyebrows and began with a contrived persona. "First of all, it's not *ma'am*. It's *miss*. And second, I saw Victor go in there, and I want to talk with him."

He shook his head. "I'm sorry. That won't be possible. Not tonight."

"No," she snapped. "It will be tonight. It will be right now. You tell Victor that I have something to say to him and that I'm not leaving until I say it." Ellie shifted her weight to her back leg and tapped her front foot against the marble. She put her hands on her hips. "Tell him he'd better come out of his little hiding place and talk with me." She stared coldly into his eyes. "Tell him *that*."

The guard was wearing an earpiece. He touched it and turned away as he whispered. He turned back to Ellie. "What's your name?"

"Sally. Sally McEntire. And if he's not out here in one minute, I'm going to start making noise."

He turned again, whispered again. "You'll need to wait a minute."

"Fine," she said, and then continued tapping her foot while she waited. The guard, unamused, continued to stare past her down the hall.

The door finally opened, and as Cruz stepped into the hallway, Ellie used the moment to glance past him into a room with wood-paneled walls and built-in bookcases filled with books and picture frames. A red-felted card table sat in the center of the room. Just before the door shut behind him, she got a glimpse of an old wooden desk on the far side of the room, directly in front of her, with a bank of flat-screen security monitors perched on top. Another security guard was standing off to the left.

Cruz looked first at the guard but received only a shrug. Cruz looked at Ellie, sizing her up and pausing briefly at the flesh of her leg, where it peeked out from the folds of her skirt. When he spoke, he sounded bored, albeit a little curious. "What?"

"Victor Cruz." Ellie's tone was vigorous, laced with irritation. "Here I am enjoying myself at Lisa's birthday party, and I see you—*you*, of all people, walking right past me! I can't think of a better way to ruin a perfectly good night."

"Do I know you?"

"No, you don't know me. But I know *you*. What are you doing in a place like this? You should still be in jail, shouldn't you?"

He blinked, caught off guard by the suggestion before twin embers started to grow hot in his eyes. "You don't know anything about me. What do you want?"

"What do I want? I'll tell you what I want. I want you to go back in time and un-break Mario's back. I want you to undo what you did." Cruz stalled at the unexpected mention of Mario's name, and Ellie kept up the charade. "I'm his sister-in-law, and I'll tell you what, Victor Cruz, I'll never forgive you. Never. Wish to God I could see *you* in a wheelchair for the rest of your life." She took a defiant step toward him, and she could see that everything inside him intended to hit her. The guard stuck a hand between them and pressed Ellie backward.

"Get out of here," Cruz said between gritted teeth.

His nostrils flared, and his fingers curled into fists at his sides. "Get the hell out of here."

"Or what? Are you going to beat me right here in front of all these people like you did to Mario?" She stepped up again, pushing hard into the guard's meaty hand.

Cruz's angry breath was whistling through his nose now, and Ellie could see that she had pressed all the right buttons. "You've had too much to drink," he said. "You need to go. Now." Cruz nodded at the guard, who kept a firm hand on Ellie. Cruz turned and scanned a key card on the side of the door.

As soon as Cruz reopened the door, the pressure in Ellie's ears changed and her body flooded with adrenaline. The bookcase next to the desk swung out, and a teenage girl wearing a terrified expression stepped into the room.

Ellie's breath caught, as if on a nail. The nail she would hammer into Victor Cruz's coffin.

Juanita's frantic eyes locked onto Ellie's just as the door to the room slammed in her face.

CHAPTER FORTY

Jet drummed his fingers across his desk. It was late, and he knew he should probably go home. But he also felt like he had just opened up a new puzzle and dumped all the pieces on his desk. They were all there; he just needed to put them together, to assemble them into a cohesive picture.

Ellie emailed back a half hour ago, informing him that she had gone ahead and checked out the locations he'd sent her. They were a bust. He was almost surprised at her quick reply, at her diligence to hunt down another lead this late at night. But it was Ellie, and he knew she wanted all this to end as much as he did.

They needed more details on Victor Cruz. If he was that close, that connected to Felipe, then certainly he was tied into another part of the organization. But Cruz was a ghost. Other than a driver's license with a now defunct address, there was no paper trail of any kind for him after he got out of prison.

Jet stood up and went over to the Keurig. He started another cup of coffee. As it dripped into his mug, an idea came to him. He returned to his desk and navigated to the website for Florida's Department of Corrections. At the bottom of the home page, he clicked on "FDC Database," and another browser opened up, taking him to a secure portal that prompted him to enter his state-issued credentials. After logging in, he typed Victor Cruz's name into the search field. It returned information on Cruz's prison term, transfer and location records, and additional information such as incident reports, notes from the parole board, a list of cellmates, and records from his medical checkups that took place during his incarceration. Jet went down the list, not sure what he was looking for.

Cruz had spent the majority of his sentence in the maximum security section of Walton Correctional in DeFuniak Springs. Jet's brows furrowed as he digested the information on the screen. He leaned forward in an unconscious attempt to validate what he was seeing. During his incarceration, Cruz had two cellmates. The last one was a Sam Webster, who was still in when Cruz was released. But the first cellmate... Jet pinched the base of his nose and tried to think through a sudden wave of cognitive dissonance—one of those truly rare moments when you don't believe your eyes and find it impossible to digest the information in front of you.

Cruz's first cellmate had been none other than Alex Serrano, the founder of Hope House.

Jet stared blankly at Alex's name. He clicked on Alex's profile, and a picture loaded on the screen. His hair was cut short, as per prison regulation, a far cry from the ponytail he sported now.

Jet sat back in his chair and rubbed at his eyes with the heels of his hands. He knew well enough that alliances were often formed in prison; an inmate with a dark imagination and starved opportunity ended up paired with one possessing the means to help him carry his out.

When Jet first met Alex here in this very office, Alex had presented himself as a reformed killer, someone whose twenty years in prison had given him ample time to reflect on how he could make amends for the wrong he had done. But now, Jet was beginning to think he, and many others, had been fed a false narrative.

He navigated to Google and performed a web search for Alex Serrano, adding the words "Hope House" to refine his results. The search returned pages of articles. He clicked on the first link. It was from last year. The leading picture showed a proud Alex in front of the shelter, shoulder to shoulder with Carlos Hernandez and several other donors.

Jet's mind felt clouded, and he couldn't understand it. If Alex was working with Cruz, if they were both complicit in Juanita's disappearance, then why hire him to find her?

He wouldn't have to wait long for an answer. At that moment, his front door swung open, and Alex Serrano stepped inside.

He was holding a gun, and it was pointed at Jet.

CHAPTER FORTY-ONE

THE DOOR SLAMMED SHUT, leaving Ellie and the guard alone at this end of the hallway. He had seen Juanita too, and just as he started to reach for his gun, Ellie slipped behind him and grabbed his wrist while throwing her free hand behind her back and slipping her fingers through her hair. They wrapped around the hilt of the knife just as he threw her hand off of his.

He froze as the cool edge of the blade pressed hard into his flesh. She applied even more pressure, and a thick drop of blood coursed down his neck, staining the rim of his white collar.

Ellie pressed her lips close to his ear. "One wrong move and I carve your throat." He didn't move, didn't flinch. Her next words came out calm, fully absent of emotion. "Your key card. Where is it?" He winced as she applied more pressure to the blade.

"Right… jacket pocket."

"When you finally get out of prison," she whispered, "I hope you remember this moment." With that, she removed the blade from his throat and shoved off of him. Before he could react, she swiveled and entered a backward spin, bringing her leg out straight and into a wide arc. The back of her heel connected hard with his temple. As she brought her leg back down and found her footing on three inch high heels, she watched as two hundred and fifty pounds of muscle crumpled to the floor. She squatted down and quickly rifled through his jacket, coming out with the key card before flipping up his blazer and slipping his weapon from the holster: a .38 Special.

She didn't have time to check his pockets for a phone, but she needed to call the police. So with expert speed, she thumbed the cylinder release and checked the load—five rounds of +P ammo—before closing the cylinder. Then she set a knee on the floor, lowered her head, extended the pistol toward the ceiling, and fired off two shots.

Down the hall, lively chatter and boisterous laughter suddenly morphed into a chaos of panic-stricken, terrified screams. Guests fell to the floor while others scurried down the front hallway, stealing quick glances in Ellie's direction as they made a frenzied escape.

Ellie paid them no attention. She stepped to the side as she swiped the key card against the reader. It beeped. She braced herself and flung open the door.

CHAPTER FORTY-TWO

ALEX'S STEELED expression was as confident as it was apathetic. His hand, clasping a semi-automatic pistol, did not tremble; there was no uncertainty in his eyes, no shake in his voice. He told Jet to lean forward and place his palms on the desk, and then, keeping the gun trained on the PI, he took several steps forward. His smile was twisted, his eyes bright and playful, as if he were enjoying the moment. Jet realized that he was seeing the former convict without his mask. "You don't look surprised to see me, Jet."

"You shared a cell with Victor Cruz." Jet's tone resembled more of a question. He was still processing the connection.

"Yes. And he was a slob. A few months in a cell with that man was enough for a lifetime. But he is a good manager. Quite skilled at operations." He clicked his tongue a few times. "How did you find Victor, anyway?"

"I don't think that matters at this point. Do you?"

"No. No, I don't guess it does. That is, unless you

told someone else. Then that would be a problem. Did you tell anyone else, Jet?"

"No," he lied. "I work alone. And I found Victor through watching that old fire station in Fort Myers." Jet was silently cursing himself for failing to lock his office door. His concealed carry rested against his right ankle, but with the position Alex had him in, there was no way he could reach it in time. "I don't understand why you hired me. Why bring in someone to investigate an enterprise you're a part of?"

"Yes," Alex smirked. "I can see the conflict from your point of view. It's simple, really. Carlos Hernández is one of Hope House's most gracious donors. When he caught wind that Juanita disappeared and the detective hit a dead end, he wrote me a check and told me to hire a private investigator. I thought with you being a new PI and three hours from Miami there was no chance that you would take my request seriously. So when you showed up at Hope House, I must say I was a bit disappointed. But," he smiled again, "my mistake." Alex nodded toward Jet. "You have a weapon on you, correct?"

There was no sense in lying about it. "Yes."

"Where?"

"My ankle. Right one."

"Please stand up and turn around. Then move away from the desk and get down on your left knee. Place your right hand behind your back."

Jet did as he was told.

"Now, use only your thumb and forefinger to pull up your pant leg and remove the gun from the holster. Toss it toward the desk." Jet complied, careful to keep his movements slow and easy. When the gun slid beneath his desk chair, Alex ordered him to return to his feet. "Empty your pockets and turn them out." Thirty seconds later, Jet's wallet, a pen, and several coins were lying on the floor.

"Now stand up and let's go outside." Jet came to his feet and slowly turned. "You're lucky," Alex said. "I was on my way to your house when I saw the light on in your office and your car out front. So let me just say that if you try anything foolish, I will continue my route to your house when I'm done with you."

Jet glared at him. Linda, his wife, was home and two of their small grandchildren were staying overnight. "Don't you dare threaten my family," he snapped.

Alex motioned toward the door with the gun. "Outside." Jet went out the door and made his way down the steps as Alex flicked off the office light and followed behind him. A white Ford Fusion was parked next to his Maxima. Alex opened the front passenger door and motioned with his gun. "Get in," he said. "You're driving."

Jet ducked his head and slid onto the seat before maneuvering his legs around the console and sitting into the driver's seat. "Where are we going?"

"Head into Cape Coral. Just stay on Pine Island Road. I'll let you know where to go after that." Alex kept his gun trained on Jet and handed him the keys. Jet started the car and pulled into the road, his mind abuzz with possible scenarios that might get him out of this alive. Alex had threatened his family, and he had no doubt that Alex was the kind of man to make good on such a promise. If Jet's time was up tonight, if this was how it all ended, he was going to make sure this deceptive monster's life ended too.

They drove in tense silence for several minutes, passing through the inky darkness covering Little Pine Island before crawling past a tucked-in Matlacha and coming over the bridge into Cape Coral. Jet stopped at the red light at Burnt Store Road, his eyes searching for a police cruiser. The light turned green, and he continued to head east, driving for ten minutes before speaking. "Why?" he asked.

"Why?" Alex repeated, as if the answer were already painted in the sky. "Jet, the prison system…" He huffed. "It's broken. They stash you away for a couple decades and expect you to come out reformed. But I did learn something while I was in there. Everyone, and I mean everyone, Jet, loves a good redemption story. The world is thirsty for them, for tangible examples that people can and do change. I'm the poster child—" Alex interrupted himself with a hearty chuckle. "Forgive the pun," he said. He cleared his throat and continued. "I am the poster child for reform. A man spends twenty years locked up for killing an old lady. Then while he's tucked away from society, he gets his college degree before getting out and starting a shelter in the very neighborhood he used to haunt. That man becomes the example of what it looks like to turn your life around. Everyone likes to point at a story like that to prove that prison makes men better." Alex grimaced and shook his head. "Well, you know, it doesn't work. Do you want to know how many times I got raped before I went to prison?"

"Alex, I—"

"None. Zero."

"You want to know how many men raped me in my first year on the inside?"

"I—"

"Eight."

"Want to know how many guards let them? I'll tell you. *All* of them. They all just stood to the side smirking, looking the other way while it all happened. So by the time Victor Cruz is thrown into my cell and tells me about a little deal he made with the devil, I asked him where I should sign."

"Your suffering in prison doesn't give you the right to turn around and harm others," Jet replied angrily. "You're still responsible for how you choose to respond."

"You're right. And I chose a good path. For me." He used his chin to point to the sign marking I-75 South. "Get on the highway," he said.

"Where are we going?"

"You'll see. I like giving surprises."

Jet turned onto the highway and accelerated to the speed limit. "Where is she?" he finally asked.

"Juanita? Ah. She's perfectly safe. Not perfectly happy. But perfectly safe." He chuckled to himself again, making Jet's chest tighten. And then, empowered by a deep-abiding hubris that has caused the fall of many, Alex made a mistake. "You know, Jet. When all this dies down, and your funeral is well behind everyone, I think I might come and get your granddaughter. She was the blonde in that picture on your desk. Am I right? What is she, about sixteen? Seventeen?"

The muscle along Jet's jawline flared up. He tightened his grip on the steering wheel, and his knuckles lost their color. A vein rose up and pulsed down his forearm like an angry garden snake. His reply needed no words. He slammed his foot on the accelerator. Within seconds the speedometer had moved from sixty to ninety-five.

"Stop!" Alex snapped. "Slow down."

Jet left his foot in place, where it lay against the pedal like a cinder block. He switched lanes to avoid slamming into the back of a late model Camry. Alex jammed the barrel of the gun into the older man's cheek and growled through his teeth. "Slow down. Now."

"I don't think so."

Alex hesitated. He couldn't shoot Jet. Not at this speed. His weapon was now as effective as poking Jet in the face with a straw. Behind them, blue and red lights pulsed, quickly fading behind them until the police cruiser accelerated enough to match their speed. Alex cursed in Spanish. "You're making me very angry, Jet."

Jet smiled. "You think I care about that, Alex?" The speedometer now read 125, and Jet lifted his foot slightly, maintaining the speed and cautiously avoiding the occasional vehicle still on the road at this late hour.

Jet could only see one way out of this. If he pulled to the shoulder, there was no doubt that Alex would shoot the officer. He knew that because of their current speed, the cruiser behind them would have already called for backup. Alex wasn't about to let himself get arrested, and Jet wasn't going to stand for a shootout. He wasn't going to put any blue in danger tonight.

There was only one way to ensure that Alex's deceptions ended tonight. One way to ensure that Fort Myers's finest got back home to their families at the end of the shift.

Alex was done selling precious souls for profit. And

he wouldn't be going back to Jet's office to cover his tracks. As the former head of the local DEA Special Response Team, Jet had trained his people how to respond in the event they were involved in a vehicle rollover. The time had come to recall his own instruction.

CHAPTER FORTY-THREE

ELLIE REMAINED in the hallway as the office door swung open, anticipating a flurry of bullets. She was not disappointed. Three rounds peppered the door, ricocheted off the door frame, and bounced off the floor, sending chips of marble speeding through the air. A fresh wave of screams issued from the other end of the hall as hysterical guests continued to vie for a hasty exit.

Moving quickly, Ellie checked the gun's load. She had three rounds left. And two men in the room. By the scattered placement of the shots, she immediately deemed the shooter inexperienced and nervous. But even more helpful, they gave away the guard's point of origin: the far right section of the room. She heard a shuffle and a cry of pain from inside the room, and she knew Juanita was struggling with Cruz.

Ellie was in a nearly impossible situation. She had to clear that room, but there was only one of her. She had no partner, no help. The rule book and common sense mandated two people to clear an active shooter from a room. Ellie subconsciously recalled the maxim she had learned years ago: *Two is one, one is none.* There were too many unknowns, too many dangerous angles for one person to clear safely, their individual degree of coverage too limited. The door was the fatal funnel—the singular point of focus for the shooter inside, and where he would concentrate all his attention and firepower.

Ellie could hear Cruz yelling angrily at Juanita but was unable to make out his words over the commotion coming from the remaining guests still fleeing behind her. With the gun wrapped in her practiced fingers, Ellie took several steps back, a move that offered her a better view of the room while keeping her behind the relative safety of the wall. Finding her axis, she mentally sliced the room into sections, stepping to the side as she cleared each one.

The door was in the center of the office wall. To the left, with the door blocking her view, were Juanita, Cruz, and the desk with the monitors. To the right, with the wall blocking that view, were the card table, two couches, and, based on the angle of the shots, the guard as well.

Ellie's focus was singular now, and she blocked out the noise behind her and Cruz's struggle with Juanita before her. She breathed in slowly, calmly, and took a step to her left.

She could see half the card table now, and behind it, a section of a couch against the wall. She took another slow and cautious step. Then she saw it. The muzzle of the guard's gun—the furthest thing from him as he held the weapon out in front of his body. The barrel was short: another revolver. Which meant he had two rounds left, to her three.

With all the agility of a former CIA special operations agent, she leaned out and pressed off a shot before moving back into cover.

She missed, the bullet flying just past his shoulder, and it was immediately answered by two more. They went wide. Ellie was already out of his angle, and the wall in front of her shielded her from view like a faithful guardian. She heard the click of the empty revolver as the guard tried to fire again. He hadn't bothered to keep track of his shot count.

She seized the moment and cautiously stepped into the doorway. The guard looked up from his empty gun, stunned that it was out of ammunition. Ellie stole a fractional glance to her left and saw Cruz. He had no weapon, and his attention was on Juanita. She was on the floor beneath him, scratching and kicking as he struggled to subdue her. Juanita's head hit the corner of the desk, and she cried out as she continued to fight for her life.

The guard was wide-eyed and fearful but suddenly smiled as though a dim bulb had turned on behind his eyes. He reached into his pocket and produced a tactical switchblade. Flipping out the blade, he made to throw it.

Ellie shouted at him to stop, ordering him to put the knife down. He didn't listen, drawing back instead and preparing to hurl it toward her.

Her final two rounds hit their mark, both in the chest, the first piercing his lung, the second tearing through his heart. He fell backward and hit the ground, his blood staining the ornate carpet. Then he lay still.

Out of bullets herself, Ellie dropped her gun and turned her full attention on Cruz. He was on his feet, still struggling to bring Juanita under his control. Juanita's fingers had found a picture frame on the bookshelf next to her, and she drew it back and hurled it into his face. He howled in pain as a sharp corner caught him directly in his dead eye. Cruz slapped her across the face with the back of his thick hand, and her head hit the floor where it remained as she let out a dazed whimper. Cruz leaned forward and threw open a desk drawer, slid his hand in, and drew out a 9mm pistol, Ellie's final cue to bring the chaos to an end.

With smooth, determined strides, she crossed the floor, and pinching at the skirts of her dress, she raised them a few inches. Cruz settled the gun into his grip and drew it up. He faced Ellie as he raised it toward her, blood now seeping down his cheek, oozing freely from the soulless eye Juanita had pierced. Ellie pivoted completely away from him, bringing her knee up high before leaning over and sending her foot plowing backward in a perfect back kick. The long, narrow heel of her shoe pierced upward through his shirt and his skin, striking high between his ribs and entering his heart. Cruz grunted as the force of the kick launched him backward off his feet, and he crashed into the bookcase, falling to the floor as Ellie snatched her leg back; the heel of her shoe now covered in a thick red sleeve of his blood.

Ellie found her balance, and as Cruz dropped the gun and gathered his hands around his chest, she grabbed his head and sent her knee into his nose. His body flopped to the side, hit the floor, and did not move. Blood bloomed wide against his shirt, and his mouth yawed back and forth like a dying fish as his heart began to shut down.

Ellie snatched up the gun and stepped over him. She moved quickly toward Juanita and kneeled before her.

The girl was on her elbows now, wincing from the pain incurred at the hands of the man now lying dead at her feet. Ellie surveyed the room and the doorway. She saw no more immediate threats. "Come here," she said, and then carefully helped Juanita to her feet. They stepped around Cruz's limp body, and Ellie assisted her to the couch, where they sat, both of them catching their breath.

Seconds later, Major appeared in the doorway, his eyes full of worry and his body tense. "Ellie." He came to her and squatted down. He looked at Juanita and his expression softened, but the concern was still there. He looked Ellie over.

"Are you okay?"

"Yes."

"Is this Juanita?"

Ellie nodded, and the girl's face lifted, surprised to hear her name. Major turned to her. "You're okay." He sounded like a worry-sick father consoling his daughter. "We're getting you out of here." He looked around and nodded at the dead guard's body. "Are there others?" he asked.

Juanita stared wide-eyed at the floor. Ellie spoke softly. "Juanita, honey. Are there others?"

She nodded quickly.

"How many?"

Her voice was no stronger than a whisper. "Eight." She shook her head. "No... seven. There are seven."

"Are there guards? Do they have guns?"

"No. No, it's just...the men." The bookcase door was open several inches, and she lifted a hand and pointed toward it. "Down there."

Ellie locked eyes with Major. His jaw was set hard,

his pupils wide, and if she had ever witnessed such rage in his eyes, she couldn't remember. And she loved him for that. He extended an open hand to Ellie. She placed the gun in it. And without a word, he walked to the bookcase door, threw it open, and disappeared behind it.

CHAPTER FORTY-FOUR

THE POLICE CRUISER was only a few car lengths behind now, its horn blaring intermittently over the rumbler siren like an angry mother-in-law.

"So what do you want me to do?" Jet asked.

Alex cursed again. "Stop the car. Just stop the car. I'll deal with this." He scowled. "You really shouldn't have done that."

Red and blue lights pulsed across the Fusion's interior, forcing Jet to squint against the visual assault. He removed his foot from the accelerator, and the vehicle started to slow as it shot down the highway on pure momentum.

He avoided the urge to tighten his seatbelt. If his plan worked properly, the seat belt retractor would automatically ratchet the belt in a couple more notches.

Alex's forehead was glistening nervous sweat, and his eyes were wide and searching as he silently worked to formulate a new plan on the fly.

"Alex," Jet said quietly. They were at 90 mph now.

"What!?"

"You're going to pay for what you've done."

80 mph.

"Shut up, Jet!"

"No. I won't shut up, *Alex*. You prey on the weak. You kidnapped an innocent girl, and you asked the wrong man to find her."

60 mph.

"Shut. Up!"

"Go ahead. Shoot me. You don't intimidate me." He turned and looked Alex dead in the eye. "Tonight, you lose."

Alex didn't get a chance to respond. Jet switched lanes and slammed the sole of his shoe into the brake pedal, sending brushstrokes of hot Firestone rubber streaking onto the pavement. The sudden loss of forward progress was enough for Alex's arm to drift toward the windshield, bringing the gun clear of Jet's body.

Jet moved with a swift and controlled finesse. He pressed his left knee hard into the steering wheel and shoved Alex's weapon further toward the windshield. Then he shot his fingers down and slammed them into Alex's seat belt release. The younger man cried out in a sudden burst of anger and panic as he drifted toward the dash.

Jet ignored him and, moving with lightning speed, crossed his hands over his own chest and grabbed his shoulders. He tucked his chin into his forearms as he flung his knee toward the center console, taking the steering wheel with it.

The car was still going forty when the front tires

caught sideways on the pavement and two tons of American steel levitated off the ground and entered a ruthless spin across the grassy median.

CHAPTER FORTY-FIVE

The lights from nearly two dozen emergency vehicles strobed across the Palm Rivers Country Club, and seven men in custom suits were sitting in the back seats of as many police cruisers. A crime scene unit was inside, collecting evidence in the girl's prison while the medical examiner snapped pictures of Miguel Zedillo's body.

Two short minutes after Major had disappeared behind the bookcase, the first frightened girl had stepped timidly into the room. She had been wrapped in a blanket, and both Juanita and Ellie stood to receive her. The remaining girls followed behind in brief intervals.

Cami had been the last to come through. She was followed by Major, who was still holding the gun and clutching a handful of thick plastic key cards. The knuckles on both his hands were bloody and already beginning to swell.

He had helped Ellie shepherd the girls from the office just as they heard the sirens from the first responders arriving out front. Major set the gun on the floor and took up the rear of the procession.

Ellie had spent the last ten minutes standing in the parking lot fielding questions from a detective. When his attention was briefly diverted by an inquiring officer, Ellie asked for a couple of minutes and stepped away. She walked over to where an ambulance was parked near the fountain. Its back doors were open, and Juanita was sitting on the bumper. A blanket was draped around her, and she huddled beneath it as though it was her one security in the world.

Ellie smiled as she approached her.

"What will happen now?" Juanita asked.

"They're going to take you to the hospital." Ellie noted the concern in the girl's eyes. "You'll have a police escort. You'll be safe." She leaned in and drew Juanita's gaze to hers. "You're safe now. It's over."

Juanita nodded weakly like she was trying to believe it.

An EMT materialized from the side of the ambulance. "It's time to go," she said.

Juanita turned back to Ellie. "Can you come with me?" Her eyes were almost pleading. "Please."

Ellie looked back toward the detective. He was waving her over. "I can't," she said. "The police have a lot of questions for me. I have to go with them for a few hours. But I'll come to you as soon as they let me leave."

"Why did you help me?"

Ellie placed a hand on her shoulder. "We've been looking for you."

Juanita's head lifted. "You were? For me?"

"Yes, sweetheart. For you."

"Why?"

Ellie moved her hand to the girl's cheek. "Because you're worth it. And no one should have to go through what you did. No one." A hot tear slid into Ellie's hand, and she smeared away the wet track with her thumb. "It's over now. You'll get to see your brother soon."

Juanita smiled. Her first real smile of the evening. "Yes," she said triumphantly. "I will."

CHAPTER FORTY-SIX

The Fusion came to rest upside down, straddling the grass and the shoulder of the northbound lane where it lay like a crumpled soda can.

The windshield was splintered with thousands of milky cracks. The tempered glass of the rear and side windows had blown out, having shattered into thousands of small pebbles and strewn across the road, the median, and the inside of the car.

Jet heard a voice. It sounded far away, like he was underwater. He couldn't make it out.

Pain ripped through every inch of his body, too much to decipher where exactly the damage was. He slowly opened his eyes, and as he waited for his blurred vision to clear, he realized he was hanging upside down.

He heard the voice again. Clearer this time, like he was out of the water but now wearing earplugs.

"Jet!"

He slowly licked his lips and tried to speak. But it only came out as a muted whisper.

"Jet!"

It took him several seconds to turn toward his door. He looked down. A face near the ground looking up at him. He knew that face. But from where?

"Can you hear me?" Yes. He could. And it was clear now.

He tried putting more into his voice. "Yes." The face—it was an officer with the Ft. Myers PD. Jet couldn't recall his name, but they had trained together at the gun range a couple of times.

"Okay. Good. We need to get you down from there but I have to wait for an EMT to get you a neck brace. Just hang tight."

While sirens grew louder in the distance, Jet cautiously turned his head in the other direction. The cruiser's floodlight lit up the inside of the car, and his vision started to clear. His eyes came to rest on Alex.

He was sprawled across his back against the inside canopy. He was unrecognizable. Blood covered his face, slicked across it like an overdone Halloween mask, and one of his arms was broken, twisted and turned back over his head. The entire right side of his chest was a wide delta of oozing blood. He wasn't breathing.

As the Fusion had completed its second roll, it kicked into the air and descended onto a mile marker. The metal entered through Alex's window and sliced into him, just missing Jet's head as it came out the other side. As it rotated upright again, the metal withdrew and left his impaled body to bounce around the car like a broken lottery ball.

Jet turned his eyes away. He couldn't feel his own face. There was too much pressure in it from hanging upside down. But he was fairly certain that, in spite of the gruesome pain pulsing through him, he was smiling.

CHAPTER FORTY-SEVEN

One Week Later

The Salty Mangrove was humming with laughter and conversation, and live music completed the tropical atmosphere. Red Fish Blue Fish, a local island band, was covering Bob Seger and Jackson Browne from a makeshift stage at the edge of the boardwalk. It was dark, and a gentle breeze floated off the water while Edison lights intermixed with Christmas lights to provide the kind of tropical ambiance that you could only find in Southwest Florida.

Major was busy serving a crowded bar, and Ellie was standing next to Tyler and enjoying much-needed laughter with Nick and Tiffany.

Behind Tyler, Ellie saw Jet hobble up the ramp from the parking lot. He went to the front of the bar, and when Major saw him, they exchanged handshakes. Ellie excused herself and walked over to him. Major was handing over a Red Stripe, and she heard him tell Jet that his money wasn't any good here.

"Hey," Ellie said.

Jet turned to her, and like she had every time she'd seen him in the last week, she wanted to wince. His left arm was resting in a sling, and deep abrasions were still healing on his cheek, forehead, and elbows. His neck was wrapped in a foam neck brace. "How do I look?" he asked.

"Major has a no lying policy around the bar, so…" She smiled apprehensively.

"Yeah. I scare my wife a little bit too. You have a minute?"

They stepped away from the bar and the music and sat at one of the picnic tables on the boardwalk. "Well," he began, "as bad cops go, they've arrested three so far. Gomez and one other from the Ft. Myers PD. And one in Miami. It seems that Zedillo had Cruz keep backups of all the video surveillance. So far they have over sixty different men. And get this, all of them are international businessmen. None of them are U.S. citizens."

Ellie sighed deeply and looked off toward the docks. The day after Ellie followed Cruz and found the girls, the FBI decided they had enough to move on Blake Duprey. They went to his house and took him away in front of a confused wife and crying little daughter.

It seemed that everything was over now. It was all wrapped up in a pretty little bow. They had not only found Juanita, but seven other missing girls too. Ellie knew that should feel like a win. And it did. The girls were safe now; they were no longer slaves, no longer someone's else property. But the darker lining: Ellie knew those girls would never be the same. They would wrestle with the effects of their trauma for the rest of their lives; they were all facing a very long road ahead.

She could only hope that with the right care from the right people the girls would one day overcome it.

"Carlos came by yesterday," Ellie said. "He's going to make sure all the girls get sent through a recovery program with Florida Abolitionist. When they're done with that, he's going to pay for ongoing counseling for them. If they want to go to college, he's going to fund it and pay for all their living expenses."

"He's a good man," Jet said. "Did he tell you about Hope House?"

"No. What about it?"

"Carlos is sending someone from one of his companies to run it." Jet winced a little as he brought out his phone. "I just got this from the caseworker. She was kind enough to send it along." He turned his phone toward her. The screen displayed a picture of a smiling Juanita clutching a happy little boy.

"That's Junior?" Ellie asked.

"It is. She turns eighteen next week, and she'll get custody of him."

"Let's go visit her together when you don't look like you just came out of a blender."

"Hey, now."

Her eyes narrowed, and she studied him. "Jet, you know I'm good at reading people."

"Sure."

"So something else is on your mind."

He chuckled. "Okay. I'll get to it. You've got a gift, Ellie. You have a knack for sniffing out the bad guys. But more than that. Your personal sense of justice is, I think, what makes you exceptional."

She said nothing, waited for the substance.

"I know you're not fully sold on becoming a private

investigator. That said, since I used to work with you at the DEA, the Department of Homeland Security reached out to me and asked what I thought of you."

She arched an eyebrow but said nothing.

"They're forming an interagency task force. Several actually. They will be focused on pushing back crime in key areas of the country: Chicago, L.A., Houston, and most of South Florida, given our coastline. I'm staying in my role as a PI, but they've also asked me to consider coming aboard in a supportive role as needed. They're interested in you in the same capacity. I said I'd have a chat with you about it."

Ellie sighed. There was a part of her that enjoyed the freedom of just helping Major around the bar and being able to go fishing and shooting as her whims dictated. But there was also the satisfaction of seeing a picture of a young lady hugging her little brother and realizing that you had something to do with that. "What do you mean by interagency?" she asked.

"Homeland, of course. ICE, some Coast Guard, and perhaps the FBI and DEA. It will depend on the threat and the concerns of the moment. They're trying to shore up some gaps in their counter-terrorism policies and practices."

"That's a lot to think about," she said. She stood up. "Are you sticking around?"

"For a little while. Want to hear the band."

"Don't leave without letting me know," she said.

Gloria was planted back on her bar stool, she and Fu having returned from their cruise two days before, and Ellie listened as Gloria recounted stories of a trip no one thought they would ever take.

"We were walking through the rain forest in Belize

to get to where we started the cave tubing. And on the way, I look off to my right and see this huge, and I mean *huge*, snake working its way up a rubber tree. The guide said it was some kind of python but that unless they're basically starving they stay away from people. And he said that a full-size python can actually eat a small mammal? A small human even, if they're hungry enough." Gloria's face contorted into a look of disgust. "A snake eating a person. Can you imagine that?"

Major's eyes narrowed. "Yes," he said slowly. "I think I've heard a story like that."

"You have any pictures of the trip?" Tyler asked.

"Oh, pictures. Of course! Come over here." Gloria retrieved her phone from the top of her swimsuit, where it lay tucked in against a heavy breast.

Ellie heard a sound behind her and turned to see Fu smiling up at them, his head bobbing a hello on his thick neck. Next to her, Tyler said, "What the…"

Ellie reached out and squeezed Tyler's forearm.

Fu, still smiling, head still bobbing, was wearing a red, sun-faded ball cap. Stitched in gray lettering was the word "Hornady," Tyler's favorite ammunition company.

"Hey…uh, Fu?" Tyler said. "Where'd you find my hat?"

"Oh," Gloria answered. "It was on the bar the night before we went on the cruise. Fu thought you didn't want it."

"Thought I didn't want it?" Tyler repeated, like maybe Gloria had just said she thought he didn't like brisket. Or Ellie.

Fu shrugged and removed the hat, handed it to Tyler.

"Thanks," Tyler said. He turned his hat over in his hands the way a treasure seeker might an ingot of gold.

"Pictures," Gloria said. "Here we are." Ellie and Tyler stepped in behind her. "This one is right after we tried snorkeling. I didn't like it, but Fu nearly blistered his back. He was out there for hours."

In the picture, holding a frozen drink in his hand and smiling broadly at the camera, was Fu, wearing Tyler's hat. Tyler shot a look toward Ellie and raised his brows to her when he saw that she was grinning

"And, oh, you guys," Gloria was saying. "This was when we rented a couple ATVs in Belize. I nearly fell off half a dozen times." She tilted the camera to show a clearly drunk Fu standing on an ATV, his tongue out, Tyler's hat turned backward on his head.

"Good lord," Tyler sighed, and looked down at his hat like he was apologizing to it.

Gloria took a sip of her drink, and Tyler asked if he could see the phone. "Oh sure." She handed it over, and Tyler started thumbing the glass. As he quickly reviewed the photos, he shook his head.

"Fu, you wore my hat the entire time?"

"Yes. Yes."

"Sunbathing...swimming...cave tubing," Tyler muttered to Ellie. "Unbelievable."

Fu leaned over and said something in Chinese to his wife.

"What'd he say?" Tyler asked Gloria.

"He asked if you want to know what else he did when he was wearing it."

"Um..."

Fu waggled his eyebrows at Tyler and followed it with a coy wink. Gloria flushed red.

Tyler cursed under his breath. "You...didn't." Beside him, Ellie had her fingers over her mouth, trying to stifle her laughter. Tyler slicked a hand down his face. "This can't be happening." He reached behind him and brought his hat out. He handed it to Fu. "It's yours."

"Tyler," Ellie whispered, and put a hand on his arm. "You can't do that. That's your *hat*."

"You heard what he just said."

She laughed freely now. "Yeah, I guess you're right."

Fu took it appreciatively and set it comfortably on his head. He nodded a thank you to Tyler, who now looked like tears were in his immediate future. But his grief was interrupted by Nick raising his voice from the other end of the bar. "If everyone could give me a minute," Nick said. "I have something I'd like to say."

"He's going to thank us," Tyler whispered to Ellie. "Because we found the people who wanted to kill him."

"We?"

Nick mentioned for Tyler to come join him, and Ellie followed behind. "You all know," Nick began, "that Tyler is my best and oldest friend." Nick nodded across the bar to Major who pressed a button on a remote control. A flat-screen television hung over the bar, and it changed from surfing on ESPN to a picture of a much younger Tyler. He was in a locker room, leaning against a bench, wearing only his underwear. He looked sicker than a hazed freshman.

"Oh, no," Tyler moaned. Beside him, Ellie had returned to her laughter.

Tyler shot a glance at Major. He tossed his hands out, feigning betrayal. "I helped you rebuild this place after the hurricane," he said.

"True," Major said. "But you didn't pull off your own version of Easter morning like Nick did."

"How do I compete with that?"

"You don't. That's why your picture is on my television."

"Unbelievable."

"Tyler," Nick called out. "You want to explain this or should I?"

"I can—"

"Great," Nick interrupted. "I'll be glad to." Everyone around the bar hushed as Nick took another pull off his beer and used it to motion toward the television. "This, ladies and gentlemen, is our distinguished Tyler Borland when he was a junior at Texas Tech. You'll notice him here in his tighty-whities. This was before he moved exclusively to Speedos." The crowd roared with laughter.

"I don't wear Speedos," Tyler murmured.

The crowd suddenly groaned and shifted as one in Ellie and Tyler's direction. "What was that?" Ellie asked.

"I think Fu just showed everyone that he wears Speedos himself."

Ellie cringed.

"This particular moment in Tyler history," Nick continued, "occurred at the end of a Red Raiders basketball game."

"Don't do this," Tyler said, but Nick paid him no mind.

"As you can imagine, Tyler had worked his way through a few beers. He even snuck a flask of whiskey into the game. Mike Jessup was Raider Red—the college mascot—and as soon as the game was over and Raider Red finished his final few antics, Tyler tackled him on his way to the locker room. Tyler stripped Mike out of the costume, then with great speed for someone in his inebriated state, slid into the outfit. But," Nick continued, "you see him here in his tighty-whities, so I'm sure you're all asking yourselves what changed between the time he turned into Raider Red and the moment this picture was captured."

From the other end of the bar, Fu started chanting: "Yes, yes, yes."

"Tyler ran back out to the stadium and started slapping any and every girl he passed on the butt." Nick paused to take another sip of his beer. Tyler looked down at Ellie.

"Ready to go?" he asked.

"Nope. Nick has my undivided attention."

"After about three or four minutes of this," Nick said, "Tyler draws up on the edge of the court and sets his hands on his knees to catch his breath. I hear him repeating, 'Too hot, too hot.' He rips off the mascot's face and grabs his stomach as he runs to the locker room. Thankfully, he made it there before throwing up. But the problem was he ran into the girls' locker room and peeled off the rest of the costume and his pants before he realized he was standing in the middle of a bunch of half-dressed cheerleaders. Then he barfed on two of them. And…about five seconds later, this picture was taken."

"I think I'd like to be on a boat right now," Tyler said. "Way out in the Gulf."

"I'll bet you do," Ellie said. "But you had that coming. Now go buy your friend a beer."

"Fine."

After Tyler walked away, Ellie found Jet still sitting at

the picnic table. She took a seat across from him, and he motioned toward the television. "You sure you want to be associated with him?" he asked.

"He's still a keeper," she smiled. "So, this squad. We'd be going after some bad apples?"

"The baddest."

"And you'll be on it?"

"And I'll be on it," he said.

She nodded thoughtfully. "Tyler and I are enrolled in a long-range shooting tournament this weekend up in Ocala. Why don't I call you when I get back, and we can set up a time for you to introduce me to the people behind it?"

"Yeah?"

"Yeah."

Jet smiled. "We're going to make a good team."

Ellie raised her beer and clicked her bottleneck to Jet's. "I'm pretty sure we already do."

THE END

HUMAN TRAFFICKING

Human trafficking is a serious problem. It's the fastest-growing organized crime activity in the United States and includes both sex and forced labor trafficking.

Most Americans don't realize that between 14,500 and 17,500 people are trafficked into the U.S. each year. Globally, it generates profits up to $32 billion every year. When it comes to children getting pulled into trafficking, perpetrators are looking for vulnerable children that they can easily control and manipulate. Lonely children who don't have a good relationship with friends or family are prime targets.

Below is a link to Florida Abolitionist, an organization based in Florida that works tirelessly to fight human trafficking in the U.S. I would urge you to visit their site, become informed, and perhaps donate or get involved somehow.

https://floridaabolitionist.org/the-problem/

FUN FOOTNOTES TO BREAKWATER

While creating a world of fiction, I root as much as I can in reality. So, should you be interested, you'll find a few links below that offer more detail on what you saw in several of the scenes:

Miami-Dade County's process for using iPads to assist families in identifying a body, HERE: https://www.miamiherald.com/news/local/crime/article24394471.html

For Ellie picking a lock with a bobby pin: Bobby Pin
　　https://www.youtube.com/watch?v=cjuT_63Ioig

For Ellie dusting for fingerprints: Fingerprints
　　https://www.scientificamerican.com/article/finding-fingerprints/

Proper positioning for a vehicle rollover: Vehicle Rollover

https://www.youtube.com/watch?v=7LFJM8kOwZc

AVAILABLE NOW

Ellie's adventures continue in *Lonely Coast* which is available on Amazon now.

ALSO BY JACK HARDIN

For those of you just entering the series with Breakwater, you can catch up from the beginning with Broken Stern. The first four books in the Pine Island Coast Series all form one larger story arc which finds its resolution in book 4. Breakwater is the first stand-alone in the series.

The Ellie O'Conner Coastal Suspense Series

Silent Ripple: An Ellie O'Conner Prequel Novella

Broken Stern (Book 1)

Shallow Breeze (Book 2)

Bitter Tide (Book 3)

Vacant Shore (Book 4)

Breakwater (Book 5)

Lonely Coast (Book 6)

18 Dragons: A TEAM 99 Novella

The Apostate: A TEAM 99 Novella

The Ryan Savage Series

Savage Coast

Savage Justice

Savage Storm

GRATITUDE

A special thank you to all of you who have corresponded with me through email, Facebook, and reviews to let me how much you love Ellie and her world. It means a lot.

I'm off to work on the next Ellie installment. Be blessed!

—Jack
jack.w.hardin00@gmail.com

LEAVE A REVIEW

I hope you enjoyed *Breakwater*. As a self-published author, reviews truly help to get my books in front of other potential readers. If you enjoyed the book, you can leave a review on the book's sales page on Amazon. Thanks so much.

Made in the USA
Coppell, TX
04 June 2021